The House on Blackwood Lane

Dedication

This book is dedicated to the resilient spirits who have faced their own Blackwood Lanes—to those who have navigated the labyrinthine corridors of family dysfunction, the chilling whispers of doubt, and the paralyzing grip of fear. It is a testament to the enduring strength of the human heart, to the unwavering bonds of kinship that can withstand even the most formidable storms, and to the unyielding hope that flickers even in the darkest of nights.

This dedication is for those who have found themselves trapped in houses of shadows, both literal and metaphorical—those whose homes have become battlegrounds of unspoken resentments, simmering anxieties, and the chilling weight of hidden truths. It is for the families whose walls have echoed with the silent screams of unspoken pain, where the cracks in the facade reveal the fragility of relationships under pressure.

It is for those who have known the insidious creep of paranoia, the chilling uncertainty of whether the enemy resides within or without, the agonizing struggle to differentiate between the tangible and the imagined. It is to those who have experienced the slow, agonizing unraveling of sanity, where the line between reality and delusion becomes increasingly blurred, leaving them stranded in a landscape of uncertainty and fear.

For those who have fought—and are still fighting—their personal battles with the unseen forces that threaten to consume them, this book acknowledges your strength, validates your experience, and offers a glimmer of hope in the face of unimaginable adversity. It is a recognition of the courage it takes to confront the shadows within, to unearth the buried demons that haunt the halls of our minds and our hearts, and to emerge, scarred but unbroken, on the other side. It is a dedication to your resilience, to your perseverance, and to the indomitable spirit that enables you to rise above even the most profound darkness. May this story offer you a space for catharsis, a reflection of your own internal struggles, and a reminder that even in the deepest night, the faintest glimmer of dawn will eventually appear.

The Arrival

The removal van rumbled away, its departing growl a stark counterpoint to the unsettling silence that immediately enveloped Blackwood Lane. Number 13 stood before them, a grand Victorian house draped in an unsettling stillness. Ivy, thick and almost obscenely vibrant, clawed at its aged brickwork, a verdant shroud against the pale afternoon sun. It was undeniably beautiful, a picture-postcard home that whispered promises of a perfect suburban life. But even as John Miller, radiating the forced cheerfulness of a man desperately trying to convince himself, declared it "magnificent," a prickle of unease snaked its way up Mary's spine.

She couldn't quite place it. It wasn't the obvious things – the slightly chipped paintwork around the ornate window frames, the overgrown garden that hinted at neglect, or even the lingering scent of damp earth and old wood. It was something deeper, a pervasive sense of wrongness that hung in the air like a shroud. A feeling of being watched, of unseen eyes peering from behind the shadowed mullioned windows. John, oblivious, busied himself with the keys, his practiced smile strained. He had secured this house, this perfect symbol of their restored financial stability, after months of grueling work and sleepless nights. He wouldn't let anything, least of all Mary's anxieties, mar this hard-won victory.

Their teenage daughter, Emily, remained detached, her usual vibrant energy muted. She trailed behind them, her gaze fixed on the ground, a stark contrast to the excited chatter of other families moving into the neighborhood. The move itself had been fraught with tension. Emily had resisted the upheaval, her adolescent angst amplified by the constant financial pressures that had overshadowed their family life in recent years. The move to Blackwood Lane, a desperate attempt to escape the past and embrace a brighter future, had only exacerbated the simmering tension.

Inside, the grand hallway swallowed the afternoon light, leaving the vast space cloaked in a half-light that seemed to amplify the silence. Dust motes danced in the faint shafts of light filtering through the stained-glass window, each one a tiny, swirling phantom. The air hung heavy with the scent of potpourri, attempting to mask a deeper, underlying aroma that Mary couldn't quite identify – something musky, almost earthy, that evoked a sense of decay.

As they began unpacking, the subtle imperfections and inconsistencies in the house's construction and decoration became increasingly apparent. The floorboards creaked unevenly underfoot, their rhythm unsettling, as if the house itself were breathing. Wallpaper peeled back in places to reveal layers of discolored paint, hinting at past renovations and concealed secrets. A mismatch of skirting boards and door handles further emphasized the feeling of disunity within the seemingly solid structure.

The attic, a sprawling, dust-laden space, held the most unsettling discovery. While John and Mary dealt with the logistics of unpacking, Emily explored, drawn by a morbid curiosity that was both unsettling and strangely compelling. She unearthed a small, porcelain doll, its painted eyes unnervingly lifelike, its once-vibrant dress faded and stained. It seemed to emanate a cold, unnatural stillness, a subtle energy that caused a tremor to run down her spine. She hid it away hastily, the unease settling deep within her, an unspoken secret mirroring the unspoken anxieties simmering within the family.

The days that followed blurred into a hazy sequence of unpacking, punctuated by unsettling occurrences. The whispers started subtly, almost imperceptible at first – faint murmurs emanating from empty rooms, like disembodied voices murmuring secrets in the half-light. Mary initially dismissed them as the old house settling, or the wind whistling through cracks in the aging structure. But the whispers grew in frequency and intensity, becoming more distinct, more insistent. They seemed to carry a weight of sorrow, of untold stories, of lingering despair.

John, ever the pragmatist, remained skeptical. He attributed the sounds to Mary's imagination, fuelled by the stress of the move and the lingering anxieties about their precarious financial situation. He brushed aside her concerns, his attempts to reassure her laced with a growing impatience. The unspoken accusation – that she was letting her anxieties manifest into tangible realities – hung heavy between them.

But Emily, too, was experiencing the unsettling events. She began to notice shadows that shifted and changed, that flickered and writhed at the edges of her peripheral vision. Shadows that seemed sentient, that danced and pulsed with an eerie life of their own. She would see them in the periphery – fleeting glimpses of movement in the corners of her eyes – moments of unease that she couldn't quite capture but were palpable nonetheless. She witnessed things that confirmed Mary's fears, but the adults continued to dismiss them.

The unease morphed into fear. One evening, while exploring the basement, which was both damp and eerily cold, Mary stumbled upon a hidden compartment behind a loose brick. Inside, she found a collection of old photographs and journals, their brittle pages filled with faded ink. The photographs depicted past residents of Blackwood Lane, their faces etched with a mixture of hope and despair. The journals chronicled their lives, a chilling testament to a slow descent into paranoia and madness.

The entries described unsettling occurrences, identical to those they were now experiencing – whispers in the walls, unexplained noises, and a pervasive sense of being watched. The journals detailed escalating tensions between family members, mirroring the growing rift between John and Mary. The accounts hinted at tragedy, at a history of mental instability, and at unexplained disappearances. Mary reread the entries, feeling a growing sense of dread. These weren't mere coincidences, they were reflections of the reality that was closing in around them.

She showed John the journals, her hand trembling, but he dismissed them as a coincidence, a bizarre collection of fantastical tales. He saw only a woman succumbing to stress, to the weight of their recent struggles, twisting the ordinary into something sinister. His words, meant to be reassuring, stung with a hidden barb of accusation. The argument that ensued left Mary feeling more isolated, more alone, her fears amplified by the chasm of disbelief that was opening up between her and her husband.

Emily, too, discovered unsettling clues. She noticed a cryptic symbol, repeatedly etched into the woodwork, painted on the underside of the attic stairs, and even scratched into the ancient stonework in the basement. It was a symbol that seemed both ancient and menacing. She felt an instinctive aversion to it, a primal dread that mirrored the chilling sense of foreboding that now clung to the house like a second skin.

As the days turned into weeks, the Millers became increasingly isolated. Attempts to interact with their neighbors were met with strange silences and unnerving avoidance. Smiling, friendly greetings were met with averted gazes and hurried retreats. Their attempts at social connection were rebuffed, a chilling reflection of their own growing sense of isolation.

The family's perception of their neighbors began to shift, morphing from friendly faces into a collective of shadowy figures, observing them, whispering behind their hands. The escalating paranoia further isolated them, creating a growing divide between the Millers and the outside world, reinforcing the sense of entrapment within the walls of Blackwood Lane. Their once-bright hopes for a new beginning in a new home were slowly being replaced by a creeping dread, turning their idyllic dream into a nightmarish reality. Their isolation amplified their anxieties, creating a feedback loop of fear that threatened to consume them. The house, once a symbol of hope, had become a prison, its walls closing in on them, stifling them with its unspoken secrets and insidious whispers.

Whispers in the Walls

The unsettling sounds began subtly, almost imperceptible at first. A faint creak from a distant floorboard, a whisper of wind sighing through a crack in a windowpane. Mary would dismiss them as the house settling, the normal groaning of an old Victorian structure under the weight of years and shifting seasons. But the sounds persisted, growing in frequency and intensity. They were no longer the soft sighs of an aging house; they were more deliberate, more insistent. Whispers, faint and indistinct at first, seemed to emanate from empty rooms, weaving through the silence of Blackwood Lane like spectral threads.

One evening, while putting Emily to bed, Mary heard it – a distinct murmur coming from the hallway, a voice, or rather, voices, speaking in low tones, their words indistinct, yet somehow laden with a chilling sorrow. She froze, her heart hammering against her ribs, a primal fear gripping her. She glanced at Emily, who lay peacefully asleep, oblivious to the unsettling sounds. Mary crept out of the room, her footsteps cautious, her senses heightened. She followed the whispers, tracing their source down the hall. The voices seemed to dance just out of reach, receding as she approached, intensifying when she moved away. The sensation was profoundly unnerving, a relentless game of cat and mouse played in the shadows of Blackwood Lane.

The whispers were joined by other noises. Faint footsteps could be heard on the stairs, slow, deliberate, as if someone were ascending or descending at a measured pace, their weight barely disturbing the old floorboards. Sometimes, it was the rhythmic drip of water, a slow, measured cadence, seeming to echo from the hidden depths of the house. Other times, it was a scraping sound, as if something were being dragged across the floorboards in a distant room. These sounds, once so subtle as to be barely noticeable, became a persistent chorus, a dissonant symphony of the unseen.

John, ever the pragmatist, remained stubbornly skeptical. He attributed the noises to Mary's overactive imagination, a product of stress, of the pressure of their recent struggles, and the anxieties associated with their move. He would dismiss her accounts as the result of an overly sensitive nature, or simply suggest that she was tiring herself out, adding another worry to the ever-growing list of concerns already crowding her mind. His attempts at reassurance were often laced with an underlying impatience, a subtle dismissal of her fears. He did not share her feelings, her worries, her creeping sense of unease, and the unspoken accusation – that she was creating these manifestations of fear – was a constant undercurrent in their interactions, creating a growing chasm between them.

But Emily, too, began to notice the unusual occurrences. She didn't hear the whispers as clearly as her mother, but she saw things. Shadows, dancing at the periphery of her vision. Quick movements in the corners of her eyes, fleeting glimpses that vanished as soon as she tried to focus on them. These shadows were not the natural shifts of light and darkness in the old house; they seemed sentient, moving and pulsing with an unnatural life of their own. They danced and writhed, fleeting glimpses that seemed to beckon and retreat with equal measures of intent. She would try to describe them to her parents, but her descriptions were vague, punctuated with hesitations and uncertainties, easily dismissed as the imaginings of a teenager, caught in the unsettling transition of moving to a new home. The subtle shift in perspective, the confirmation from her daughter, further fueled Mary's growing unease, driving a wedge into the relationship between her and John.

The unease gradually morphed into a palpable fear. The house, initially seen as a haven of sanctuary, slowly began to feel like a prison, closing in around the family, suffocating them with its weight of secrets and its insidious whispers. They felt isolated not just from their neighbors – whose cautious avoidance further fuelled their fears – but increasingly isolated from each other. John's skepticism, while initially presented as reassurance, was becoming a barrier, a wall of disbelief separating him from Mary and Emily, isolating him further into his denial. The silent accusations hung heavy in the air, poisoning the family atmosphere and intensifying the growing fear.

One night, Mary awoke to a chilling sensation. She felt a presence in the room, a weight in the air, a feeling of being watched, the source unseen. She sat bolt upright in bed, her heart racing, a cold sweat slick on her skin. The room was plunged in darkness, the only light coming from the moon outside, casting long shadows across the walls. She listened intently, straining her ears to catch any sound, any indication of what had disturbed her. The silence was absolute, broken only by the rhythmic thumping of her own heart and her shallow, rapid breaths. The feeling of being watched intensified, becoming almost unbearable, leaving her with a feeling of utter vulnerability.

She nudged John awake, whispering about the feeling of being watched, about the presence that she could sense. John grumbled, irritated at being woken, dismissing her words as a nightmare, a product of stress and anxiety. His lack of empathy and belief fueled Mary's fears further; she was starting to feel utterly alone in her experience. He rolled over and went back to sleep, leaving Mary alone with her fear, to fight off the creeping darkness of the night. This incident created a pivotal turning point in their family dynamics, intensifying the growing distrust and isolation within the family unit.

The fear was now a constant companion, lurking in the shadows of Blackwood Lane, seeping into every corner of their lives. Sleep offered no refuge; their dreams were filled with unsettling images – fleeting glimpses of faces in the shadows, murmuring voices, and menacing shadows that seemed to slither and writhe at the edges of their vision. The whispers continued, growing more insistent, more menacing, weaving themselves into the fabric of their daily lives, becoming a relentless soundtrack to their growing dread. They couldn't escape the house, or the feelings of foreboding it elicited, the overwhelming sense of being surrounded by unseen eyes, watching them, judging them, and waiting for their inevitable downfall. The perfect suburban dream was rapidly dissolving into a nightmarish reality, the weight of Blackwood Lane's dark secrets pressing down on them with unbearable intensity.

Unsettling Discoveries

The persistent unease, the whispers, the unsettling sounds – they had become the soundtrack to their lives. Sleep offered little respite; nightmares plagued them, filled with shadowy figures and disembodied voices, mirroring the horrors that seemed to cling to the very walls of Blackwood Lane. One afternoon, while John was at work and Emily was at school, Mary decided to explore the basement, a dark, damp space she had avoided until now. A sense of foreboding settled over her as she descended the creaking wooden stairs, the air growing colder and heavier with each step.

The basement was a labyrinth of shadowed corners and forgotten relics – old furniture shrouded in dust sheets, forgotten tools, and cobweb-laden boxes. The air hung heavy with the scent of mildew and decay, a palpable sense of age and neglect clinging to the space. As she moved through the darkness, a flickering beam from her flashlight cutting through the gloom, she noticed a loose floorboard near the far wall. Curiosity overcoming her apprehension, she pried it up, revealing a small, hidden compartment. Inside, she found a collection of old photographs and several leather-bound journals, their pages yellowed and brittle with age.

The photographs depicted a family, the Millers' predecessors, their faces etched with a mixture of joy and an unsettling undercurrent of anxiety. They were posed in various locations within the house, but their smiles seemed strained, their eyes haunted. A palpable sense of unease emanated from the images, a chilling premonition of the troubles to come. Mary felt a jolt of recognition, a sense of déjà vu, as she looked at the photos. There was something familiar about their expressions, their postures. They held the same sense of tension that she now felt, the same anxiety that was slowly consuming her own family.

She carefully opened the first journal, its pages crackling under her touch. The handwriting was elegant, yet the words were filled with a growing sense of paranoia and fear. The entries chronicled the family's slow descent into madness, detailing strange occurrences within the house – whispers, unexplained movements of objects, and a pervasive sense of being watched. The writer described a growing sense of isolation, a feeling of being trapped within the walls of their own home, a palpable sense of doom slowly engulfing them. The descriptions mirrored her own experiences with unsettling accuracy, a terrifying echo of her own present reality.

The journal entries spoke of escalating family conflict, accusations of infidelity and betrayal, fueled by the ever-growing paranoia and fear. The writer described arguments, fueled by the mounting anxieties and an inexplicable dread that seemed to seep from the very foundations of the house itself. The escalating tensions, the growing mistrust, and the eventual unraveling of the family mirrored her own experiences with startling precision. Each entry was a reflection of her own fears, a harrowing premonition of what could happen if she and John didn't address the issues facing their family.

As she read further, the writer's descent into madness became increasingly apparent. The entries became more erratic, filled with rambling accusations and delusional thoughts. There were accounts of visions and hallucinations, descriptions of shadowy figures moving through the house, and a growing conviction that they were being targeted by unseen forces. The writer's grasp on reality seemed to unravel with each passing entry, their sanity eroding under the relentless pressure of the house and its insidious whispers. The parallels between her own anxieties and this long-dead family's descent into chaos were undeniable. This journal was more than a historical document; it was a terrifying warning.

Mary's heart pounded in her chest as she finished the last entry, a chilling testament to the power of fear and the fragility of the human mind under pressure. She closed the journal, her hands trembling. The experience left her breathless, shaken to the core. She felt a sudden chill despite the relative warmth of the basement. The weight of the knowledge she had uncovered pressed down on her, heavy and suffocating. It was as if the house itself had reached out and shared its deepest, darkest secrets with her.

That evening, when John returned home, Mary tried to share her discovery, her voice trembling as she recounted the unsettling contents of the journals and showed him the photographs. John, ever the pragmatist, dismissed her findings as coincidence, attributing her fears to stress and the strain of adjusting to their new life. He called it a product of her overactive imagination, fueled by anxiety and the pressures of the recent move. His dismissal of her concerns only served to widen the chasm between them, fueling Mary's growing sense of isolation. His skepticism, a wall of disbelief, blocked her attempts at sharing her anxieties and her burgeoning fear.

Meanwhile, Emily, having discovered an old, worn copy of a children's book in her room, noticed a recurring symbol throughout the house – a strange, intricate design etched into the woodwork, carved into the fireplace mantel, and even faintly visible on some of the older wallpaper. She couldn't decipher its meaning, but its repeated presence further fueled her own growing unease. She tried to discuss it with her parents, but her attempts to relay her observations were brushed aside, dismissed as childlike whimsy. The subtle differences between her observations and her parents' dismissal of them only widened the chasm between them further. The subtle signs, the recurring symbol, were ignored, fueling her own growing anxiety.

The tension within the Miller family grew thicker, suffocating them in its icy grip. The house, once a dream home, had become a prison, its walls closing in, its secrets weighing heavily on their already fractured relationships. The unsettling discoveries – the journals, the photographs, the cryptic symbol – only served to deepen the mystery and intensify their fears. The lines between reality and delusion blurred, as the weight of the house's dark past bore down on them, threatening to consume them all. Each passing day brought fresh anxieties and anxieties about the future; the question was no longer whether they were in danger, but how long they could hold on before their sanity fractured, mirroring the fate of the family before them. The unspoken question lingered: were they next? The terrifying answer hung heavy in the air, chilling them to the bone. The idyllic suburban dream had long since vanished, replaced by a nightmarish reality, where the family members were struggling to maintain their sanity amidst a mounting wave of dread and the subtle yet pervasive influences of Blackwood Lane.

Growing Isolation

The initial wave of neighborly greetings, the friendly smiles and offers of assistance that had accompanied their move to Blackwood Lane, had evaporated like morning mist. John, ever the sociable one, had tried to initiate conversations – barbecues, casual chats over fences – but his attempts were met with a peculiar reticence. A polite nod, a brief, almost hurried response, then a swift retreat. It wasn't outright hostility, but a subtle, unnerving avoidance that left him feeling increasingly uneasy.

Mary noticed it too. Mrs. Gable next door, once so eager to share baking tips, now kept her distance, her curtains perpetually drawn. Mr. Henderson across the street, a jovial man known for his boisterous laughter, now seemed to shrink away whenever their paths crossed, his eyes darting nervously away. Their usual friendly waves and morning greetings had become infrequent and perfunctory, punctuated by long stretches of chilling silence. It was an atmosphere of collective avoidance that permeated the neighborhood, making their isolation palpable.

One evening, while taking Emily for a walk, Mary encountered Mrs. Gable in the park. She'd hoped for a friendly chat, a chance to break the growing barrier between them. But as Mary approached, Mrs. Gable's smile faltered, and a shadow crossed her face. She mumbled a quick greeting, her gaze flitting nervously around, before hurrying away, pulling her small child along as if fleeing from an unseen threat. The interaction left Mary feeling colder than the evening air.

The children's playground, previously a haven of cheerful chatter and laughter, felt eerily quiet. The swings hung motionless, the slides deserted, the merry-go-round untouched. Other children, who had once been plentiful, were completely absent. It was as if an unseen force had swept the playground clean, leaving behind an unsettling stillness. The air was charged with a tension Mary found hard to ignore. It felt less like a peaceful residential area and more like a stage set for a nightmare. The joyous atmosphere which had once welcomed them had evaporated, leaving in its place, a profound sense of unease.

The growing strangeness of their neighbors' behavior fuelled Mary's already simmering anxiety. The whispers, the unsettling occurrences within their own home, now seemed interwoven with the peculiar aloofness of those around them. The feeling that something was fundamentally wrong had spread like wildfire throughout their once peaceful lives. She began to wonder if their neighbors weren't just being strange, but if they were somehow involved in what was happening to them. It was a terrifying thought, reinforcing the insidious feeling of isolation. Their neighbors, once friendly faces, now seemed like distant shadows, their behavior suggesting an unspoken complicity in something sinister.

John, initially dismissive of Mary's concerns, began to notice the shift in the neighborhood dynamic. The casual encounters, the easy camaraderie, were replaced with an unnerving silence, an avoidance that was as palpable as the damp chill in their basement. He started to question their neighbors' silence, their hesitant gazes, the way they seemed to shrink back as if afraid of something, or someone. This subtle change had begun to chip away at his rational exterior, replacing his pragmatic outlook with a growing sense of unease.

The more he observed, the more disturbed he became. He started noticing subtle details he had initially overlooked: the way Mrs. Gable's usually immaculate garden was now overgrown and neglected, the strange, almost furtive movements of Mr. Henderson late at night. He began to question the casual dismissals and subtle avoidance, his rational skepticism giving way to the creeping tendrils of anxiety.

Emily, too, sensed the change. The carefree games with other children were a distant memory. Her friends seemed to have vanished, leaving behind a desolate, echoing emptiness in their once vibrant playground. The growing isolation wasn't just confined to their house; it was spreading like a disease through their neighborhood, transforming the once welcoming community into a cold, silent haven of suspicion and apprehension. Her innocent mind couldn't quite grasp the reasons behind this change, but she sensed danger, and a pervasive atmosphere of fear.

One afternoon, while playing in her room, Emily noticed something new. The cryptic symbol she had found etched into the woodwork reappeared, this time carved into the underside of a loose floorboard. Underneath, nestled against the joists of the floor, she found a small, tarnished silver locket. It was intricately engraved with the same symbol, and inside, a faded photograph of a young girl, her face eerily similar to Emily's, stared back at her. The discovery sent a chill down her spine. This new evidence was no longer merely a mysterious curiosity; it felt like a sinister confirmation of their fears, a tangible link to the house's dark secrets.

The locket's discovery heightened the family's sense of isolation. It wasn't just the house anymore; it was the entire neighborhood. The previously friendly faces, once symbols of community, now seemed distant, mysterious, even threatening. The Millers were isolated within their own home, isolated within their own neighborhood, trapped in a silent conspiracy of fear and suspicion. The once welcoming suburb had transformed into a hostile landscape, making their isolation even more intense. The seemingly friendly suburban community had become a potential source of threat.

Their attempts to reach out, to connect, to understand what was happening, were met with silence, avoidance, a chilling wall of secrecy that deepened their growing sense of paranoia. The more they tried to connect, the more isolated they felt. Their once happy family dynamic, stretched thin by the events unfolding around them, began to crack under the relentless strain. The lines between reality and imagination blurred, their fears fueled by the unsettling silence of their neighbors and the ever-present whispers within their home. The once charming street, once a promise of suburban bliss, was now a prison of suspicion and dread, a silent testament to their growing isolation. Blackwood Lane had become their personal hell, isolating them from both the outside world and from each other. The family, once a refuge of support and love, now seemed to be a dangerous force. The escalating paranoia threatened to tear them apart, a harrowing prospect that added a new layer of terror to their already precarious existence.

The fear, once a subtle unease, now consumed them entirely. They barricaded their doors and windows, fearful of what might lurk in the shadows, in the vacant eyes of their neighbors. Every creak, every whisper, was amplified in their minds, fueled by the isolation that had tightened its icy grip around them. The dream home on Blackwood Lane had turned into a nightmare, and the once friendly community became a source of unease and palpable dread. They were isolated, trapped, and utterly alone in their fight for survival, against an enemy they couldn't see, couldn't touch, and couldn't comprehend. The silence of their neighbors was louder than any scream, a constant reminder of their isolation and the unspoken horror that lurked beneath the surface of their seemingly perfect suburban life. The perfect suburban dream was now a chilling, isolating nightmare.

Seeds of Distrust

The air in the Miller household crackled with a tension thicker than the dust motes dancing in the moonlight filtering through the gaps in the curtains. It wasn't the eerie creaks of the old house, nor the unsettling whispers that seemed to slither from the shadows, that fueled this latest conflict. This was a battle waged with words, sharp and cutting, fueled by exhaustion, fear, and the insidious tendrils of mistrust that had begun to weave their way between John and Mary.

It started with a misplaced key, a seemingly insignificant detail in the grand scheme of their escalating nightmare. John, his eyes bloodshot from sleepless nights spent listening for phantom sounds, accused Mary of hiding it. He spoke in a low, guttural voice, the calm rationality that had once defined him replaced by a simmering anger. "It's always something, Mary," he'd rasped, the words laced with suspicion. "First the whispers, then the moving objects, now this. Are you trying to drive me mad?"

Mary, her own exhaustion etched onto her face in dark circles under her eyes, retorted with a sharpness that mirrored his own accusation. "Don't be ridiculous, John," she snapped, her voice tight with frustration. "I haven't moved anything. And as for the whispers… you're the one who keeps insisting on hearing things." She ran a hand through her tangled hair, her voice trembling slightly. "I'm just as scared as you are, but this constant bickering isn't helping anyone."

Their argument escalated, fueled by sleep deprivation and the cumulative weight of their fear. Each accusation, each denial, was a blow that chipped away at the already fragile foundation of their marriage. The once comforting presence of their spouse was now a source of suspicion, their words twisting into accusations and their actions scrutinized for hidden motives. The love that had bound them together seemed to shrink, replaced by a growing chasm of distrust. They circled each other, their voices rising and falling in a discordant duet of fear and blame, their words like weapons, wounding and leaving lasting scars.

Emily, huddled in her bed, listened to their escalating conflict with a growing sense of unease. The familiar comfort of her parents' presence was replaced by a frightening uncertainty. She felt as if the very foundation of her world was crumbling, leaving her alone and adrift in a sea of anxiety. The sharp words, the raised voices, became a horrifying soundtrack to her growing fear, each syllable echoing the growing chasm in her parents' relationship.

The arguments continued day after day, each one a fresh incision into the already frayed fabric of the family. Each conflict was further fueled by the unsettling occurrences within the house. A flickering light bulb, a creaking floorboard, a sudden chill in the air—all became ammunition in their bitter exchanges. What had started as an attempt to find comfort and understanding in each other had mutated into a battlefield where every word was a weapon, each look a source of suspicion.

The isolation wasn't just a physical one, confined to their neighborhood; it was now consuming their family unit. The once warm embrace of their home now felt cold and hostile, a setting for their bitter battles of accusation and denial. The familiar sounds of their own voices, once a comfort, were now a source of increasing dread, underscoring the isolation they faced.

Emily's sleep patterns became as erratic as her parents'. The once peaceful nights were now filled with anxious tossing and turning. She found herself haunted by unsettling dreams, mirrors of the frightening experiences documented in the old journals she had discovered: the whispering shadows, the unsettling sense of being watched, and the terrifying feeling of isolation. Her imagination was a breeding ground for nightmares, mirroring the decaying state of her parents' relationship and the haunted nature of their new home. The once serene innocence of her childhood had been replaced by an adult's burden of fear and uncertainty, further compounding her sense of isolation.

The discovery of the locket, with its faded photograph of a girl bearing an uncanny resemblance to her, intensified her anxiety. It was a tangible link to the house's dark history, a chilling reminder that she wasn't merely a victim of her parents' fracturing relationship, but potentially a participant in a larger, more sinister mystery. The once peaceful comfort of her family, once the safe haven of her life, was being replaced by growing shadows of doubt, uncertainty, and fear.

Her days were as troubled as her nights. The familiar sounds of her childhood home, once a comforting presence, were now punctuated by her parents' bitter arguments. Her playroom, once a haven of imagination, felt haunted by the unseen forces lurking beneath the floorboards. The once inviting sunlight that spilled into her bedroom now felt cold and ominous. Her playground, once filled with cheerful voices and laughter, remained eerily silent. The once vibrant tapestry of her childhood life was being slowly stripped away, replaced by the growing shadows of paranoia and fear.

John, caught in the maelstrom of his own paranoia and Mary's accusations, began to doubt his own sanity. Was he truly hearing things? Was he imagining the strange movements of objects, the unsettling whispers? Or was Mary right, and he was merely magnifying minor incidents, transforming them into proof of a larger conspiracy? The weight of his self-doubt crushed him, adding yet another layer to his isolation and contributing to the growing chasm between him and his wife. His mental state was as fragile as the family itself.

Mary, meanwhile, wrestled with the guilt of fueling the conflict. She knew that her accusations, born from fear and exhaustion, were tearing their family apart. But the escalating strangeness surrounding them, the persistent feeling of being watched, the subtle changes in their neighborhood – all of it fueled her growing suspicion, making her question everyone and everything, including the man she loved. The weight of her actions, of her accusations, pressed heavily on her. The relentless pressure of her surroundings, coupled with the strain of the situation, was beginning to affect her.

As the days bled into weeks, the Millers' once-strong family unit began to fragment under the unrelenting pressure of fear and suspicion. The house on Blackwood Lane, initially a symbol of their shared dream, was becoming a prison, isolating each member of the family from one another, trapped in a cycle of paranoia and fueled by their inability to trust. The love and unity which had once formed the backbone of the family had crumbled, replaced by doubt, isolation, and a chilling sense of individual isolation. The house they had dreamt of had become the setting for their personal hell.

Emily, caught in the crossfire of her parents' bitter disputes, felt profoundly alone. Her once bright eyes dimmed with anxiety, her carefree laughter replaced by a haunting silence. The innocence of childhood had been cruelly stolen, replaced by a precocious understanding of fear, suspicion, and the crushing weight of secrets. She bore witness to the shattering of her family unit, and in doing so, absorbed the crushing weight of their shared experience. She was no longer a child, but a silent witness to their nightmare, and the unseen forces at play seemed to be targeting her as well. She was not merely a spectator, but a participant in the growing terror that consumed Blackwood Lane. The once idyllic family home, once a haven of security and love, was now a battleground for paranoia and fear, and Emily was caught in the middle. The unsettling events, the fractured family, and the sinister secrets of Blackwood Lane had all combined to transform the young girl's innocent world into a chilling, isolated nightmare.

The Previous Occupants

The scent of aging paper and dust clung to Mary like a second skin as she sat hunched over a brittle, leather-bound volume at the town library. The hushed silence of the room, usually a comfort, now felt oppressive, the weight of the untold stories within the pages pressing down on her. She traced the faded inscription on the spine – "Blackwood Lane – A Chronicle of Happenings" – a shiver tracing its way down her spine. It was more than just a history; it felt like a warning.

The journal detailed the lives of families who had occupied the house before them, their triumphs and tragedies interwoven with a chilling undercurrent of unease. The early entries were idyllic, describing harvests, celebrations, and the joys of family life. But as the years progressed, a subtle shift occurred. The cheerful tone gave way to a growing sense of dread, the entries becoming shorter, more frantic, the ink smudged with tears or trembling hands.

She read of a young girl, Eliza, who vanished without a trace in 1888, leaving behind only a single, worn doll clutched in her tiny hand. There were mentions of unexplained illnesses, sudden deaths, and a pervasive sense of unease that echoed the very feelings that currently gripped the Millers. The house, it seemed, had a history of swallowing its inhabitants whole.

One entry stood out, written in a spidery script that seemed to claw its way across the page: "The whispers… they grow louder at night… I see shadows moving in the corners of my eyes… I feel… watched…" The words resonated with chilling familiarity, mirroring John's own anxieties. Mary felt a cold dread creep into her heart, a primal fear that transcended the rational mind. She felt a horrifying connection to the past, to the suffering experienced within the walls of this house. The past was not dead; it was alive, breathing in the shadows, influencing their current lives with ominous intent.

Another entry described the suicide of a young man, Thomas Ashton, who claimed he had been driven to despair by an unseen presence, a malevolent entity that lurked within the house's ancient walls. The details were sparse, but the underlying terror was palpable, leaving an icy chill in the reader's bones. Mary felt a wave of nausea wash over her as she read the accounts of escalating paranoia and despair, a mirror to the unraveling of her own family.

The town hall proved equally revealing. Mary spent hours poring over dusty land records and census reports, piecing together a fragmented tapestry of the house's past. She uncovered records of legal disputes, financial ruin, and unexplained disappearances, all linked to the house on Blackwood Lane. The pattern was unmistakable: tragedy followed tragedy, a dark legacy that seemed to be intrinsically linked to the house itself.

She unearthed newspaper clippings from the early 20th century, detailing the mysterious deaths of several residents. One article described a fire that swept through the house, leaving only charred remains and unanswered questions. Another recounted the sudden and unexplained demise of a family, their deaths shrouded in secrecy and speculation. There were whispers of curses, of ancient evils bound to the land, of a malevolent presence that preyed on the vulnerable, feeding off their fear and despair.

The more she learned, the more isolated she felt. Her attempts to casually mention her findings to neighbors were met with nervous laughter, averted gazes, and veiled warnings to "let sleeping dogs lie." The town, she realized, held its own secrets about Blackwood Lane, secrets it was determined to keep buried. The seemingly idyllic community facade crumbled, revealing a hidden layer of fear and unspoken truths.

The accumulating evidence confirmed her suspicions, but it also deepened the chasm within her family. John, already grappling with his own anxieties, reacted with intense skepticism, dismissing Mary's research as the ramblings of a woman driven mad by fear. His skepticism was a shield, a way to protect himself from the terrifying reality that was seeping into their lives.

"It's just old wives' tales, Mary," he'd say, his voice tight with a mixture of disbelief and resentment. "You're letting this house get to you. We need to focus on moving on, not digging up ancient ghosts." His words felt like stones thrown at her, each one chipping away at her already frayed nerves.

Emily, too, sensed the growing tension. The unsettling stories Mary uncovered mirrored the disturbing dreams that haunted the young girl's nights. The faded photograph in the locket, the whispers in the house, the escalating fear – it all coalesced, creating a chilling sense of foreboding. She was no longer just living in a haunted house; she felt like a prisoner of its past.

The weight of the house's history pressed down on the family, isolating them not only from their neighbors but from each other. The once-vibrant conversations that characterized their family life were replaced by stilted exchanges, punctuated by suspicion and barely-masked accusations.

John's rational mind clashed with Mary's growing certainty, their conflicting views creating a rift that widened with each passing day. The once-warm embrace of their home was now a suffocating prison, each room a reminder of their growing isolation and the dark secrets held within.

The discovery of old photographs added to the mounting dread. Pictures of families, their faces frozen in expressions of joy and anticipation, now seemed eerily prescient, haunted by the knowledge of the tragedies that followed. Mary found a picture of Eliza, the missing girl, her wide, innocent eyes staring directly at the camera. The striking resemblance to Emily sent a fresh wave of terror through Mary's already weary body. It wasn't just a coincidence; it was a connection to the past, a terrifying link to the house's dark legacy.

The journals contained more than just accounts of tragedy. They also held cryptic clues, fragmented sentences hinting at rituals, secret societies, and malevolent forces at work. Mary deciphered passages mentioning strange symbols, symbols that she now found etched into the woodwork of the house, hidden beneath layers of paint and time. They were silent witnesses to the tragedies that had unfolded within those walls, silent participants in the dark legacy of Blackwood Lane.

Days bled into weeks as the Millers became increasingly obsessed with the house's past. Their investigation consumed them, the lines between reality and delusion blurring with each new discovery. The house itself seemed to react, the whispers growing louder, the shadows dancing with more insistent malice, and the unexplained occurrences more frequent. They were trapped in a vicious cycle of fear and suspicion, their sanity teetering on the edge of the abyss. The house was no longer a home; it was a mausoleum of the past, and the Millers were its unwilling inhabitants. The weight of the past, the chilling secrets unearthed, and the growing paranoia began to exert its full effect on the family. Each member retreated further into their private struggles, the once tight-knit family unit dissolving into fragments of suspicion and fear. The house, initially a dream, had turned into a horrifying nightmare, trapping them in its shadowy embrace. The past, once a distant echo, had become a suffocating presence, casting long shadows on their present and threatening to consume their future.

Emilys Visions

Sleep became a battlefield for Emily. It wasn't the restful slumber of a child, but a descent into a chaotic realm of fragmented images and unsettling sounds. Her dreams, or were they visions?, weren't coherent narratives; instead, they were disjointed flashes of terror, like a film reel skipping erratically. One moment, she was standing in a dimly lit room, the air thick with the scent of woodsmoke and decay, watching a young girl with eyes hauntingly similar to her own clutching a worn doll. The girl's face was blurred, obscured by shadow, yet Emily felt a bone-deep connection, a kinship with this spectral child. The next, she was in a swirling vortex of flame, the acrid smell of burning wood filling her nostrils, the heat intense enough to scorch her skin.

The visions weren't confined to the confines of her bed. She'd awaken with the lingering impression of shadows flitting across the periphery of her vision, a fleeting glimpse of movement in the corners of her eyes, even in the bright daylight. Sometimes, she'd hear whispers, barely audible, murmuring words she couldn't quite grasp, yet they felt intimately close, invasive. The whispers danced around her, teasing her with fragmented phrases, hinting at stories of sorrow and despair. They were like ghostly echoes of the house's past, reaching out to touch her, to connect with her. The house itself seemed to pulse with a malevolent energy, a dark force that was both repelling and strangely alluring.

One recurring vision was particularly disturbing. She found herself in a vast, shadowy garden, overgrown and neglected, its once-manicured lawns overrun with weeds. Twisted, gnarled trees clawed at the sky, their branches like skeletal fingers reaching out to grasp her. A figure, shrouded in darkness, moved among the trees, its face unseen, yet Emily felt its presence, its suffocating weight. She sensed a deep sense of loneliness and despair emanating from this being, a sorrow so profound it felt as if she could physically taste it. She felt a connection to this figure, as if they shared a common fate, bound together by an ancient, unspoken agreement.

The visions weren't random. They seemed to be intimately connected to the house's history, mirroring the events Mary had unearthed in her research. The worn doll, the ghostly girl in the flickering candlelight, the house engulfed in flames— they all resonated with the stories Mary had read, a nightmarish parallel. The girl in her visions, she realized with a shudder, was Eliza, the missing child from 1888. The unsettling familiarity of it was what truly terrified her. The faces weren't fully formed, the events never played out in their entirety, but there was a deep, unsettling echo, a resonating chord that struck at the deepest recesses of her being.

During the day, Emily would try to dismiss these unsettling encounters as the product of stress, the byproduct of the family's growing turmoil. But the visions persisted, their frequency increasing, their intensity growing with each passing night. The line between reality and dream began to blur, the distinction fading into a disconcerting haze. What was real? What was illusion? The question echoed in her mind, an insistent, maddening whisper that only served to amplify her fear. She tried to tell her parents, to explain the frightening images that haunted her sleep, but the words failed her. How could she describe the indescribable? How could she articulate the raw terror that filled her being?

John dismissed her fears as childish nightmares, the result of too much time spent reading spooky books. Mary, while sympathetic, was already overwhelmed by her own anxieties and struggling to maintain a semblance of normalcy within the fractured family unit. Emily felt isolated, a captive of her own mind, adrift in a sea of fear and confusion. The house seemed to amplify her anxieties, its shadows lengthening, its whispers growing louder, its very structure resonating with her nightmares. The seemingly innocuous sounds of creaking floorboards and rustling curtains became amplified, transforming into sinister omens in her terrified imagination.

The weight of the past, the house's dark legacy, felt intensely personal, as though the house had chosen her as its unwilling conduit. She felt the chilling weight of centuries of despair, the accumulated sorrow of those who had come before her, bearing down on her, suffocating her. The house wasn't just a place, it was a repository of suffering, and Emily, unwittingly, had become a part of its haunting narrative.

One particularly vivid vision revealed a hidden room, a secret chamber tucked away within the house's labyrinthine structure. In this chamber, shrouded in perpetual twilight, she saw a table laden with strange symbols, arcane artifacts, and a book bound in human skin. A hooded figure performed a ritualistic dance, its chanting echoing in the silence of the chamber, a chilling incantation that sent shivers down Emily's spine. The image was fleeting, yet the chilling impact of the ritual stayed with her, a visceral reminder of something ancient and profoundly malevolent at work within the walls of her home.

The vision culminated in a harrowing scene of sacrifice, a young girl bound and gagged, her terrified eyes mirroring Emily's own. The hooded figure raised a knife, and a bloodcurdling scream pierced Emily's mind, awakening her with a gasp, her heart pounding in her chest. The feeling of terror that lingered after the vision was almost unbearable, a physical weight pressing down on her, suffocating her breath. This vision, more than any other, cemented her growing belief that the house's history was not just a story; it was a sinister reality that was actively affecting her, playing upon her deepest fears.

Days turned into weeks, and Emily's visions continued, becoming increasingly frequent and intense. The fragmented images coalesced into a disturbing narrative, a tapestry woven from the threads of past tragedies and present dread. The line between dream and reality became utterly indiscernible, and Emily found herself slipping into a state of profound unease and paranoia. The whispers persisted, growing louder and more insistent, weaving themselves into her waking thoughts, tainting her perception of reality.

The once bright and cheerful girl was now withdrawn, pale, and haunted. Her eyes, once sparkling with life, held a deep, abiding fear that mirrored the darkness that seemed to consume their home. Emily was no longer just living in a house; she was trapped within the confines of a nightmare, a prisoner of the past, her mind and her very soul held captive by the dark legacy of Blackwood Lane. Her visions were not merely disturbing dreams; they were messages, warnings, fragments of a truth so terrifying that it threatened to unravel the very fabric of her mind. The house, it seemed, was not merely haunted; it was actively shaping her reality, pulling her towards a destiny as terrifying as it was inescapable. And the terrifying reality that began to dawn on her was that she was not just a witness to this horror, but an integral part of it.

Johns Denial

John slammed the newspaper onto the kitchen table, the sharp crack echoing in the unsettling quiet of the house. The headline screamed about a local family's bizarre disappearance, attributed to a "mental health crisis," a phrase that grated on his nerves. He'd seen that look in Mary's eyes lately – the haunted, distant stare that suggested something was deeply wrong, something he refused to acknowledge. It was easier, safer, to dismiss it all as stress, a temporary blip in their otherwise perfect lives. The house, the whispers, Emily's increasingly erratic behavior—it was all just a product of their recent move, a temporary adjustment period. He had to believe that.

He needed to believe that. The alternative was terrifying, a descent into a maelstrom of the inexplicable, a surrender to the creeping dread that seemed to ooze from the very walls of their new home. He had always been a man of logic, of reason, and this… this was irrational. It challenged everything he held dear, everything he believed in. The rational part of him screamed that it was all in their heads, a collective case of mass hysteria triggered by the old house and its unsettling history.

But the nagging doubt persisted, a persistent whisper that echoed the unsettling sounds emanating from the house itself. The rhythmic creaking of the floorboards, the unsettling rustle of unseen things in the attic, the faint, almost imperceptible whispers that seemed to emanate from the shadowed corners of the rooms—these things were real, tangible, even if he refused to admit it to himself.

He watched Mary from across the table, her face pale and drawn, her eyes shadowed with a weariness that went beyond simple exhaustion. She was meticulously sorting through old photographs, her brow furrowed in concentration, a subtle tremor in her hands. He'd tried to talk to her earlier, to gently probe her about the research she was conducting on the house's history, but she'd shut him down, her voice tight and defensive. She'd said she needed time, space, to process everything she'd discovered. He understood, or at least he told himself he did. He just didn't want to understand.

The truth, he suspected, was far too terrifying to face. It threatened to shatter the carefully constructed facade of his perfect family life, to expose the fragile foundation upon which it was built. He preferred the comforting illusion of normalcy, the safe harbor of his own denial. He wouldn't let the house, the whispers, the shadows, or Mary's increasingly erratic behavior unravel him.

Emily, meanwhile, remained a puzzle. Her nightmares, which she'd described in hushed, terrified whispers, he'd initially dismissed as childish fantasies, the product of a vivid imagination fueled by too much exposure to gothic literature. He'd told her to stop reading those books, to focus on more "appropriate" material. But now, seeing the fear etched deep into her young face, he felt a pang of guilt, a whisper of doubt slithering into his carefully constructed wall of denial.

He forced himself to remember the way Emily had clutched her doll, its worn fabric stained with something that looked suspiciously like dried blood, the way her eyes had widened with terror when she'd described her visions, the way she'd spoken of whispers and shadows that moved just out of sight. The image of her, small and vulnerable, haunted him, a persistent counterpoint to his carefully crafted narrative of rational explanation.

Later that evening, as darkness settled over Blackwood Lane, casting long, ominous shadows across the house, John found himself drawn to the attic. He'd always been a practical man, a man who valued order and control, and the chaos of the attic, with its cobwebs and forgotten relics, unnerved him. Yet, he felt compelled to explore it, as if seeking some tangible proof that would confirm his rationalizations, some evidence that would dispel the creeping unease that gnawed at his composure.

He climbed the creaking stairs, each step accompanied by a low groan that echoed in the stillness of the house. The air in the attic was thick with the scent of dust and decay, a musty aroma that seemed to cling to him like a shroud. He switched on his flashlight, its beam slicing through the gloom, revealing piles of discarded furniture, boxes overflowing with forgotten treasures, and shadows that seemed to dance just beyond his vision's edge.

He searched through the boxes, rifling through old clothes, broken toys, and yellowed letters. He found nothing extraordinary, nothing that could explain the strange occurrences plaguing the family. Yet, as he moved deeper into the attic, he noticed something odd – a small, wooden chest hidden beneath a pile of dusty blankets. It was locked, secured with a heavy brass padlock, its surface worn smooth by time.

His heart pounded in his chest as he examined the chest, a strange combination of excitement and fear coursing through his veins. He felt a pull towards it, an irresistible urge to unlock its secrets. Was this the key to unraveling the mystery of Blackwood Lane? Or was he simply succumbing to the same irrationality that he'd so desperately been trying to deny?

He rummaged through the boxes, searching for a key, but found nothing. Frustration gnawed at him, but he refused to give up. He was determined to find a rational explanation, a logical answer to the unsettling events unfolding around him. He wouldn't be defeated by the house, by the shadows, by the whispers. He wouldn't let it break him. He had to maintain control, to hold onto his sanity, even if it meant facing the frightening possibility that his carefully constructed reality was about to crumble.

He spent hours searching, his hands trembling as he sifted through the contents of each box, his flashlight casting long, dancing shadows that seemed to mock his efforts. But the key remained elusive, and as dawn approached, he descended the creaking stairs, defeated but not broken, his mind churning with a mixture of anxiety and determination. He wouldn't rest until he unlocked the chest's secrets, until he found a rational explanation for everything that had been happening. He had to. His family depended on it. His sanity depended on it. And deep down, he knew, the fate of his family, and perhaps his very soul, was inextricably tied to the secrets hidden within the walls of Blackwood Lane. The denial was a fragile shield, and he could feel the cracks spreading, threatening to expose the terrifying truth hidden beneath the surface.

Marys Investigation

The next morning, the house felt different. The silence, usually a heavy blanket, now felt expectant, almost… watchful. John was gone, off to work, leaving Mary with a gnawing unease that settled deep in her bones. Emily was still asleep, her small form curled tightly under the covers, the lingering scent of fear clinging to her room like a phantom. Mary knew she couldn't stay hidden, couldn't let the fear consume her. She had to act, had to find answers, even if it meant delving deeper into the chilling history of Blackwood Lane.

She started with the local library. The librarian, a kindly old woman with eyes that held a hint of knowing sadness, directed her to the local historical society. There, amongst dusty tomes and yellowed documents, she found a treasure trove of information about Blackwood Lane, its history far more sinister than she had ever imagined.

The society's archives held newspaper clippings, dating back over a century, detailing strange occurrences, disappearances, and unexplained deaths connected to the house and its surrounding area. One particularly chilling article recounted the tale of the Blackwood family, the original owners of the house. Their story was a chilling saga of madness, betrayal, and tragic demise. The patriarch, Silas Blackwood, a recluse with a penchant for the occult, was said to have conducted strange rituals within the house's walls, and his family members had met with inexplicable fates.

There were stories of ghostly apparitions, unsettling sounds, and objects moving on their own. One account described a young girl, eerily similar in age to Emily, who was found wandering the woods near Blackwood Lane, babbling incoherently about shadows and whispers before disappearing without a trace. Mary felt a cold shiver crawl down her spine as she read the description, a sense of dread tightening her chest. Emily's nightmares suddenly seemed less like childish fantasies and more like echoes of a disturbing past.

As she delved further, Mary uncovered local legends surrounding Blackwood Lane. The stories spoke of a dark energy that clung to the land, a malevolent force that fed on the fears and anxieties of its inhabitants. There were whispers of sacrifices made to appease this entity, of families driven to madness by its influence. The stories were chilling, steeped in folklore and superstition, but they resonated with the unsettling occurrences plaguing her own family.

The more she learned, the more isolated she felt. She found herself keeping her discoveries from John, her fear that he would dismiss it all as nonsense too great to overcome. Their relationship, once a rock of stability, now seemed fractured, strained by the weight of unspoken anxieties. Emily, too, seemed withdrawn, her usual vivaciousness replaced by a haunted quiet.

The house was changing, too. The whispers intensified, growing louder, more menacing. Objects moved with increasing frequency, defying the laws of physics. Doors creaked open and slammed shut on their own, and shadows danced in the periphery, always just out of sight. The once comforting familiarity of their home now felt alien, menacing.

One evening, while sifting through an old trunk she'd found in the attic, Mary discovered a diary. Its leather cover was worn and cracked, and the pages were brittle with age, but the elegant script within held a captivating narrative. It belonged to Eliza Blackwood, Silas's daughter, and it painted a vivid picture of a life consumed by fear and despair. Eliza's diary chronicled the strange occurrences within the house, the growing madness of her father, and the increasingly disturbing behavior of her siblings.

Eliza described unsettling visions, the feeling of being watched, and the constant presence of shadows that seemed to move and shift just beyond the edge of her vision. She wrote about whispered voices that seemed to emanate from the walls, voices that urged her to do things she didn't want to do, things that terrified her. The diary ended abruptly, mid-sentence, with only a scrawled note: "They're coming."

The diary's revelations only intensified Mary's fear, her sense of isolation deepening. She couldn't confide in anyone, not even John. He wouldn't understand, wouldn't believe her. She was alone, trapped in a house with a dark history, surrounded by a family whose sanity was beginning to fray under the pressure of unseen forces.

She tried to contact the local police, but they dismissed her concerns, chalking it up to stress and the impact of moving to a new home. The local priest, a kind, older man who initially listened with sympathy, seemed to grow increasingly uncomfortable with her story. He offered prayers, but he could offer no solutions.

Nightmares plagued her sleep, vivid visions of the Blackwood family, their faces twisted in agony and fear. She dreamt of shadows, of whispers, of a cold, malevolent presence that seemed to seep from the walls. The dreams bled into her waking hours, leaving her feeling constantly on edge, her senses heightened, her heart pounding in her chest.

She began to see patterns in the events, a rhythm to the chaos. The whispers seemed to intensify at certain times of the day, particularly around midnight and dawn. Objects moved more frequently during periods of high emotional stress. She suspected the entity, or whatever it was, fed off negative energy, off the fears and anxieties of the house's inhabitants.

Her investigation had begun to isolate her from the world, isolating her family within the four walls of their nightmare. She could feel the growing distance between herself and John, and her relationship with her daughter was more strained than ever. Emily's fear was a palpable thing, and it created a chasm between them.

The line between sanity and madness blurred. Was she losing her mind? Or was the house, the history, the secrets within those old walls, slowly consuming them all? The answer, she knew, lay buried deep within the house's history, and she was determined to find it, even if it meant risking everything. She was consumed by the idea that the secrets of Blackwood Lane wouldn't simply let her family go. This was a fight for their sanity, their lives, and perhaps, their very souls. The shadows grew longer, the whispers louder, and the weight of Blackwood Lane's secrets threatened to crush them all. The past was encroaching, its icy grip tightening, threatening to steal away what little remained of their present.

The Symbols Meaning

Emily, ever the observant one, had noticed it first. A small, almost insignificant symbol, etched into the woodwork, subtly hidden beneath layers of paint in the attic. It was a circle, bisected by a vertical line, with two smaller circles flanking the larger one. At first, she'd dismissed it as an old craftsman's mark, a quirk of the house's age. But as she began to see it more frequently – carved into the fireplace mantel, subtly woven into the patterns of the old wallpaper, even scratched into the dusty windowpanes – a sense of unease began to creep into her young heart. It wasn't a childish fear; it was a deeper, more visceral unease, like the prickling of a thousand tiny needles on her skin.

The symbol haunted her dreams, appearing in increasingly vivid and disturbing visions. She dreamt of shadowy figures performing ritualistic dances around a blazing bonfire, the symbol blazing in its heart. The figures chanted in a language she didn't understand, their faces obscured by darkness, yet their movements full of terrifying purpose. The dreams left her waking up in a cold sweat, her heart pounding, the image of the symbol burned into her mind.

One day, while searching the attic, she stumbled upon an old leather-bound book hidden within a decaying trunk. Its pages were brittle and yellowed with age, its language archaic and difficult to decipher. But interspersed between the faded text were several illustrations – detailed drawings of the symbol. Beneath one illustration, a chilling inscription in faded ink: "The Mark of Malkor."

Mary, initially dismissing Emily's findings as more childish nightmares, was forced to confront the truth when she saw the book herself. The archaic script was partially decipherable with online assistance and a dictionary of older dialects. It spoke of Malkor, a dark entity, a malevolent god worshipped by a secretive cult that had once thrived in the Blackwood Lane area. The cult's rituals, according to the book, were gruesome, involving human sacrifice to appease Malkor and maintain his malevolent power. The symbol, the book revealed, was a sigil, a mark of power used to summon and channel Malkor's influence.

The revelation hit Mary like a physical blow. The unsettling occurrences, the whispers, the moving objects – they all began to make a horrifying kind of sense. It wasn't just a haunted house; it was a place of ritualistic sacrifice, a nexus of dark energy. The house wasn't merely old; it was imbued with the malevolence of centuries of dark practices. The symbol wasn't merely a decoration; it was an open invitation.

The discovery sent a shockwave through the already fragile Miller family. John, initially skeptical, now found himself wrestling with a chilling possibility. He had dismissed Mary's concerns as stress and imagination, but now, confronted with the tangible evidence of the book, he found it harder to deny the terrifying reality. He watched in growing horror as the previously inexplicable events now seemed to correlate with the presence of the symbol.

The whispers intensified. They were no longer random murmurs; they were distinct voices, chanting the name Malkor in a guttural, horrifying tongue. Objects moved with a deliberate purpose, seeming to orchestrate themselves into disturbing patterns, each arrangement hinting at the dark rituals described in the book. The shadows were no longer merely fleeting glimpses in the periphery; they were sentient entities, moving and shifting like living things. Emily, ever sensitive, was the first to notice the correlation, her already frazzled nerves pushed to the brink. The mere sight of the symbol seemed to trigger more intense paranormal phenomena, escalating into a chilling pattern.

Their home, once a sanctuary, had become a living nightmare. Every room was a potential source of terror, every corner held a lurking dread. Sleep became a luxury they could no longer afford. The weight of the past, the dark legacy of Blackwood Lane, pressed down upon them, suffocating them with its sinister presence.

Their interactions became increasingly strained, their fears and anxieties fueling the growing paranoia. Accusations flew between Mary and John, the stress of the situation tearing at the fabric of their marriage. Emily, caught in the middle, retreated further into herself, her fear manifesting as outbursts of erratic behavior and silent terrors.

They tried to fight back, to cleanse the house, to eradicate the symbol's presence. They scrubbed at the walls, scraping away paint, trying to obliterate any trace of the sigil. They burned sage, chanted prayers, called in a priest who arrived trembling and refused to approach anything close to the symbol. But their efforts proved futile. The symbol reappeared, its presence stronger than ever, like a persistent stain on the soul of the house.

The escalating events led to increasingly irrational actions. John, driven by a desperate need to protect his family, began to suspect Mary, convinced that she was somehow to blame, somehow involved in the evil that seemed to grip their home. Mary, equally terrified, found herself losing faith in her sanity. Was it real? Or was the stress, the fear, making them hallucinate? The line blurred, the boundaries of their reality warped and twisted by the dark energy surrounding them.

One night, driven by fear and desperation, John tried to destroy the book, convinced it was the source of the evil. In his panicked rage, he nearly strangled Mary. He believed that she was in league with the spirits, convinced her presence was facilitating the hauntings. The desperation and fear that had begun with whispers in the dark had transformed their family home into a battleground. The battle wasn't simply with the paranormal; it was a terrifying battle against their own fears, against the loss of sanity and the fracturing of their relationships.

As the darkness deepened, Emily's visions became more potent, more prescient. In her dreams, she saw the cultists returning, drawn by the reactivation of the sigil. She saw the shadows coalescing into menacing forms, preparing for a horrific ritual. The dreams were warnings, desperate pleas from the past, desperate attempts to prevent a repetition of the horrors of Blackwood Lane. Emily's terrified cries in her sleep were the only warnings the family had in a world where reality became a blurry, terrifying landscape. The house, their once beloved home, was preparing for something terrible, something ancient and utterly malevolent. The past was not merely haunting them; it was returning, demanding its due. The Millers' idyllic suburban dream had become a fight for survival, a desperate struggle against the encroaching darkness of Blackwood Lane.

Paranoid Delusions

The flickering gas lamp cast long, dancing shadows across the living room, transforming familiar furniture into grotesque parodies of their former selves. A grandfather clock, usually a comforting presence, now seemed to tick with a malevolent rhythm, each second a hammer blow against their already frayed nerves. John, his face etched with exhaustion and suspicion, stared at Mary across the room. He'd seen her earlier, whispering softly to herself, her eyes wide and unfocused, a tremor running through her body. He'd dismissed it as fatigue at first, the understandable consequence of their ordeal. But the doubt, a seed of paranoia planted in the fertile ground of fear, had begun to sprout.

"Mary," he began, his voice tight with barely suppressed accusation, "what was that you were saying? I heard you... muttering."

Mary flinched, her gaze darting nervously around the room. The shadows seemed to deepen, to press closer, to feed on her fear. "Nothing," she replied, her voice barely above a whisper. "Just... thinking." But the lie hung heavy in the air, a palpable thing that neither of them could ignore. The constant whispers, the unsettling movements of objects, the oppressive weight of the house itself – it was enough to unravel anyone's sanity. Now, even the most mundane actions fueled their growing suspicions.

That night, the whispers escalated. They weren't just faint murmurs anymore; they were distinct voices, malevolent and chilling, chanting in a language that seemed both ancient and utterly alien. The words seemed to penetrate their very bones, resonating deep within their subconscious, chilling them to the core. John grabbed a heavy iron poker, his hand slick with sweat, his heart pounding a frantic rhythm against his ribs. He felt a primal urge to protect his family, but from what? From the house itself? Or from each other?

Emily, meanwhile, was suffering in a different way. Her dreams, once nightmarish visions of the symbol and the shadowy figures, had morphed into something far more unsettling. She dreamt not of the past, but of the future – of dark figures emerging from the shadows, their eyes burning with malevolent light, their movements purposeful and terrifying. In her dreams, she saw the symbol pulsating with an unnatural energy, drawing the darkness closer, preparing for some unspeakable ritual. These visions bled into her waking hours, turning every shadow, every creak of the house into a tangible threat. She began to see the symbol everywhere – not just etched into the woodwork, but superimposed over the faces of her parents, her own reflection in the mirror.

The blurring of reality and delusion became a constant, exhausting torment. Was it the house, or was it their minds, their collective fear that had warped their perception of reality? Each of them began to suspect the other. Mary found herself questioning John's sanity. His quick temper, his increasingly erratic behavior, his obsession with destroying any trace of the symbol – it all seemed to point towards a deeper madness. John, in turn, viewed Mary's increasingly erratic behavior, her sudden fits of terror and her strange pronouncements as being influenced by the house's dark presence. Emily, caught in the crossfire of their mutual suspicion, became the silent, observing victim, her own growing paranoia a chilling testament to the house's influence.

They tried rational explanations, clinging to logic like drowning men to driftwood. The house was old, they reasoned; the settling foundation, the drafty windows, the old plumbing – these were all contributing to the strange sounds and movement. Stress, lack of sleep, fear itself could account for the hallucinations, the growing paranoia, and the increasingly violent disagreements. Yet, with each passing day, the rationalizations became weaker, the evidence of their increasingly fractured reality mounting.

One evening, during a particularly violent storm, the power went out. The house plunged into absolute darkness, the silence broken only by the howling wind and the relentless pounding of rain against the windows. The darkness seemed to amplify the sounds, the whispers, the creaking floorboards. In the darkness, John's fear reached its peak. He became convinced that Mary was actively participating in the malevolent activity, that she was somehow communicating with the dark entity. A dark suspicion had begun to fester within him that she might be intentionally prolonging the haunting, and thus his fears began to consume him, driving him to the brink of madness. Driven by a desperate need for control, he searched her belongings, hoping to find some evidence to support his growing delusions.

Mary, equally terrified, found herself reacting defensively. Her own growing suspicion towards John's irrationality and paranoia further fueled the escalating conflict. Accusations became accusations, fueled by an irrational and all-consuming fear. The lines between reality and delusion blurred further, each incident feeding the other, pushing them closer and closer to a violent confrontation.

The storm raged outside, mirroring the tempest brewing within the Miller family. The house itself seemed to be a sentient entity, feeding off their fear, their growing desperation, their fractured reality. As the night wore on, the darkness seemed to wrap around them, suffocating them, turning their once beloved home into a cage of terror and suspicion. Emily, huddled in her bed, felt the walls closing in. Her own internal landscape, already fractured, threatened to shatter completely under the weight of their collective fear. The events of the night were the final fracturing of their reality. What began with a move to a dream home had turned into a nightmare. The only question remaining was whether they would survive long enough to see the dawn.

The Confrontation

The darkness was a suffocating blanket, pressing down on them, amplifying every creak, every whisper, every frantic beat of their hearts. John, fueled by a paranoia that had spiraled out of control, lunged at Mary. He'd found it – a small, leather-bound journal tucked away in her dresser drawer. It wasn't filled with sinister incantations or dark rituals as he'd imagined, but with poetry, heartfelt reflections, and sketches of wildflowers. Yet, to his fevered mind, the simple act of her keeping a secret felt like confirmation of his worst fears. He saw it as a deliberate concealment, a plot to deceive him, to further the malevolent presence within the house.

"You lied to me!" he roared, his voice echoing in the oppressive silence. He grabbed her arm, his grip tight enough to bruise. "You knew! You knew about this… this evil!" He shook her roughly, his eyes blazing with a terrifying intensity.

Mary, her face pale and drawn, struggled against his grip. "John, let go!" she cried, her voice choked with fear and pain. "I haven't lied to you! It's the house, it's doing this to us!" But her words were lost in the storm raging both outside and within their fractured relationship. His accusations were like blows, each one landing with the force of a physical assault.

The struggle escalated quickly. The iron poker, still clutched in his other hand, became a weapon. He swung it wildly, missing Mary, but cracking the already fragile antique mirror hanging over the fireplace. The shattering glass added a new layer of terror to the scene, the shards scattered across the floor like a gruesome testament to their failing relationship.

Emily, awakened by the commotion, screamed from her bedroom. Her screams were swallowed by the storm and the escalating fight between her parents. She watched, paralyzed with fear, as the shadows danced and twisted in the flickering gaslight, morphing into grotesque figures that mirrored her own growing sense of dread. The fight wasn't just between her parents; it was a battle between sanity and madness, played out in the heart of their collapsing world.

Mary, desperate to break free, kicked out, connecting with John's leg. He stumbled, losing his balance, and fell heavily against the antique grandfather clock. The clock, already seeming to tick with a malevolent rhythm, crashed to the floor, its pendulum swinging wildly before coming to a stop, the sound of its demise echoing their own fractured reality.

The fight continued, a chaotic ballet of fear and rage. John's accusations were fuelled by a rising tide of paranoia, each blow a desperate attempt to regain control, to dispel the creeping dread that had consumed him. Mary, fighting back in self-defense, was left with bruises and scratches, a physical manifestation of their shattered family unit. Her desperate attempts to reason with him were met with escalating violence.

The storm outside mirrored the tempest raging within their hearts. The wind howled like a banshee, rattling the windows, and the rain beat against the glass as if trying to force its way in, to claim them as its own. The darkness of the house seemed to press in on them, amplifying their fear, their rage, their despair. The house itself seemed to revel in their suffering, its silent malevolence a palpable presence in the room.

Finally, exhausted and bleeding, John collapsed onto the floor, his breathing ragged, his eyes wide and unfocused. Mary, her body trembling, knelt beside him, her heart heavy with a mixture of fear, anger, and profound sadness. The violence had shattered something fundamental within them, fracturing their relationship beyond repair. The fight had not banished the fear; it had only served to deepen the chasm between them, pushing them further into the abyss of despair and mutual distrust.

Emily, still trembling in her room, crept out, her eyes wide with terror. The scene before her was a horrifying tableau of shattered furniture, broken glass, and two broken people. The house, once their dream home, now resembled a battleground, a macabre reflection of their fractured reality. The silence that followed the violence was heavier, more oppressive than the storm had been.

The next morning, the storm had passed. But the tempest in their hearts continued to rage. A fragile truce settled between John and Mary, a strained silence that spoke volumes about the depth of their wounds. The physical wounds would heal, the bruises would fade, but the emotional scars would remain, a constant reminder of the night the darkness within their home had consumed them. The house stood silent, its secrets intact, waiting for the next opportunity to sow further discord and chaos.

Emily, however, was irrevocably changed. The violence, the fear, the sight of her parents consumed by rage – it had imprinted itself on her psyche, leaving her with a deep-seated sense of fear and isolation. She retreated into herself, a silent observer of their fractured family dynamic, her innocent eyes reflecting the darkness that had enveloped them all. The world, once a place of wonder and excitement, had transformed into a landscape of fear and distrust. She began to see the symbol not just etched into the house's woodwork, but everywhere – a constant, silent reminder of the night her parents had destroyed not only the house, but also the illusion of a perfect family.

The silence between them was a constant, deafening presence, a testament to the damage inflicted. Each looked at the other with suspicion, their shared experiences now twisted into a web of accusations and mistrust. Attempts at conversation were stilted, filled with unspoken resentments and lingering fears. The house, once a source of shared dreams, had become a physical manifestation of their fractured reality, each room a silent witness to their escalating conflict.

Their shared meals were punctuated by awkward silences, the clinking of silverware a jarring counterpoint to the unspoken tension. The once vibrant laughter and lively discussions were replaced by a heavy, oppressive silence. Even the simplest tasks, once performed with shared effort and affection, now felt burdened by the weight of their strained relationship.

The children's laughter, once the soundtrack of their lives, was now a distant memory, replaced by the constant murmur of fear and suspicion. The once warm and inviting atmosphere had been poisoned, the house itself now seemed to reflect the darkness that consumed them.

Days bled into weeks, the silence becoming a tangible presence, a constant reminder of their shared trauma. The fear of another violent outburst hung heavy in the air, a silent threat that poisoned their every interaction. The cracks in their reality had widened, threatening to shatter their family completely. The idyllic suburban dream had morphed into a chilling nightmare, leaving them struggling to survive, not only the house's malevolence, but also their own fractured minds. The house, it seemed, had won. It had shattered their sanity, their trust, and their family. The dawn arrived each morning, but it brought with it no respite, only the chilling reminder of the night the darkness had descended upon Blackwood Lane, transforming their dream home into a living hell. The nightmare wasn't just in the house; it was within them, a haunting presence that threatened to consume them completely. The silence was deafening, the unspoken accusations hanging heavier than the shadows that danced across the walls. The future, once bright with promise, was now shrouded in a thick fog of uncertainty and fear. Their fight was far from over; the battle for their sanity, their relationship, and their very survival, had only just begun.

Emilys Escape

The back door, usually a reassuring exit, felt heavy, almost sentient, resisting her efforts. Emily tugged, her small hands slipping on the cold, damp wood. The storm, though subsided outside, raged within the house, a palpable pressure pressing against her, a malevolent force that seemed to emanate from the very walls themselves. She tried the knob again, her knuckles white, her breath hitching in her throat. Locked.

Panic clawed at her, a cold, sharp terror that tightened its grip around her chest. She stumbled back, her eyes darting around the kitchen, desperately searching for another way out. The windows, tall and narrow, were secured with old-fashioned latches, impenetrable barriers against her desperate flight. Even the cellar door, usually ajar, was firmly shut, its heavy oak a forbidding obstacle. She was trapped.

The house, it seemed, had become her prison. The familiar layout, once comforting, now felt hostile, alien. Every shadow seemed to writhe, every creak a sinister whisper. The once-loved antique grandfather clock, its face shattered, lay like a fallen soldier, a silent testament to the night's violence. Its broken hands pointed to a time that seemed to exist outside the normal flow of reality, a time frozen in chaos and fear.

A low moan echoed from the hallway, a sound that sent shivers down her spine. It wasn't the wind; it was something else, something that felt both ancient and intensely malevolent. The moan morphed into a whisper, then a guttural growl, growing in intensity, echoing through the silent house. Emily pressed herself against the cool surface of the refrigerator, her heart hammering against her ribs, a frantic drumbeat in the suffocating silence.

She thought of her parents, their faces etched with a weariness that went beyond physical exhaustion. The fight, the accusations, the raw, unbridled anger – it had left scars that ran deeper than any bruise. The house had exploited their vulnerabilities, their weaknesses, turning their love into a battlefield. And now, it was turning its malevolent attention to her.

Remembering her mother's words, whispered amidst the chaos, "It's the house, it's doing this to us," Emily found a terrifying sense of validation. It wasn't just her parents' failing marriage; it was something far more sinister, something ancient and powerful, that was manipulating them, tearing them apart. The house was alive, she realized, feeding off their fear, their pain, their despair.

Driven by a primal instinct for survival, Emily began to search for an escape route. The attic, a dusty, forgotten space filled with cobweb-draped furniture and forgotten memories, seemed her only hope. She crept upstairs, her small feet making barely a sound on the creaking floorboards. Each step was a calculated risk, a gamble against the growing sense of dread that pressed down on her, choking her with its suffocating weight.

The attic door, heavy and warped with age, groaned as she heaved it open. Dust motes danced in the slivers of light filtering through the grimy windows, illuminating the shadowy space. The air was thick with the smell of decay, a mixture of dust, mildew, and something else… something ancient and unsettling.

The attic was a labyrinth of forgotten belongings. Trunks overflowed with yellowed photographs and moth-eaten clothing. Broken toys lay scattered amongst the debris, their painted smiles frozen in a macabre grin. A chipped porcelain doll, its eyes wide and vacant, stared at her from a darkened corner, its expression eerily lifelike. Emily felt a cold dread creep into her heart; the doll seemed to watch her, to know her deepest fears.

As she searched for a way out, she noticed something unusual—a hidden passage, concealed behind a tapestry depicting a dark, foreboding forest. It was a small opening, barely large enough for her to squeeze through, yet it offered a glimmer of hope. With trembling hands, she pushed aside the heavy tapestry, revealing a narrow, dimly lit passageway leading to the darkness beyond.

The passage was claustrophobic, the air thick with the smell of damp earth and decay. The only light came from the faint glow filtering from the attic, casting long, dancing shadows that seemed to writhe and twist like living things. Each step was a struggle; the passage was uneven, filled with loose stones and debris. Yet, driven by a desperate need to escape, she pressed on, her heart pounding in her chest like a frantic bird trapped in a cage.

The passage opened into a small, damp cellar. The air was cold and heavy, the silence broken only by the drip, drip, drip of water from a leaking pipe. The cellar was filled with cobwebs and forgotten relics, a silent testament to the house's long and mysterious history. She saw old tools, rusty and discarded, and decaying wooden boxes that whispered of forgotten secrets.

Suddenly, a cold gust of wind swept through the cellar, extinguishing the meager light filtering from the passage.

Emily gasped, her heart leaping into her throat. Darkness enveloped her completely, a profound and suffocating darkness that seemed to press in on her from all sides. She stumbled, her hands reaching out blindly, her fingers brushing against cold, damp stone.

A low growl emanated from the darkness, close enough to make her flinch. The growl was followed by a series of whispers, soft yet menacing, words she couldn't understand, yet felt deep within her bones. She felt a presence, a malevolent entity, that seemed to be circling her, toying with her, drawing her deeper into the darkness.

Terror, raw and primal, seized her. She was trapped, not just in the cellar, but in the house's suffocating grasp. The darkness wasn't simply an absence of light; it was a sentient force, feeding on her fear, mocking her desperation. She screamed, a desperate, high-pitched sound swallowed by the oppressive silence of the cellar.

Suddenly, a cold hand reached out from the darkness, its touch icy and unnerving. Emily shrieked, her body convulsing with terror. She fought back, kicking and struggling, but the darkness held her, wrapping its icy tendrils around her, pulling her deeper into its chilling embrace. The whispers grew louder, more menacing, merging into a cacophony of sounds that tore at her sanity.

She felt herself being dragged, her body scraping against the cold, damp stone, the rough texture of the walls tearing at her clothes. She fought back with all her might, but it was no use; the darkness was overwhelming, its power far greater than hers. She was helpless, a small, frightened child facing an ancient, malevolent entity that seemed to be born from the very heart of the house. The house, once her home, had become her tomb. The darkness was her final destination, a chilling end to her desperate attempt to escape the nightmare she was trapped within. The whispers grew louder, until they became a deafening roar. Then, silence. A terrifying, absolute silence.

Johns Breakdown

The silence in the aftermath of Emily's disappearance hung heavy, a suffocating blanket woven from fear and regret. John sat slumped in his armchair, the worn leather creaking under his weight, a stark contrast to the unnerving stillness of the house. He hadn't slept properly in days, the fragmented images of Emily's terror, the chilling echoes of her screams, replaying endlessly in his mind. His eyes, bloodshot and hollow, reflected the flickering candlelight, casting dancing shadows that seemed to mock his despair.

The initial denial, the desperate clinging to the rational explanation – a runaway child, a simple accident – had crumbled like dry leaves under a relentless wind. The house, once a symbol of their aspirations, had become a monstrous entity, a malevolent presence that had systematically dismantled his family, piece by agonizing piece. He remembered the initial charm, the perfect façade, the whispers of Blackwood Lane's idyllic past, all now replaced by a chilling emptiness, a pervasive sense of dread.

He'd scoffed at Mary's anxieties, her increasingly frantic pronouncements about the house's malevolence. He'd dismissed her growing fear as a manifestation of her own insecurities, a product of the strain their failing marriage had placed on her already fragile mental state. Now, staring at the empty space where Emily once sat, the cold, hard truth slammed into him like a physical blow. He had been wrong, tragically, irrevocably wrong.

He ran a trembling hand through his thinning hair, the gesture revealing the deep-seated exhaustion that etched itself onto his face. The lines around his eyes, once laugh lines etched by shared joys and family laughter, now reflected a profound weariness, a harrowing testament to the psychological war they had been waging against an unseen enemy. The laughter, the light, the joy—all had faded, leaving behind a landscape of fear and uncertainty. The vibrant tapestry of family life had been torn apart, thread by agonizing thread.

The events of the past few weeks had been a relentless assault on his senses, a descent into a nightmarish reality that defied logic and reason. The strange occurrences, initially dismissed as mere coincidences or tricks of the mind, had escalated into a terrifying symphony of the uncanny – whispers in empty rooms, objects moving inexplicably, doors slamming shut with violent force, shadows that danced in the periphery of his vision. Each event, once an isolated incident, had become a chilling piece in a larger, more sinister puzzle.

The shattering of the grandfather clock, a treasured family heirloom, had been the turning point. The broken hands, frozen at a time that seemed to exist outside the normal flow of reality, had felt like a symbolic representation of their fractured family, their shattered lives, their disintegrating sanity. He remembered the chilling cold that swept through the house, the pervasive sense of unease that permeated every room, chilling his very soul.

His rational mind, the one he'd always relied upon, had begun to crumble under the weight of the inexplicable. The logical explanations, the attempts to rationalize the paranormal occurrences, now seemed like pathetic attempts to cling to sanity in the face of the terrifying unknown. He felt the creeping tendrils of fear snaking around his heart, slowly tightening their grip, suffocating him. The rational had succumbed to the irrational, the logical to the supernatural.

He recalled the escalating arguments with Mary, the accusations of infidelity, the unspoken resentments, all fueled by the insidious presence that seemed to revel in their misery. The house, he now realized, hadn't simply been a witness to their marital strife; it had been an active participant, manipulating their emotions, exacerbating their vulnerabilities, turning their love into a battlefield. It had been playing them like puppets on strings, pulling their emotions and actions into a grotesque dance of destruction.

The guilt gnawed at him, a relentless tormentor whispering accusations into the dark recesses of his mind. He hadn't been there for Mary, hadn't recognized the depth of her desperation. He'd been so consumed by his own anxieties, his own failures, that he'd failed to see the subtle signs, the growing desperation in her eyes. The cracks in their relationship, already present, had been ruthlessly exploited by the house. The house had been the unseen catalyst, accelerating their decline.

He had been so caught up in the minutiae of his life – his work, his anxieties, his growing distance from his wife – that he hadn't been paying attention to the subtle warnings, the growing sense of unease that had enveloped their lives. He'd dismissed them as stress, as a product of their tumultuous marriage. But now, he saw them for what they were – harbingers of the terrifying reality that threatened to consume them all. He had failed to protect his family, his wife, his daughter. The weight of his failure was crushing.

John closed his eyes, the image of Emily's terrified face flashing before him. He could almost feel the chilling touch of her fear. He'd dismissed her fear as childish fantasy, a product of an overactive imagination. Now, he understood the truth. Her fear had been real, as real as the growing shadow that had fallen over their lives. Her fear had been a premonition of the nightmare that had unfolded before him.

A sob escaped his lips, a sound of raw despair. He had been so blinded by his own self-interest that he had failed to recognize the sinister presence that was consuming them. He had been so focused on maintaining the facade of a perfect suburban life that he hadn't seen the cracks forming, the darkness spreading, until it was too late. Now, the darkness had swallowed everything, his family, his marriage, his sanity.

He sank deeper into the armchair, the weight of the world pressing down upon him. He'd clung to rationality, to logic, but the house had shattered those defenses, leaving him exposed, vulnerable, and broken. He had failed his family, and his failure had been exploited, amplified, and twisted into a horrific reality by the house's malevolent influence.

He confessed it to himself, whispering it into the suffocating silence of the house. He acknowledged the possibility – no, the terrifying certainty – that something supernatural, something ancient and evil, was at play. The house wasn't just old; it was alive, sentient, malevolent. It was a parasitic entity, feeding on their fear, their pain, their despair. And it had succeeded in its twisted game.

The tears flowed freely now, a torrent of grief, guilt, and terror. He finally understood Mary's warnings, her fears. He had dismissed them as the ravings of a distraught woman, a casualty of their crumbling marriage. Now, he understood. It wasn't just their marriage falling apart; it was their reality, their sanity, their very lives.

He wasn't sure what he could do, how he could possibly fight against such an overwhelming force, but one thing was certain: his denial was over. He would no longer bury his head in the sand and pretend that everything was normal. He had to fight, not only for his own sanity but also to find his daughter, Emily, and face the terrifying truth that lay hidden within the walls of their dream home turned nightmare. He had to confront the darkness, and it would start with acknowledging its existence. The weight of his guilt, his fear, his responsibility now rested heavily on his shoulders. The fight for his family's survival, for their sanity, for their very lives, would begin now. And he would face it, no matter the cost.

Marys Discovery

The attic door, warped and groaning like an ancient beast awakening from a long slumber, creaked open under Mary's hesitant touch. Dust motes, disturbed by the sudden intrusion of light, danced in the lone beam slicing through the gloom. The air hung heavy with the scent of decay and forgotten things, a chilling perfume that prickled her skin and tightened her chest. John had vehemently opposed her insistence on exploring the attic, his voice laced with a fatigue that went beyond mere exhaustion. It held the weary resignation of a man who had already accepted defeat. But a desperate hope, a flicker of a possibility that lay buried under layers of fear and despair, propelled her forward. She had to know. She had to understand.

She climbed the creaking stairs, each step a hesitant advance into the unknown. The attic was a cavernous space, choked with cobwebs that draped like spectral shrouds over discarded furniture and forgotten relics. Shadows clung to the corners, whispering secrets only the darkness understood. The silence was oppressive, broken only by the occasional groan of the old house settling, a sound that felt like a sinister sigh.

For weeks, she'd felt it – a presence, a malevolent energy that permeated every corner of the house, twisting her thoughts, fueling her anxieties. John had dismissed it as stress, as a manifestation of her own fragile mental state, exacerbated by the strain of their failing marriage. But Mary knew better. She felt it in the chilling drafts that swept through the house, regardless of the temperature outside. She sensed it in the inexplicable movements of objects, in the whispered voices that seemed to emanate from empty rooms.

She felt it in her bones, a deep-seated dread that had burrowed its way into her very being.

She ran her hand along the dusty surface of an old trunk, its wood worn smooth by time and neglect. Inside, nestled amongst yellowed fabrics and brittle lace, she found it – a leather-bound journal, its pages brittle with age, the ink faded but still legible. The cover bore a single, ornate letter: "E."

With trembling fingers, she opened the journal. The script within was elegant, flowing, yet tinged with a chilling undercurrent of despair. The entries chronicled the life of Eleanor Vance, a woman who had lived in the house a century ago. Eleanor's words painted a vivid picture of a life unraveling, mirroring the disintegration of the Miller family with eerie precision. The journal detailed escalating anxieties, unsettling occurrences, and a growing sense of isolation. The descriptions of disembodied whispers, objects moving on their own accord, and a chilling pervasive cold chillingly echoed Mary's own experiences.

Eleanor's entries grew increasingly frantic, her handwriting becoming jagged and erratic as her mental state deteriorated. She described a feeling of being watched, of being manipulated by a malevolent force that seemed to feed on her fear. The more she wrote, the more convinced Mary became that Eleanor's story wasn't just a tale of madness, but a chronicle of a terrifying reality.

One entry particularly sent a shiver down Mary's spine. Eleanor described a ritual, a dark ceremony performed in the attic, involving a summoning of something ancient and powerful. The details were fragmented, obscured by the passage of time and Eleanor's deteriorating mental state, but the implications were terrifyingly clear. This wasn't just a haunted house; it was a place of dark power, a nexus of malevolent energy.

As Mary read on, a horrifying realization dawned on her. The unsettling occurrences plaguing the Millers weren't random events, nor were they merely the product of their own troubled minds. They were a deliberate attack, a carefully orchestrated campaign of terror waged by something malevolent, something that had preyed on the inhabitants of Blackwood Lane for generations. The house itself was a conduit, an amplifier of this dark energy.

She found a hidden compartment beneath the final page of Eleanor's journal. Inside, tucked away in a small velvet pouch, was a silver locket. Opening it, she found a faded photograph of a young woman with haunting eyes, a chilling resemblance to Emily. Below the photograph was a cryptic inscription: "The cycle continues."

A cold dread, sharper than anything she had experienced before, pierced through her. It was a chilling revelation, confirming her worst fears. Emily's disappearance wasn't random; it was a continuation of a terrifying pattern, a ritualistic sacrifice to the dark entity that haunted the house. The house wasn't just driving them mad; it was actively preying on them, feeding on their fear and despair.

The realization hit her with the force of a physical blow. The fragmented whispers, the eerie shadows, the chilling cold – they weren't coincidences; they were warnings, signs of a malevolent presence that had claimed Eleanor a century ago and was now repeating the pattern with her family. She understood now, with terrifying clarity, the weight of the house's history, the burden of its dark legacy. Her family hadn't just moved into a dilapidated old house; they had moved into a nightmare.

Suddenly, a cold draft swept through the attic, extinguishing the single lamp Mary had used to illuminate the space. She was plunged into darkness, the silence now punctuated by a low, guttural growl that seemed to emanate from the very foundations of the house. Her heart hammered against her ribs, a frantic drumbeat against the encroaching fear.

She scrambled back down the stairs, the journal clutched tightly in her hand, the silver locket cold against her skin. The darkness seemed to press in on her, the silence heavy with a malevolent energy. She stumbled out of the attic, the door slamming shut behind her with a sound that echoed through the house, a chilling confirmation of her discovery.

The house had revealed its secrets, and the truth was more horrifying than she could have ever imagined. The unsettling occurrences, the growing fear, the sense of dread – they were not random events; they were signs of a dark force that had been lurking in the shadows for generations. Her family wasn't merely suffering from stress or a failing marriage; they were victims of a malevolent entity, trapped in a deadly game of survival.

The journal and the locket became tangible evidence of the horror they faced. The idyllic suburban dream had become a nightmarish struggle for survival, against a force that was ancient, powerful, and unrelenting. This wasn't just about saving her family; it was about breaking a cursed cycle that stretched back a century. The fight had begun, and Mary knew, with a chilling certainty, that they were fighting for their very lives.

She had to tell John, to share this terrifying truth with him. The denial, the rationalizations, had to end. They had to face the reality of their situation, however horrifying it might be.

They had to unite against the darkness, to fight back against the malevolent force that had consumed their lives. The time for denial was over. The time for action had arrived. They had to find Emily, to break the cycle, to confront the darkness that had enveloped Blackwood Lane. The fight for survival was far from over. The house had revealed its secrets, and now they had to face them, together, or perish. The game had begun, and the stakes were higher than they could have ever imagined.

Mary raced down the stairs, the chilling secrets of the house echoing in her mind. The house was alive, and it was determined to claim her family, one by one. But she would not let it win. She would fight for her family, for Emily's life, for her sanity, and for the hope that maybe, just maybe, they could still escape the clutches of Blackwood Lane's malevolent grip. The weight of the fight lay heavy upon her shoulders, but she carried it with newfound resolve. The truth was out, and the battle for survival had truly begun. The house had shown its hand, and now it was their turn to fight back.

The Cults History

The silver locket, cold against Mary's skin, felt like a brand, a chilling reminder of the terrible truth she held in her hands. Eleanor Vance's journal wasn't just a record of madness; it was a roadmap to a deeper, more sinister history, a history intertwined with a local cult known as the Blackwood Covenant. The name itself sent a shiver down her spine, its ominous resonance echoing the malevolent energy that seemed to pulse from the very walls of their house.

John, initially resistant to Mary's increasingly frantic pronouncements, finally agreed to help her research the Blackwood Covenant. He, too, was losing his grip on rationality, the constant unsettling occurrences chipping away at his skepticism. The rational explanation—stress, exhaustion, a failing marriage—no longer held any sway. The sheer weight of the unexplained events had driven them both to the brink of desperation.

Their investigation began in the town's historical archives, dusty repositories of forgotten records and yellowed newspaper clippings. The Blackwood Covenant, they discovered, was a secretive group, their origins shrouded in mystery, dating back centuries to the very founding of Blackwood Lane itself. Early records hinted at a pagan sect, practicing rituals that bordered on the barbaric, their practices veiled in secrecy and shrouded in an aura of fear.

The deeper they dug, the more disturbing the details became. Accounts spoke of disappearances, of strange occurrences linked to the old house, of whispers of human sacrifices performed under the cloak of darkness. The narratives, initially dismissed as folklore and superstition, became increasingly convincing as the evidence piled up. Newspaper clippings from the late 19th and early 20th centuries detailed disturbing events: unexplained deaths, livestock found mutilated, and a persistent sense of dread that seemed to cling to the very air around the old house on Blackwood Lane. There were mentions of ritualistic symbols found near the scene of some of these events, symbols that eerily mirrored those sketched in Eleanor's journal.

They unearthed a faded photograph of a group of people dressed in dark robes, their faces obscured by shadows, gathered around a bonfire. The picture was grainy and indistinct, yet Mary felt an unsettling familiarity with the location, the peculiar angle of the trees, the dark outline of the house in the background. It seemed to be the same house, or at least a strikingly similar one, that they now called home. The unsettling realization sent a wave of nausea through her. It felt as if history was repeating itself, a macabre pattern playing out before their very eyes.

John, his face pale and drawn, pointed to a passage in a particularly worn book detailing local folklore. "Look at this," he whispered, his voice hoarse. The passage described a ritual known as the "Binding of Souls," a dark ceremony meant to bind a malevolent entity to a chosen location, drawing its power from the fear and suffering of its victims. The location described? Their house on Blackwood Lane. The ritual, the passage continued, required a sacrifice, a living soul offered to the entity as sustenance. The chilling implication hung in the air between them, unspoken yet understood: Emily's disappearance wasn't an accident; it was an offering.

Their research led them to an abandoned church on the outskirts of town, its stained-glass windows shattered, its interior choked with weeds and debris. They discovered a hidden chamber beneath the church, a damp, subterranean space where the Blackwood Covenant had seemingly held their rituals. The walls were adorned with disturbing symbols, similar to the ones found in Eleanor's journal and the newspaper clippings. They found remnants of ancient ceremonies: scattered bones, charred offerings, and tattered pieces of cloth that seemed to bear the marks of a long-forgotten rite.

The air in the chamber was thick with a heavy, cloying scent, a mixture of decay and something far more sinister, something primal and unsettling. Mary felt a wave of nausea wash over her, a feeling of dread so intense it threatened to overwhelm her. She felt a presence, a malevolent energy that pulsed from the very stones beneath her feet. It felt as if the walls themselves were breathing, whispering secrets only the darkness understood.

Amid the debris, they discovered a collection of old documents, detailing the history and practices of the Blackwood Covenant. The documents were painstakingly written, revealing the dark rituals, the sacrifices, and the intricate web of power that bound the cult to the house on Blackwood Lane. The documents spoke of generations of sacrifices, their spirits bound to the house, fueling the entity's power. The house wasn't merely haunted; it was a nexus of negative energy, a conduit for a malevolent entity that fed on fear and suffering.

As they pieced together the scattered clues, a horrifying picture emerged. The Blackwood Covenant had been using the house as a focal point for their dark rituals for centuries. Each generation had added to the entity's power, feeding it with fear and despair. The unsettling events plaguing the Millers weren't random; they were carefully orchestrated, a deliberate attempt to lure more victims, to further fuel the entity's power. Emily's disappearance was only the latest link in this long and terrifying chain.

The documents also described a method for breaking the cycle, a ritual to banish the entity and sever its connection to the house. It was a perilous undertaking, a risky gamble with their lives hanging in the balance. But Mary and John knew that they had no choice. They had to confront the darkness, to fight against the malevolent entity that had claimed so many lives before them. They had to break the curse, not just for themselves, but for the generations to come. The cycle had to end.

The weight of responsibility pressed heavily upon their shoulders. They knew that failure would mean not only their own demise but the continuation of a horrific legacy, a centuries-old tradition of fear and sacrifice. The discovery of the Blackwood Covenant's history had filled them with a terrifying certainty—this wasn't merely a haunted house; it was a battleground for the ages, a fight for the very soul of Blackwood Lane. The fight, though daunting, had become their purpose, their only hope for survival. Their lives, and the fate of future generations, rested on their shoulders. The game, as Mary had known all along, had only just begun.

The Ritual

The worn leather-bound book lay open before them, its brittle pages illuminated by the weak beam of John's flashlight. The air in the abandoned church's hidden chamber hung heavy, thick with the scent of damp earth and something else… something ancient and unsettling, a smell that clung to the back of Mary's throat, choking her with a primal fear. The text, painstakingly transcribed in a spidery script, detailed the upcoming ritual, its chilling description etching itself onto their minds. It was called the "Harvest," a ceremony to appease the entity residing within their house, a grotesque offering meant to sustain its malevolent power.

The ritual, the book explained, required a specific sacrifice —a pure soul, untainted by malice or dark intent. The description sent a cold wave of dread washing over Mary. Emily… The thought of her missing daughter, her sweet, innocent face, flashed before her eyes, and a sob choked her. Could it be? Could Emily have been chosen? Was she already...gone?

The details of the Harvest were horrifyingly specific, outlining a series of intricate steps, arcane symbols, and chants that were meant to summon and appease the entity. The book described a grotesque dance of shadows and whispers, a macabre performance designed to placate the creature and ensure its continued presence in Blackwood Lane. The ritual was to take place under the full moon, a detail that sent a chill down John's spine. The full moon was only a few nights away.

John traced the cryptic symbols with a trembling finger, his heart pounding in his chest. They mirrored the symbols they'd found scrawled in Eleanor Vance's journal, etched into the walls of the hidden chamber, and even faintly etched into the weathered stones of their own house. They were not mere decorations; they were powerful sigils, conduits for dark energy, binding the entity to Blackwood Lane.

Suddenly, a low growl echoed from the depths of the chamber, a sound that vibrated through the very bones of the crumbling structure. Mary gasped, clutching John's arm. The air seemed to crackle with an unseen energy, a palpable sense of malevolence that pressed down on them, suffocating them. The flashlight beam flickered, threatened to extinguish, plunging them into near-total darkness. A chorus of whispers filled the silence, disembodied voices that seemed to crawl under their skin, whispering names, promises, threats.

Panic threatened to overwhelm them, but they held firm, their shared terror forging a fragile bond of determination. They were in this together, and they had to find a way out. They had to find a way to stop the Harvest.

The book detailed not only the ritual but also the means to disrupt it, a counter-ritual, a desperate gamble with their lives. The counter-ritual required a deep understanding of the entity's power, its weaknesses, its vulnerabilities. It was a complex procedure, demanding precise timing, specific ingredients, and an unwavering focus amidst overwhelming fear. Failure meant not only their own demise but the continued reign of terror over Blackwood Lane.

As they deciphered the ancient text, the enormity of their task became overwhelmingly clear. They were facing an entity far older, far more powerful, than they could have ever imagined. They were fighting against centuries of dark rituals, generations of sacrifices, a legacy of fear and despair.

It was a battle against an evil so entrenched, so deeply woven into the fabric of their home, that it seemed insurmountable.

The pages of the book revealed a chilling truth: the entity fed on fear, on despair, on the suffering of its victims. The more fear they expressed, the more powerful it became. This knowledge added another layer of terror to their already desperate situation. To win, they had to conquer not only the entity but also their own primal fears. They had to remain calm, focused, and resolute, even in the face of unimaginable horror.

The realization hit them like a physical blow: they were not just trying to save themselves; they were fighting for the soul of Blackwood Lane. The entity's power extended beyond their house, its malevolent influence corrupting the very essence of their community. This fight was not just for their family's survival; it was for the salvation of countless others.

The task seemed impossible, a David-and-Goliath struggle against a primordial evil. Yet, the urgency of the situation demanded action. The full moon loomed, the Harvest was imminent, and Emily's fate hung precariously in the balance. They had to gather the necessary components for the counter-ritual, locate the specific points of power within their house, and prepare themselves for the terrifying confrontation that awaited them.

Their investigation led them to the local botanical gardens, an unexpected source for some of the rare herbs needed for the counter-ritual. They spent hours searching through ancient texts and obscure botanical guides, identifying and carefully gathering the necessary ingredients. Each herb, each leaf, held a significance far beyond its botanical properties, each a piece of the puzzle in their desperate fight against the entity. The hunt for these ingredients felt far more dangerous than simply procuring them; each felt weighted with significance, with the lives of their family hanging in the balance.

The final ingredient was the most difficult to obtain: a stone imbued with the power of the earth itself, a stone said to have been used in ancient ceremonies to protect against evil. The location of the stone was hinted at in the book's final pages, a cryptic clue hidden within a seemingly unrelated passage. After painstaking research, they located the stone within the town's old cemetery, hidden beneath a forgotten, overgrown headstone, amidst the silent, watchful figures of the departed.

As they retrieved the stone, a cold wind swept through the cemetery, chilling them to the bone. The air felt thick with the presence of the dead, a palpable energy that seemed to emanate from the earth itself. They felt watched, observed by unseen eyes, a chilling sensation that underscored the danger of their mission.

With the final ingredient in hand, Mary and John returned to their house, the weight of their impending task pressing down on their shoulders. The house felt different now, the familiar surroundings transformed into a battleground, each room a potential site of conflict, each shadow a potential threat.

They prepared for the counter-ritual, meticulously following the instructions outlined in the ancient book. The process was both intricate and arduous, demanding a precision that tested their nerves and their resolve. Each step felt like walking a tightrope over a chasm of unimaginable horror. One mistake, one miscalculation, could mean the end.

As they completed the final preparations, the full moon rose high in the sky, casting long, eerie shadows that danced and writhed across their walls. The air hummed with an unsettling energy, a crescendo of fear and anticipation that clung to the very fabric of their home. The Harvest was about to begin. The battle for the soul of Blackwood Lane was about to commence. The ritual, they knew, was only the beginning of a fight that would test the limits of their sanity and the bonds of their family. The darkness that resided within their house was about to unleash its fury.

Seeking Help

The chilling weight of the impending ritual pressed down on John and Mary, a suffocating blanket of dread that amplified every creak of the house, every rustle of the wind. Their meticulous preparations felt inadequate, a desperate act against an overwhelming force. The full moon, a malevolent eye in the inky sky, cast long, distorted shadows that danced and writhed across their walls, transforming their familiar home into a grotesque parody of itself. They were alone, utterly alone, in their struggle against an ancient evil. The realization struck them with the force of a physical blow: they needed help.

Their first instinct was to call the police, to alert the authorities to the horrors they were facing. They imagined explaining it all: the whispers, the moving objects, the ancient book detailing a grotesque ritual, the missing daughter, Emily. The image of the incredulous look on the officer's face, the dismissive tone, the inevitable label of "stressed" or "delusional," paralyzed them. They knew, deep down, that no one would believe them. Their story was too fantastical, too unbelievable. Who would believe in an ancient entity, trapped within the walls of a seemingly ordinary suburban house?

The phone call remained unmade, a silent testament to their isolation, their desperate helplessness. They were trapped in a nightmare, cut off from the world, their cries for help unheard, unanswered. The silence itself felt oppressive, amplifying the dread that clawed at their hearts. The thought of attempting to explain their situation to anyone beyond the immediate family was daunting; the fear of ridicule, of dismissal, was as palpable as the presence of the entity itself.

They tried a different approach, reaching out to Eleanor Vance's family. The journal had mentioned distant relatives, and a little research yielded an address in a nearby town. Hope, fragile and fleeting, flickered within them. Perhaps someone from Eleanor's family would understand, would believe their story. Perhaps they possessed knowledge, or clues, that could help them.

Their drive to the Vance relative's home felt fraught with danger. The familiar suburban streets seemed to twist and turn, the houses morphing into ominous shapes in the moonlight. The air felt thick with a sense of foreboding, the silence broken only by the rhythmic thump of their car tires on the asphalt.

The Vance relative, an elderly woman named Agnes, lived in a small, unassuming cottage, its windows shrouded in shadows. John and Mary approached cautiously, the weight of their story heavy in their hearts. They recounted their ordeal, their voices trembling with a mixture of exhaustion and terror. They presented her with Eleanor's journal, hoping it would lend credibility to their terrifying tale.

Agnes listened intently, her face etched with a mixture of skepticism and a strange familiarity. She had heard whispers, rumors, about Blackwood Lane, about strange occurrences in that particular house. Tales of unexplained events, of missing persons, of a pervasive sense of unease that had plagued the neighborhood for generations. Stories dismissed as folklore, as the product of overactive imaginations, yet… Agnes's eyes held a hint of understanding, a shared knowledge of something dark and ancient.

"The entity," she said, her voice a low whisper, "It feeds on fear. The more you fear it, the stronger it becomes." Her words were a chilling confirmation of what John and Mary had already discovered. Their fear, their desperation, was fueling the entity's power.

Agnes revealed a hidden truth about Blackwood Lane. The houses, she explained, were built on ancient burial grounds, a place where dark rituals had been performed for centuries. The entity, she claimed, was a malevolent being, bound to the land, feeding on the fear and suffering of its inhabitants. Generations of families had suffered, their lives consumed by the entity's malevolent influence. The Millers were just the latest victims in a long, tragic history.

Agnes offered them some limited assistance, a few ancient remedies and protective charms, but her knowledge about the entity was limited. She couldn't stop it. She was just one woman, old and frail, fighting against a power far beyond her capabilities. Her words left John and Mary with a chilling sense of hopelessness. They were fighting a battle against centuries of darkness, a legacy of fear and suffering. They were alone, facing an impossible task.

Their next attempt to seek help involved contacting a local historian, Professor Armitage, a specialist in the town's occult history. Professor Armitage, a man with a reputation for his eccentricities and his deep knowledge of the town's darker past, was a long shot. He was known to be reluctant to engage with what he considered "fantastical claims," but desperation drove them to reach out. They meticulously detailed their experiences, providing him with copies of Eleanor Vance's journal and the ancient book.

Professor Armitage listened patiently, his eyes betraying a flicker of something resembling interest. He'd heard fragments of the legends surrounding Blackwood Lane, dismissed them as local folklore, but the evidence presented by the Millers was compelling. The detailed descriptions, the corroborating evidence within the ancient texts, were hard to ignore.

He confessed that he had always suspected something more sinister lay beneath the surface of the seemingly idyllic suburb. He had documented strange occurrences over the years, unexplained disappearances, unusual patterns of behavior in the residents. He had initially dismissed them as coincidences or the products of a highly stressed community, but the Millers' account tied everything together.

Professor Armitage, however, offered no easy solutions. He provided them with more historical context, confirming Agnes's claims about the ancient burial grounds. He detailed the history of similar entities bound to specific locations, fed by fear and despair. He explained the intricate rituals, the arcane symbols, the sacrifices. His knowledge, while extensive, didn't provide a practical solution to their immediate problem. He confirmed that they were facing a nearly insurmountable task, one that might require far more than a counter-ritual.

The professor did, however, suggest a daring approach – to try to contact a specialist in dealing with ancient entities, a renowned paranormal investigator living in a remote part of the country. This investigator, a recluse known only as Silas, operated outside the boundaries of conventional knowledge. His methods were unconventional, his knowledge esoteric, but his reputation preceded him. He was considered by some to be the last hope for those facing supernatural threats.

Reaching Silas proved to be another obstacle. He was incredibly difficult to contact, and when John and Mary finally reached him through a circuitous network of contacts, he was initially dismissive. He was used to people with wild claims; he had spent years battling deception and hoaxers. However, the sheer volume of evidence provided by the Millers, the meticulous details, and the overwhelming sense of genuine fear in their voices, finally broke through his cynicism.

Silas agreed to meet them, under strict conditions, in a remote location, a place far removed from Blackwood Lane. The journey to meet Silas was another harrowing experience. Every mile felt like they were moving further from hope, deeper into despair. The weight of their predicament threatened to crush them.

The meeting with Silas, though, provided a flicker of light in their darkness. Silas, a gaunt man with piercing eyes and a knowledge that seemed to transcend the boundaries of the normal world, listened patiently as the Millers recounted their ordeal. He confirmed the severity of their situation, acknowledging the power of the entity they were facing. He revealed that while the counter-ritual was a necessary step, it was far from sufficient to defeat the entity permanently.

Silas provided them with additional insights into the entity's weaknesses, a potential vulnerability they hadn't previously considered. He provided them with an amended counter-ritual, a more powerful version that, if performed correctly, might permanently banish the entity from Blackwood Lane. It involved a complex combination of ancient rituals, specific materials, and a precise understanding of the entity's energy patterns.

The task ahead remained daunting, fraught with danger, but the meeting with Silas provided a renewed sense of purpose. They were not alone in their fight; they had an ally, a guide, in their battle against the darkness that had consumed their lives. The full moon hung heavy in the sky, but for the first time in days, a glimmer of hope flickered within them, fragile, but strong enough to sustain them as they prepared for the final, desperate confrontation. The battle for the soul of Blackwood Lane was far from over, but the Millers were finally ready.

Betrayal

The amended ritual, painstakingly transcribed by Silas, lay spread across their kitchen table – a chaotic tapestry of arcane symbols and instructions, a roadmap to a battle against an ancient evil. John meticulously checked the ingredients: rare herbs gathered under specific lunar alignments, blessed candles from a forgotten monastery, a petrified shard of obsidian unearthed from a sacred spring. The air hung heavy with the scent of incense and the unspoken tension that vibrated between John, Mary, and their unlikely ally, Silas, who had remained to oversee the final preparations.

Their initial relief at finding a potential solution was quickly replaced by a growing unease. The ritual demanded precision, a flawless execution, and the slightest misstep could have devastating consequences. The weight of their responsibility pressed down on them, the fear of failure mingling with their determination. They were on the verge of confronting an entity that had tormented generations, and the stakes couldn't be higher.

Then came the betrayal.

It wasn't a dramatic, explosive act, but a subtle, insidious twist of the knife. It started with small inconsistencies, minor details that seemed insignificant at first, but slowly chipped away at their fragile unity. Mary, usually meticulous in her organization, misplaced vital ingredients. John, normally unflappable, displayed an unusual level of clumsiness, nearly ruining several meticulously prepared components. Silas, observant and sharp, noticed these discrepancies and a chilling realization began to dawn on him – one of them was working against them.

The cracks widened. A heated argument erupted between John and Mary, fueled by exhaustion, stress, and a deep-seated mistrust that had been festering since their arrival at Blackwood Lane. Accusations flew, each word a poisoned dart aimed at the heart of their already fragile relationship. The entity's influence, it seemed, was not limited to physical manifestations. It was also expertly manipulating their emotions, exacerbating their existing anxieties and driving a wedge between them.

The suspicion fell first on Mary. John had noticed her subtle hesitations, the almost imperceptible flinches when he spoke of the ritual. He'd seen her lingering near the window, her gaze fixed on the dark, ominous woods that surrounded their house, a sense of almost feverish anticipation clouding her eyes. The thought of Mary, his beloved wife, actively undermining their efforts filled him with a cold, icy dread. The betrayal felt like a betrayal not only of their plan but of their marriage, their entire life together.

Mary, in turn, suspected John. His sudden bursts of anger, his fits of absentmindedness, his strange obsession with the details of the ritual, all seemed to point to a hidden agenda. She recalled the way he had nervously consulted the ancient book, his fingers lingering over certain passages longer than necessary. The possibility that John, the rock of their family, had been swayed by some unseen influence, was equally horrifying. The idea that he might be complicit, even unknowingly, in their destruction chilled her to the bone.

Silas, the experienced paranormal investigator, observed the unfolding drama with a grim expression. He knew that the entity wouldn't simply allow them to perform the counter-ritual without interference. It would use their fears, their doubts, their weaknesses against them, sowing the seeds of discord and undermining their collective strength. The betrayal was a calculated move, a sophisticated tactic designed to disrupt their efforts and ensure its continued reign over Blackwood Lane.

He realized that the culprit's identity was almost irrelevant. The important thing was to identify their vulnerability and prevent it from disrupting the ritual. This wasn't just a battle against a supernatural entity; it was a battle against the very fabric of their family, against their trust, their love, and their ability to work together.

The situation deteriorated rapidly. The arguments escalated into accusations and bitter recriminations, the trust that had once held them together splintering into fragments. Their combined efforts had faltered. The ritual, originally scheduled for the next full moon, now seemed impossibly far away. Every delay increased the risk; every fight drained their collective strength.

Silas attempted to mediate, but his words fell on deaf ears. John and Mary, blinded by suspicion and exhaustion, were beyond reason. Each saw the other as the enemy, a threat to their survival. Their combined fear, their suspicion of each other, was now the ultimate weapon against them, feeding the entity's power, increasing its influence.

Days turned into a nightmarish blur of arguments, accusations, and near-misses. The house seemed to amplify their discord, every creak and groan a mocking reminder of their failing efforts. The whispers grew louder, the shadows more menacing. The entity, sensing their weakness, pushed harder.

But amidst the chaos, a flicker of realization began to dawn. A detail overlooked in their mutual accusations, a seemingly minor inconsistency that held the key to their predicament. It was revealed in a moment of unexpected clarity, a quiet moment of reflection during the lull between battles, a shared understanding that transcended the chaos. The betrayal wasn't by either John or Mary against the other, but by a third, unseen player.

A figure from Blackwood Lane's past, a vengeful spirit, a ghost of a previous inhabitant, was skillfully manipulating their minds. This unseen force wasn't merely lurking in the shadows; it was actively orchestrating their downfall. It wasn't John or Mary but a force far more malicious and cunning, using them against each other to weaken their resolve and ultimately, prevent the ritual from being successfully performed.

This revelation brought an eerie sense of relief. The sense of personal betrayal, of a loved one's perfidy, shifted, revealing a larger enemy that played a far more intricate game. This enemy's sophistication in manipulating their emotions and their relationships made their previous battles seem child's play.

Their fight became more than merely a ritual to banish an ancient entity. It became a fight for survival, a battle against a more insidious, more cunning antagonist who sought to not merely prolong its reign of terror over Blackwood Lane, but also to destroy the family that dared to challenge it.

The realization of this larger, more malevolent force, galvanized them. The shared understanding of a mutual enemy, a common threat, surpassed their suspicion. The focus narrowed, their fear transformed from fear of each other, to fear of this larger entity and its power to manipulate them.

The joint recognition of their shared enemy fostered a renewed sense of unity. The fractured trust began to mend, a delicate process as they grappled with the reality of this insidious plot. The ritual, originally a desperate attempt to banish an entity from their house, had shifted to a battle against a more intricate and cunning force than either of them could have initially imagined. They worked tirelessly to compensate for the missed steps of the interrupted ritual, the cooperation a stark contrast to the days of recriminations that preceded it. It was a race against time, a final push against an enemy that played a much deeper game than they initially anticipated. The amended ritual, now a symbol of their renewed alliance and a testament to their resilience, awaited them. The battle for Blackwood Lane had reached its crescendo.

The Confrontation II

The old, gnarled oak at the edge of the Blackwood Lane woods seemed to watch them, its branches like skeletal fingers clawing at the bruised twilight sky. John, Mary, and Silas stood before it, the amended ritual almost complete, the air thick with the scent of woodsmoke and fear. The full moon, a malevolent eye in the inky blackness, cast long, distorted shadows that danced and writhed like restless spirits. This wasn't just the culmination of their struggle against the entity; it was a confrontation with the architect of their torment, the leader of the cult that had plagued Blackwood Lane for generations.

Silas, his face etched with years of battling the unseen, adjusted the obsidian shard, its cold surface a stark contrast to the sweat beading on his brow. He'd spent countless nights poring over ancient texts, deciphering cryptic symbols, piecing together the fragmented history of the house and its sinister inhabitants. He'd seen the horrors that lurked within these woods, felt the chilling breath of the entity on his neck, but nothing had prepared him for the confrontation that awaited them.

A chilling whisper, barely audible above the rustling leaves, slithered through the air, a voice devoid of warmth, ancient and cruel. It spoke of betrayal, of broken promises, of the inevitable triumph of darkness. The ground beneath their feet seemed to tremble, the trees groaning in an eerie symphony of dread. From the shadows of the woods, a figure emerged, tall and gaunt, cloaked in darkness, its face obscured by a deep hood. This wasn't the faceless entity they'd been battling; this was its puppet master, the one who pulled the strings, the source of the insidious evil that had infiltrated their lives.

The leader of the cult, as Silas later described him in his chilling account, possessed an unnerving stillness, a predatory grace that belied the darkness within him. His eyes, when they finally emerged from the shadows, burned with an unholy light, reflecting the malevolent energy that pulsed from him. He moved with a silent, deliberate purpose, each step measured and precise, as if he were stalking his prey.

He spoke, his voice a low growl that resonated deep within their bones. He spoke of Blackwood Lane's history, a history of rituals and sacrifices, a history stained with blood and despair. He revealed the true nature of the entity, a malevolent spirit bound to the land, its power fueled by the fear and despair of its victims. And he revealed how he had meticulously orchestrated their discord, exploiting their vulnerabilities, feeding on their anxieties, turning their love and trust into weapons against them.

John, his face pale but resolute, stepped forward. The fear was still there, a cold knot in his stomach, but it was overshadowed by a steely determination. He had faced his own demons, confronted his deepest fears, and emerged stronger, more focused. He no longer saw Mary as an enemy, but as an ally, a partner in this desperate fight for survival.

Mary, too, had undergone a transformation. The initial suspicion, the gnawing uncertainty, had been replaced by a fierce protectiveness, a burning desire to protect her family, to reclaim their lives from the clutches of this malevolent force. She stood beside John, their hands clasped, their shared strength a beacon in the encroaching darkness.

The ensuing battle wasn't a clash of swords and sorcery, but a struggle of wills, a war waged in the realm of the mind and spirit. The cult leader unleashed a torrent of psychic attacks, attempting to shatter their resolve, to exploit their fears and drive them to madness. He conjured illusions, manipulating their perceptions, twisting their memories, trying to break their unity.

John fought back with the strength of his unwavering love for Mary and his determination to protect his family. He used the power of his will to shield himself from the psychic onslaught, his love for Mary and his fierce determination acting as a protective barrier, a shield against the encroaching madness. Mary, drawing strength from her deep-seated faith and her resolve to protect her family, countered the attacks with fervent prayers and focused visualizations. Her resilience was a testament to her inner strength, her spirit unflinching against the waves of psychic attacks. Silas, armed with his knowledge of ancient rituals and his unwavering belief in the power of good, guided them, directing their energies, helping them withstand the onslaught of the dark force.

The confrontation wasn't merely physical. It was a psychological battle, a war within their own minds, a struggle for their very sanity against this master of manipulation. The fight raged on, their shared love and unwavering commitment sustaining them through the psychic assaults.

The leader's attacks became increasingly erratic, his power waning as John, Mary, and Silas fought back with a newfound unity and focus. He attempted to sow seeds of doubt, whispering lies meant to exploit their vulnerabilities. But their shared understanding of the larger threat neutralized his attacks, their bond unbreakable against the storms of deception. They were no longer battling each other, but a common enemy, and in their unity, they found their strength.

As the moon reached its zenith, the balance shifted. The ritual, meticulously performed despite the chaos, began to take effect. The ancient symbols glowed with an ethereal light, drawing power from the moon, from the earth, from the very essence of life itself. The leader's power faltered, his form flickering and wavering as the combined strength of John, Mary, and Silas pushed back against him.

His final attack was a desperate, frenzied assault. He tried to overwhelm them with a wave of pure, unadulterated fear, trying to exploit the primal fear of mortality, the fear of the unknown, aiming to shatter their will with a wave of terror meant to crush them utterly. Yet, their shared love and the realization of their mutual enemy fortified them, rendering them immune to his attempts at subjugation. Their shared strength became a bulwark against his attacks, unyielding and resolute.

He screamed, a sound of pure agony and despair, as his power was finally broken. His form disintegrated, his essence dissolving into the night, leaving behind only a chilling silence, a vacuum where malevolent energy once pulsed. The oppressive weight of the entity's influence lifted, replaced by a sense of calm and tranquility. The whispers ceased, the shadows retreated, the trees ceased their mournful groan.

The battle was won, but the scars remained. The experience had left its mark on them, altering their perceptions, etching a permanent sense of unease into their being. The house, once a symbol of their dream life, now stood as a testament to their arduous struggle against supernatural forces. The lingering tension between them was a reminder of their shared ordeal, a constant undercurrent in their lives. They left Blackwood Lane behind, their family unit reshaped and irrevocably changed. The scars of the confrontation would remain, but they had emerged from the darkness, battered but unbroken. They had faced their demons, both internal and external, and in doing so, they had found a strength they never knew they possessed. Their victory came at a price, a profound understanding of their vulnerability and the fragility of the human spirit. Yet, they emerged with a renewed bond, a shared understanding that transcended the fear and suspicion that had once threatened to tear them apart. They had faced the darkness, and they had emerged victorious. But the memory of Blackwood Lane, of the confrontation, would forever haunt their dreams.

Desperate Measures

The lingering silence after the confrontation with the cult leader was more unsettling than the preceding chaos. The woods, once alive with malevolent energy, were now eerily still, the air thick with the scent of damp earth and something else… something akin to ozone, a metallic tang that prickled their nostrils and left a strange taste on their tongues. John, Mary, and Silas stood amidst the remnants of the ritual, the obsidian shard lying inert on the ground, its cold surface reflecting the pale moonlight. The weight of what they had just endured settled upon them, heavy and suffocating.

The escape from the immediate threat didn't signify an end to their ordeal. The house itself, Blackwood Manor, remained a malevolent presence, a nexus of dark energy that pulsed beneath the surface of their seemingly normal lives. They knew, with a chilling certainty, that the fight was far from over. The entity, though weakened, was still bound to the house, its influence still clinging to the walls, the floors, the very air they breathed. Their victory had been pyrrhic, a temporary reprieve in a protracted war.

Their immediate priority was survival. The house had to be neutralized, the entity contained, if not eradicated entirely. But how? They had exhausted their knowledge of ancient rituals, their arsenal of arcane defenses depleted. Desperation fueled their brainstorming session, huddled together in the battered car as they drove away from Blackwood Lane, leaving behind the house that had consumed their lives for far too long.

John, pragmatic and ever-resourceful, suggested contacting experts – paranormal investigators, exorcists, anyone who might possess the knowledge and skills to deal with the entity. He'd scoured the internet in the aftermath of the confrontation, finding fragmented accounts of similar occurrences, of houses that had claimed the sanity of families who dared to inhabit them. Yet, none of these accounts provided definitive solutions. The cases were shrouded in mystery, the entities nameless, faceless, their motives inscrutable. The information, scattered and unreliable, offered no concrete answers.

Silas, though exhausted from the psychic battle, remained the voice of reason. He cautioned against approaching such individuals without careful vetting. He knew, from his years of research, that not all who claimed expertise in the paranormal were genuine. Some were charlatans, others possessed dark agendas, and some were potentially worse. Finding a trustworthy ally in this fight, one who wasn't fueled by their own malicious intents, was a near-impossible task.

Mary, although shaken, focused on the practicalities of their situation. They needed a plan, a systematic approach to deal with the lingering threat. Their home, their sanctuary, was now a haunted battlefield, a place where every shadow held a threat, every creak of the floorboards a harbinger of dread. They needed a place of refuge, a safe space, where they could regroup and plan their next move, while simultaneously securing their future.

Their initial plan involved neutralizing the entity's power source – a seemingly impossible task, but it was the only viable strategy they could envision at the moment. Based on Silas' research, the house itself was the source of the entity's power; its malevolent energy was intrinsically linked to the house's foundation, its history stained with dark rituals and untold suffering. Their task was to sever that connection, to break the nexus that sustained the entity. They needed a way to sever the entity's link to Blackwood Manor, its earthly anchor.

They began with the mundane – securing the house, preventing further intrusion. John, using his skills as an architect, devised a plan to reinforce the security, making the house virtually impenetrable. He installed high-tech security systems, motion detectors, and cameras, transforming their dream house into a fortress. It wasn't foolproof, but it was a start, a layer of protection against the unseen forces.

Mary delved into the house's history, researching deeds, census records, and historical archives, trying to unearth any information that might offer a clue to the entity's origins or weaknesses. She unearthed disturbing stories of disappearances, inexplicable accidents, and a long-standing pattern of misfortune. Each piece of information added another layer of complexity to the puzzle, each detail painting a darker picture of Blackwood Manor's chilling history.

Silas concentrated on the spiritual aspect of the situation. He spent hours studying ancient texts, searching for rituals or spells that could weaken or banish the entity. He discovered forgotten incantations, cryptic diagrams, and whispered prayers, each fragment offering a tiny piece of the puzzle. He experimented with various protective talismans and amulets, hoping to discover something that would offer protection against the house's malevolent energy.

The weeks that followed were a blur of frantic activity, a race against time and against the ever-present threat that lurked within Blackwood Manor. They were living on edge, their nerves frayed, their sleep disturbed by nightmares and the constant awareness of the supernatural threat that surrounded them. Their relationship, strained during the previous conflict, had been solidified by their shared ordeal. The deep understanding of their mutual vulnerability had fostered a bond that transcended the fear and suspicion that had once threatened to tear them apart.

Their desperate measures were not limited to esoteric rituals and technological defenses. They understood the entity was a master manipulator, and its attacks were not solely paranormal. The entity manipulated their emotions, exploited their vulnerabilities, and intensified the existing tensions between them, trying to undermine their unity. To counter this strategy, they focused on maintaining open communication, ensuring they were aware of the entity's manipulative tactics.

Mary, ever the vigilant observer, recognized the subtle shifts in their behavior, the moments when the entity attempted to sow discord. She'd interrupt the insidious whispers of doubt and suspicion with gentle reminders of their shared goal, their shared strength. John, in turn, channeled his energy into tangible tasks, using his architectural skills to make the house safer, providing a sense of control amid the chaos. And Silas remained a constant source of information, constantly piecing together fragments of knowledge, helping them understand the nature of their adversary.

Their attempts to banish the entity were met with fierce resistance. The house seemed to fight back, responding to their efforts with a surge of paranormal activity. Objects moved inexplicably, whispers echoed from empty rooms, and shadows danced in the corners of their vision. The entity's efforts to sow discord among them intensified; suspicions were planted, accusations were made, but their bond held. They learned to recognize the entity's manipulations, to ignore the whispers of doubt, to focus on their shared goal: survival.

The final confrontation was not a dramatic, Hollywood-style showdown. It was a quiet, methodical process, involving a complex series of rituals, technological safeguards, and unwavering willpower. They slowly, methodically, weakened the entity's grip on the house, severing its connection to the earth, until finally, the presence was completely gone. The house became eerily quiet, the weight that had pressed upon them lifting, leaving behind an unnerving silence that was in stark contrast to the preceding chaos. They had won, but the victory was tinged with the knowledge that their life had been irrevocably changed. The memory of Blackwood Lane, of their desperate fight for survival, would forever linger, a testament to the fragility of the human mind and the enduring power of family in the face of unimaginable horror.

Supernatural Conflict

The air crackled with unseen energy, a palpable tension that tightened the muscles in their chests. The obsidian shard, still pulsing faintly with residual power, lay between them and the remaining cult members, their faces contorted in a mixture of rage and fear. They had underestimated the entity's reach, its ability to manipulate and control. The cult, acting as unwilling puppets, were now the final obstacle, their blind faith a terrifying weapon in the entity's arsenal.

John, his architect's mind surprisingly calm in the face of impending chaos, positioned himself strategically, using his knowledge of the terrain to their advantage. He had studied the layout of the woods, identifying potential escape routes, cover, and weaknesses in the cult's formation. His calm demeanor, a stark contrast to the escalating horror around them, offered a sense of control that anchored Mary and Silas amidst the encroaching pandemonium.

Mary, ever the pragmatist, assessed the situation with a chilling efficiency. She had learned to decipher the subtle shifts in the entity's influence, the way it subtly manipulated the cult members' behavior, twisting their loyalty into a weapon. She understood the cult's desperate devotion wasn't simply blind faith; it was a parasitic bond, fueled by the entity's power, a terrifying testament to the entity's ability to manipulate and control minds.

Silas, his face pale and drawn from the exertion of the previous psychic battle, focused his energy inward, drawing strength from his connection to the earth. He felt the entity's malevolent presence pulsating through the woods, a dark tide threatening to engulf them. He knew this was more than a physical fight; it was a battle of wills, a clash of energies. His task was to protect them, to shield them from the entity's psychic attacks, even as he channeled his own energy to counter its influence.

The fight began not with a roar, but a chilling whisper, a chorus of distorted voices emanating from the shadowy depths of the woods. The cult members, their eyes glazed over with fanaticism, lunged at them, their movements erratic and unpredictable, guided by the entity's invisible hand. John reacted instinctively, using his architectural knowledge to create makeshift barriers, diverting the cult members' attacks. He used fallen branches and boulders to funnel them into chokepoints, buying precious time for Silas to work his magic.

Silas, channeling his energy, created a shimmering shield of protective energy around the family, deflecting the initial assault. The psychic energy throbbed, a counterpoint to the chaotic energy of the cult members. His face contorted in pain as he fought against the entity's influence, its attempts to break through his defenses, to overwhelm his mind and body. Mary, meanwhile, moved with a deadly grace, using her knowledge of the entity's manipulative tactics to exploit the weaknesses in the cult's formation, turning their fanaticism against them. She spoke softly, her words carefully chosen, disrupting their focus, sowing seeds of doubt in their minds, creating fissures in their otherwise unwavering unity.

The battle raged for what felt like an eternity, a terrifying dance of shadows and light, of faith and fear, of human will and supernatural power. The forest floor became a battleground, littered with broken branches, scattered stones, and the fallen forms of the cult members, their devotion seemingly shattered. The air was thick with the smell of ozone and something far more sinister, a scent of decay and despair that clung to the very air they breathed.

As the fight progressed, Silas realized the entity wasn't merely manipulating the cult; it was feeding on their fear, their pain, their desperation. The more they fought, the stronger the entity became. He knew they couldn't win by brute force; they had to find a way to sever the connection between the entity and its human pawns.

Mary, recognizing the shift in Silas's strategy, focused her attention on disrupting the flow of energy between the entity and the cult. She targeted their emotional vulnerabilities, exploiting their fears and doubts, creating a ripple effect that weakened the entity's hold over them. She spoke to them, not as an enemy, but as someone who understood their pain, their misguided devotion. Her words were a balm, a counterpoint to the entity's malevolent influence, slowly but surely eroding the entity's control.

John, seeing the change in the battle, focused his efforts on creating strategic advantages. He employed his knowledge of the terrain, diverting and isolating the cultists, preventing them from forming a cohesive unit. He utilized the natural defenses of the woods, manipulating the shadows and the uneven ground to their advantage.

The tide turned subtly at first, a shift in the energy that was almost imperceptible. The cult members' attacks became less ferocious, their movements less coordinated, their eyes showing glimmers of doubt and confusion. The entity, its power source diminished by the erosion of its control over the cult, began to weaken. Silas felt the pressure lessen, the weight on his soul lifted.

The final confrontation wasn't a dramatic showdown, but a slow, methodical dismantling of the entity's power. Mary continued her quiet, subtle manipulation of the cultists' minds, weaving doubts and uncertainties into the fabric of their belief. Silas channeled his energy, reinforcing the protective shield, pushing back against the entity's weakened attacks. John, ever the pragmatist, ensured they remained strategically positioned, making use of the terrain to their advantage.

The obsidian shard, its malevolent energy depleted, lay inert on the ground, a testament to their victory. The entity, weakened and vulnerable, retreated, its presence fading into the background, leaving behind only a lingering sense of unease. The cult members, their minds finally freed from the entity's control, collapsed, exhausted and bewildered, their devotion shattered.

The aftermath was a strange mix of relief and exhaustion. The woods, once alive with a malevolent energy, were now strangely quiet, the only sound the gentle rustling of leaves in the night breeze. They had won, but the cost had been high. The experience had changed them, leaving its mark on their minds and souls. Their bond, forged in the crucible of this terrifying ordeal, was stronger than ever, but the scars of the night remained. They had survived, but the fight for survival had irrevocably changed them. The lingering silence was a testament to their victory, a stark contrast to the preceding chaos, but also a constant reminder of the horrors they had faced. The journey back to their lives wouldn't be easy. The house, Blackwood Manor, still stood, a silent testament to the darkness they had confronted, waiting for them to resume their lives, forever changed by the fight for their survival. The fight was over, but the echoes of their ordeal would remain, a constant reminder of the fragility of the human mind, and the strength of the human spirit when faced with the unimaginable.

Sacrifice

The silence that followed the retreat of the entity was heavier than the chaos that had preceded it. The air, still thick with the lingering scent of ozone and decay, pressed down on them, a suffocating blanket of exhaustion and relief. John, his usually sharp features etched with fatigue, slumped against a moss-covered boulder, the obsidian shard lying inert in his palm. He looked at his family, their faces pale and drawn but alive, and a wave of profound gratitude washed over him. They had survived.

Mary, her eyes still wide with the lingering shock, knelt beside Silas, who was breathing heavily, his face pale and clammy. His body trembled, the remnants of the psychic battle still coursing through his veins. The earth, his usual source of strength, seemed to have withdrawn, leaving him drained and vulnerable. He had shielded them, absorbing the brunt of the entity's psychic attacks, sacrificing his own well-being for their safety. The cost, Mary knew, would be significant.

"Silas," she whispered, her voice thick with emotion, her fingers gently tracing the lines of his face. His eyes fluttered open, meeting hers with a weak smile. "We did it," he rasped, his voice barely a whisper. "We won."

But even as the words escaped his lips, Mary felt the chilling realization sink in. Silas's connection to the earth, the very source of his power, was severed. The entity, in its desperate struggle to survive, had not merely attacked them; it had targeted Silas's life force, severing his connection to the earth's energy, leaving him profoundly weakened, possibly permanently. The victory had come at a terrible price. His face was not just pale; it had taken on a greyish hue, indicating an alarming lack of vitality.

John, understanding the gravity of the situation, carefully checked Silas's pulse. It was weak, erratic, a stark contrast to the steady rhythm he usually possessed. Silas's body trembled from exhaustion, the effort of drawing on the earth's power, of shielding his family, had drained him to the point of collapse. He was fading, his life force slowly ebbing away. The fight for survival had not only changed them; it had stolen a part of them, a vital part of their family's strength.

The weight of this realization hit Mary with the force of a physical blow. Silas, their unwavering protector, their anchor, was failing. The silence stretched, punctuated only by Silas's labored breathing. The victory felt hollow, tainted by the impending loss. The joy of survival was overshadowed by the looming specter of death. John's silence spoke volumes of his own distress as he attempted to help his brother-in-law in a way that a trained architect was ill-equipped to do.

A wave of despair threatened to engulf her, but she fought it back. They had come too far, endured too much, to succumb to despair now. Silas's sacrifice, his unwavering commitment to protecting his family, had given them this victory. She wouldn't let it be in vain. She wouldn't let him die.

Drawing on her own inner reserves, on the strength that had sustained her throughout the ordeal, Mary turned her attention to Silas, her focus laser-like. She felt the faintest flicker of life within him, a spark of resilience struggling against the encroaching darkness. She didn't know how, but she would find a way to rekindle it, to reignite his connection to the earth, to save him.

The night stretched into an agonizing eternity. John, his architectural precision now applied to creating a makeshift shelter, carefully collected fallen branches and leaves to shield them from the night's chill. He worked silently, his movements efficient and focused, his mind grappling with the enormity of the situation. His usually calm demeanor was replaced by a tense alertness, reflecting the gravity of the crisis. His practical skills were of little use in addressing Silas's rapidly deteriorating condition. He could build a house; he could not restore a man's life force.

Mary, meanwhile, remained by Silas's side, channeling her energy into him, whispering words of encouragement, her voice a fragile lifeline in the face of impending death. She spoke not of the battle, not of the entity, but of their life together, of their shared memories, of the laughter they had shared, of the bond that tied them together. She attempted to re-establish the link to the earth, a subconscious connection that could possibly help Silas recover. She coaxed and pleaded, not with words, but with a silent transfer of energy, a desperate attempt to revive his weakening life force. She knew time was slipping away, each breath Silas took becoming shallower, more strained.

As dawn approached, painting the eastern sky with hues of pink and gold, a subtle shift occurred. A faint warmth spread through Silas's body, a glimmer of life flickering in his eyes. His breathing, though still labored, became a little steadier, a little less strained. He stirred, his eyelids fluttering, his fingers twitching slightly.

He awoke to Mary's touch and the warmth of the rising sun. His eyes, though still weak, held a flicker of recognition. He saw the worry etched on their faces and the exhaustion in their bodies. His lips trembled, but a faint smile graced his face.

The journey back was arduous. The return to Blackwood Manor was a silent testament to their shared ordeal. The house, once a symbol of their suburban dream, now stood as a stark reminder of their struggle for survival. The physical scars would heal, but the emotional wounds, the memories of the fight, the sacrifice, the near-death experience would linger forever.

Silas's recovery was slow and painstaking. The connection to the earth was not fully restored, leaving him weaker than before. His recovery was a testament to his determination, to the unbreakable bond of their family, and the unwavering love that had sustained him through the darkness. The scars remained, visible and invisible, serving as a constant reminder of their ordeal, a mark of their shared sacrifice, their fight for survival, and the strength of the human spirit in the face of unimaginable terror. The suburban dream had vanished, replaced by a shared reality forged in the crucible of a harrowing battle, binding them together in a way that no idyllic life could ever have achieved. The house remained, but the fight for their survival had changed them forever. Their family unit had survived, but it had been profoundly transformed. The silence that once signified fear now symbolized resilience. The scars of the night remained, but they stood together, a family united by the shared trauma, each member bearing the weight of the sacrifice made to ensure their collective survival.

The Escape

The escape was less a dramatic sprint and more a stumbling, disoriented retreat. The oppressive weight of the house, the suffocating presence of the entity, seemed to linger even as they stumbled through the overgrown woods bordering Blackwood Lane. Each rustle of leaves, each snap of a twig, sent jolts of fear through them, echoing the phantom touches and whispers they'd endured within the manor's walls. Silas, his face ashen, leaned heavily on John, his usual strength replaced by a debilitating weakness. Mary, her eyes darting nervously, kept a watchful eye on their surroundings, her hand instinctively reaching for the obsidian shard still clutched in her pocket – a tangible reminder of their harrowing ordeal.

The air hung heavy with the scent of damp earth and decaying leaves, a stark contrast to the suffocating, cloying odor of the house. Yet, even here, in the relative safety of the woods, the sense of unease persisted. The silence, broken only by their ragged breathing and the occasional rustle of unseen creatures, was more terrifying than any scream. The trauma of the night's events hung over them like a shroud, heavy and inescapable. They moved as if in a dream, their bodies reacting on autopilot, their minds still grappling with the surreal horror they had just witnessed.

John, despite his architectural background, felt utterly unprepared for this type of survival situation. His usually precise mind struggled to process the raw, primal fear that gripped them. He found himself relying on instinct, on the basic survival skills he had never needed to employ in his carefully ordered life. The stark reality of their predicament stripped away the veneer of his sophisticated existence, revealing the raw, vulnerable human beneath. He was a man out of his element, relying on Mary's intuition and Silas's remaining strength to guide their escape.

The escape route itself was treacherous, a labyrinth of tangled undergrowth and hidden pitfalls. Thorns snagged at their clothing, branches whipped at their faces, and the uneven terrain tested their already weakened bodies. Each stumble, each fall, served as a painful reminder of their physical exhaustion and the psychic toll the night had taken. Yet, they pushed on, driven by a primal instinct for survival, a shared determination to escape the suffocating grip of Blackwood Manor and the sinister cult that had claimed it.

As the first rays of dawn broke through the canopy, painting the forest floor in streaks of ethereal light, they stumbled upon a barely visible path. It was a deer trail, barely wide enough for them to pass, but it offered a glimmer of hope, a route out of the suffocating darkness of the woods. They followed it, their weary bodies fueled by a mixture of adrenaline and sheer desperation.

The path led them to a quiet country road, far from the imposing presence of Blackwood Manor. As they emerged from the woods, a wave of relief washed over them, so potent it was almost overwhelming. They were free, at least for now. But the relief was short-lived, replaced by a chilling realization: their ordeal was far from over.

They found refuge in a small, deserted cabin on the edge of the property. It wasn't much – a ramshackle structure with a leaky roof and cobweb-laden walls, but it offered shelter from the elements and a modicum of privacy. Exhaustion finally claimed them; they collapsed on the dusty floor, their bodies aching, their minds reeling from the trauma they had endured.

The following days were a blur of exhaustion, fear, and the slow, agonizing process of recovery. Silas's condition remained precarious. His connection to the earth, severed during the confrontation with the entity, had left him weak and vulnerable. Mary tended to him with unwavering devotion, drawing on a reservoir of strength she didn't know she possessed. John, though still shaken, channeled his anxiety into practical tasks, finding solace in the familiar rhythm of building a makeshift fire and scavenging for food.

Their escape hadn't brought an end to the nightmares. The memories of the ritual, the chilling presence of the entity, the unsettling familiarity of the cultists' faces haunted their dreams, leaving them exhausted and emotionally drained even during their waking hours. The idyllic suburban dream had shattered, leaving behind a fractured reality populated by fear and uncertainty. They were survivors, but their survival had come at a steep price.

The trauma had profoundly altered them. Silas, once the strong, silent pillar of their family, was now frail and withdrawn, his once vibrant connection to the earth severed, leaving him dependent on the others' support. Mary, once the loving wife and mother, had developed an almost hyper-vigilance, her senses constantly on alert, her mind forever searching for threats. John, once the rational, composed architect, struggled with the lingering anxiety and lingering sense of helplessness, the realization that his meticulous planning could not guarantee safety against supernatural forces.

Their escape was a victory, a hard-fought battle against overwhelming odds. Yet, the battle had changed them, etching deep scars onto their souls. The Millers had survived the house, but the house had survived within them, its dark legacy imprinted on their minds and hearts, a constant reminder of the fragility of life and the enduring power of fear. The escape had been physical, but the true fight for survival was just beginning, a battle against the lingering trauma, the shattered fragments of their former lives, and the insidious whispers of the past that continued to echo in the silence. The journey back to normalcy, if such a thing even existed for them now, would be long and arduous, filled with the shadows of Blackwood Manor and the chilling reminder of their near-death experience. Their lives were irrevocably changed, and the scars, both visible and invisible, would forever bear witness to their harrowing escape. They had survived, but at what cost? The question lingered, an unspoken weight shared by all, a silent testament to the darkness they had confronted and the indelible mark it had left upon their souls. The fight was over, but the journey to healing had only just begun.

Aftermath

The dilapidated cabin offered little comfort, its rough-hewn walls whispering tales of forgotten inhabitants. The silence, once a welcome reprieve from the house's oppressive atmosphere, now felt heavy, pregnant with unspoken anxieties. Silas, his face gaunt and pale, lay huddled beneath a patchwork quilt, his breaths shallow and ragged. The vibrant energy that had once flowed through him, connecting him to the earth, was now a faint flicker, a dying ember. He drifted in and out of consciousness, his whispers, when they came, fragmented and unintelligible, haunted by images only he could see.

Mary, her eyes shadowed with exhaustion but her spirit unwavering, sat beside him, her hand resting gently on his forehead. The obsidian shard, a grim memento of their escape, lay nestled beside her, a cold comfort in the chilling silence of the cabin. She had always been the anchor of the family, the glue that held them together. Now, her strength seemed stretched thin, yet she persevered, fueled by an unwavering devotion to Silas and a fierce determination to help him heal. The normally meticulous tidiness of her nature was gone; the cabin reflected their disarray, a tangible representation of the fractured state of their lives.

John, meanwhile, moved restlessly around the cabin, his architect's mind struggling to adapt to this brutal reality. The methodical precision that had once defined his life felt inadequate, almost childish, in the face of the primal fear that still clung to them like a shroud. He busied himself with practical tasks, foraging for food, gathering firewood, trying to establish a semblance of order in the chaos. His movements, once fluid and purposeful, were now jerky and tense, punctuated by moments of paralyzing fear that would send him scrambling back to Silas's side. The carefully constructed walls of his rational mind were crumbling, replaced by a raw, unfiltered emotion he had never known before.

Days bled into weeks. The physical wounds healed, but the emotional scars remained, deep and festering. Silas's recovery was slow, agonizingly so. His connection to the earth, the source of his strength and vitality, remained severed, leaving him weak and vulnerable. He struggled to speak, his thoughts a jumbled mess of terrifying visions and fragmented memories. The once vibrant green of his eyes had dulled, reflecting the turmoil within.

Mary's tireless devotion began to take its toll. The constant vigilance, the unending fear, etched lines of worry around her eyes and stole the light from her smile. She slept little, her dreams haunted by the chilling images of the ritual, the faceless cultists, and the malevolent entity that had sought to consume them. Her hyper-vigilance extended beyond Silas; she scanned their surroundings with an almost animalistic intensity, perpetually on the alert for any sign of danger. Her once warm and nurturing nature was overshadowed by a constant, simmering anxiety.

John, despite his efforts to maintain a semblance of normalcy, wrestled with a debilitating anxiety. The escape had shattered his sense of control, the bedrock of his existence. His meticulous planning, his rational approach to life, had proven useless against the overwhelming power of the supernatural. He found himself paralyzed by indecision, plagued by the haunting realization that he could not protect his family from forces beyond his comprehension. His nights were filled with unsettling dreams, replays of their ordeal, intensified by the feeling of his own helplessness.

The silence within the cabin was broken only by the occasional creak of the floorboards, the crackling of the fire, and the rustling of leaves outside. The oppressive weight of their shared trauma hung heavy in the air, an unspoken barrier between them. The bond that had once held them together, strong and unbreakable, was now strained, fractured by the events they had endured. Accusations, unspoken and yet palpable, lingered between them, ghosts of doubt and mistrust fueled by their shared trauma and the lingering fear that the darkness was not truly behind them.

Their escape had been a physical liberation, a flight from immediate danger, but it had not brought peace. The house, Blackwood Manor, seemed to have taken up residence within them, its oppressive atmosphere permeating their lives, its sinister presence a constant reminder of their ordeal. The trauma had reshaped them, twisting their personalities, disrupting the delicate balance of their family dynamic.

Therapy offered a lifeline, a path towards healing, but the journey was long and arduous. They relived their trauma again and again, each session peeling back layers of fear and despair. Silas slowly began to reconnect with the earth, his energy returning in fits and starts, though the deep scars remained. Mary's hyper-vigilance eased, although her capacity for trust had been significantly diminished. John, while still wrestling with his anxiety, began to reclaim his sense of control, focusing on tangible tasks – rebuilding their lives, brick by brick, metaphorically and literally.

The road to recovery was not linear; setbacks were frequent and agonizing. There were nights filled with terror, days when the memories threatened to overwhelm them, and moments when the fragile threads of their family unit seemed on the verge of snapping. Yet, amidst the darkness, a flicker of hope persisted. Their shared experience, the terrifying ordeal that had nearly destroyed them, became the foundation for a new bond, stronger and more resilient than before. The Millers had survived Blackwood Manor, but more importantly, they were surviving the aftermath, inching towards healing, supporting one another through the darkest hours, their bond, though scarred, forged in the crucible of unimaginable horror. The fight for survival had transformed them, but it had not broken them. Their journey towards healing, a testament to the resilience of the human spirit, was just beginning. The whispers of Blackwood Manor might linger, but they were no longer the defining force in their lives. They were survivors, their strength forged in the fires of trauma, their bond deepened by shared adversity. The scars remained, a permanent reminder of their harrowing experience, but they also served as a testament to their enduring spirit and unwavering commitment to one another. The fight for survival was over; the fight for life, for healing, and for a new beginning, had just begun.

Traumas Grip

The rebuilt cabin, though sturdy and warm, felt strangely alien. The scent of pine and freshly cut lumber couldn't quite mask the lingering odor of fear that clung to the walls, a ghostly echo of their ordeal. Silas, while physically healed, remained a shadow of his former self. The vibrant connection to the earth that had once defined him was a fragile thread, easily snapped by a sudden noise, a fleeting shadow. His eyes, though regaining some of their former green, held a haunted look, a deep well of unspoken terror. He'd started painting again, but the canvases were filled with swirling, chaotic imagery, a stark reflection of his tormented mind. The landscapes were distorted, the colors muted and unsettling, often featuring shadowy figures lurking in the background. He wouldn't speak about them, wouldn't explain the meaning behind the haunting visions that bled onto the canvas. The art was a silent scream, a visual manifestation of his trauma.

Mary's unwavering strength, the rock upon which the family had rested, had begun to crumble. Her hyper-vigilance, once a protective shield, had morphed into a crippling anxiety. Every creak of the floorboards, every rustle of leaves outside, sent a jolt of adrenaline through her. Sleep offered little respite, her dreams a relentless replay of the terrifying ritual, the chanting voices, the cold, dead eyes of the cultists. The sharp obsidian shard, once a symbol of their escape, now felt like a constant reminder of the horror they had faced. She found herself flinching at unexpected touches, avoiding eye contact, her trust irrevocably broken. She'd begun to isolate herself, finding solace only in the repetitive tasks of tending to the small garden she'd planted near the cabin, her hands finding comfort in the earthy soil.

John, the pragmatic architect, found his carefully constructed world reduced to rubble. His rational mind, once his sanctuary, had been invaded by a relentless tide of anxiety and self-doubt. He'd embraced his work, designing a new cabin that was both functional and comforting – a stark contrast to the unsettling structure of Blackwood Manor. He drew upon his skills to create a haven for his family, focusing his energy on tangible results. Yet the nightmares remained, each more vivid than the last. He saw himself paralyzed, unable to protect his family, watching helplessly as the darkness consumed them. He'd found himself reaching out to Silas and Mary with a newfound tenderness, an attempt to rebuild the bridges that had been destroyed. But the chasm between them remained, wide and deep, echoing with unspoken anxieties and recriminations.

The therapy sessions, initially a source of hope, became a grueling journey through the darkest recesses of their minds. Each session unearthed new layers of trauma, forcing them to confront the horrors they had endured. Silas's fragmented memories gradually coalesced, revealing the extent of the ritualistic abuse, the manipulation, the psychological torment. His recollections were shrouded in terrifying imagery, visions of ancient symbols, unsettling rituals, and the cold, chilling presence of a malevolent entity that seemed to feed off their fear. The therapists struggled to make sense of it all, to categorize and understand the nature of the evil they had encountered.

Mary's sessions focused on her feelings of guilt and self-blame, her inability to protect Silas and her pervasive sense of failure. She grappled with the weight of her trauma, the constant fear of recurrence and the lingering shadow of the faceless cultists. She spent long hours alone, carefully studying books on cults and occult practices, desperately trying to understand the forces they had faced and what drove them. This obsessive need to know felt like a way of gaining control over her life and escaping the feeling of helplessness that engulfed her.

John's therapy revolved around his feelings of inadequacy and helplessness. He constantly replayed the events in his mind, dissecting his actions, searching for a moment where he could have done better, could have prevented the ordeal. The architect's sense of control had been shattered, and he battled with his inability to rationalize his experiences. The sessions were less about unraveling the past and more about reclaiming his life, rebuilding his confidence, and learning to trust again. He was learning that some things are beyond human control. He started volunteering, offering his architectural skills to rebuild homes for the underprivileged, a way to channel his newfound sense of purpose and to contribute something positive.

Their individual struggles were interwoven with a shared, unspoken trauma that cast a long shadow over their lives. The bonds that had once held them together were strained and fragile, easily fractured by moments of fear, anger, or sadness. Arguments erupted spontaneously, fueled by the anxieties and resentments that had accumulated over the years. They accused one another of not doing enough, of not being strong enough, their words sharp and barbed, each fueled by the unspoken terror that still hung in the air. The slightest disturbance, even the most mundane event, could send them spiraling back into the depths of their trauma. Simple sounds, shadows, and even specific smells, would trigger vivid flashbacks, plunging them into the chilling reality of their ordeal.

As weeks turned into months, the wounds of the past began to heal, though the scars remained. The physical scars were reminders of their struggle, but the psychological wounds were deep, invisible, and sometimes more debilitating. The family therapy sessions became crucial. They learned to express their anxieties, their fears, their guilt. They began to understand that they weren't alone in their pain. The therapeutic setting provided the environment they needed for safe healing and growth.

They practiced mindfulness exercises, coping mechanisms, and learned how to regulate their emotional responses to triggers and environmental cues. Gradually, they were able to create a safe space where they could communicate without fear. They discovered a new level of empathy and understanding. Their shared trauma had created a deeper bond, but it was a bond forged in the fires of adversity and marked by deep scars.

The healing process was not linear. There were days when the darkness threatened to consume them, when the nightmares returned with renewed intensity, and when the fear of relapse hung heavy in the air. But they persevered. They leaned on one another, offering comfort and support, rebuilding their lives brick by brick. Their collective strength proved that the human spirit, though wounded, was ultimately resilient. The memory of Blackwood Manor, though a permanent fixture in their lives, no longer held the power to define them. They were survivors, forever changed, but not broken. They were a family, bound not only by blood but by the shared crucible of unimaginable horror, their story a testament to the enduring power of love, resilience, and the unrelenting human spirit's capacity to heal. The road to healing was long, but the promise of a new dawn, however faint, shone brightly on the horizon.

Rebuilding Trust

The silence in the rebuilt cabin was a different kind of silence than the one that had haunted Blackwood Manor. There, it had been a suffocating, pregnant silence, thick with unspoken dread. Here, it was a fragile silence, easily shattered by a cough, a sigh, or the creak of a floorboard. It was a silence that held the potential for healing, but also for the resurgence of old wounds. The air, though clean and fresh, still carried the phantom scent of fear, a lingering ghost of their shared ordeal.

Mary found herself constantly searching for reassurance, a desperate need to know that she was safe, that they were safe. Her hands, once steady and capable, now trembled slightly. The garden, her sanctuary, offered a semblance of control, but even there, the shadows seemed longer, the rustling leaves more menacing. She'd started keeping a journal, meticulously documenting their progress, charting their moods, noting the triggers that sent them spiraling back into the darkness. It was a desperate attempt to quantify their recovery, to translate the intangible into something concrete and measurable. The entries chronicled not only their struggles but also the small victories: Silas's first truly restful night's sleep, John's return to a semblance of normalcy, the rare moments when laughter, genuine and unburdened, filled the cabin.

Silas, though his paintings were slowly losing their chaotic energy, replacing the swirling vortexes with calmer landscapes, still struggled with the residual effects of the trauma. His nightmares were less frequent, but their intensity remained unchanged, vivid and horrifying. He'd started attending a support group, a hesitant step towards sharing his experiences, towards finding solace in the shared vulnerability of others who had endured similar ordeals. The group provided a safe space for him to talk about things he couldn't bear to mention to his family, to acknowledge the lingering shame and self-blame that still gnawed at him. He found a strange comfort in the shared pain, a sense of camaraderie forged in the fires of shared trauma.

John, despite his efforts to maintain a façade of normalcy, found himself overwhelmed by a wave of profound exhaustion. His meticulously crafted plans for the cabin, his architectural drawings, his attempts to reclaim his life, they all felt like a desperate act of self-preservation, a way to stave off the encroaching despair. He noticed the subtle shifts in Mary's demeanor, the way she flinched at sudden movements, the way her eyes darted nervously, constantly scanning the room for potential threats. He saw the quiet desperation in Silas's gaze, the way his hands would clench into fists when he was struggling to control his emotions. The weight of their shared trauma bore down on him, threatening to consume him.

Their attempts at communication were tentative at first, fraught with unspoken anxieties and underlying resentments. Arguments, though less frequent, were more intense, fueled by the accumulated frustration and the lingering distrust. Simple misunderstandings were magnified, blown out of proportion by the fragile state of their emotional equilibrium. Accusations, however unintentional, stung with the venom of unhealed wounds. They would find themselves retracting their words, apologizing profusely, only to have the cycle repeat itself in a painful and relentless loop.

Family therapy, however, became a crucial turning point. The therapist, a kind and insightful woman with a gentle but firm demeanor, helped them navigate the treacherous waters of their shared trauma. She taught them to identify their triggers, to develop healthy coping mechanisms, and to communicate their needs and anxieties without fear of judgment or condemnation. She facilitated a safe space for them to express their anger, their grief, their guilt, without the threat of reciprocation. The sessions weren't always easy; there were tears, there were screams, there were moments of intense emotional upheaval. But amidst the chaos, a fragile sense of hope began to emerge.

Slowly, painstakingly, they started to rebuild their trust. It wasn't a quick or easy process. It required conscious effort, unwavering patience, and a deep commitment to understanding one another. They learned to listen, truly listen, without interrupting, without judgment, without the need to offer immediate solutions. They learned to validate each other's feelings, acknowledging the pain, the fear, the anger, without trying to minimize or dismiss it. They learned to forgive, not just for the sake of reconciliation, but for their own well-being.

Silas began to share his paintings with his family, explaining the symbolism, the emotions he had poured onto the canvas. The landscapes, once bleak and disturbing, slowly transformed, revealing a glimmer of hope, a sense of peace that had previously been absent. His artwork became a tool for healing, a means of externalizing his inner turmoil, a visual representation of his journey towards recovery.

Mary found solace in sharing her journal entries with John, reading aloud the accounts of their struggle, highlighting their triumphs and acknowledging their setbacks. It was a way of acknowledging the journey they had taken, of celebrating the progress they had made. The act of sharing, of putting her emotions into words, helped her to process her trauma, to come to terms with her experiences. The meticulous documentation became a testament to their resilience, a tangible record of their healing journey.

John, in turn, started sharing his architectural plans with his family, explaining his design choices, outlining his goals. The act of creating, of building something tangible, helped him to regain a sense of control, a sense of purpose. He found that his architectural skills were a means of expression, a way of manifesting his inner healing. The design of the new cabin, originally a desperate attempt to escape the past, now became a symbol of their collective strength, a testament to their ability to rebuild and create something beautiful from the ashes of their trauma.

The rebuilding of their relationships was a long and arduous process, marked by setbacks and moments of profound despair. There were days when the darkness threatened to engulf them, when the memories of Blackwood Manor resurfaced with renewed intensity. But amidst the struggle, their love for one another, the powerful bond that had been forged in the crucible of trauma, remained. They learned to rely on one another, to support each other, to celebrate each small victory, and to acknowledge each painful setback.

They began to find joy in simple things: a shared meal, a quiet evening by the fireplace, a walk in the woods. They rediscovered their shared interests, rekindled their laughter, and began to create new memories, memories that were not overshadowed by the terror of Blackwood Manor. Their shared trauma had left an indelible mark on their lives, but it didn't define them. They were survivors, scarred but not broken, a testament to the enduring power of love, forgiveness, and the unwavering human spirit's capacity for healing. Their story wasn't one of escape, but one of resilience, a journey of rebuilding trust, brick by brick, and piece by painful piece. The road ahead was long, but they walked it together, hand in hand, toward a future defined not by the darkness of the past, but by the light of their shared love and unwavering hope. The silence in the cabin, once fragile and tentative, now held the promise of peace, a peace hard-won, but richly deserved.

Seeking Help

The initial sessions with Dr. Evelyn Reed were excruciating. The weight of their collective trauma pressed down on them, a suffocating blanket woven from fear, guilt, and a profound sense of loss. John, ever the pragmatist, tried to compartmentalize, to present a clinical, almost detached account of their ordeal at Blackwood Manor. He detailed the unsettling occurrences, the escalating paranoia, the fracturing of their family unit, as if describing a complex architectural problem demanding a methodical solution. But his carefully constructed facade crumbled under the weight of Dr. Reed's gentle probing. The carefully controlled cadence of his voice cracked, revealing the underlying tremor of fear. His eyes, usually sharp and focused, became clouded with a weariness that went beyond simple exhaustion. The meticulously crafted mask he'd worn for so long began to slip, revealing the raw, vulnerable man beneath.

Mary's struggle was different. She didn't attempt to distance herself from the emotional maelstrom; she was submerged in it. Tears flowed freely, washing away the carefully constructed barriers she'd erected to protect herself and her sons. She spoke of the pervasive sense of dread that clung to them like a second skin, the constant feeling of being watched, the unsettling whispers that seemed to emanate from the very walls of the house. She relived the moments of terror, describing them with a painful vividness that left the room heavy with unspoken fear. Her voice, initially a trembling whisper, grew stronger as she spoke, finding solace in the act of verbalizing her suppressed emotions. The sharing, the unburdening, became a form of catharsis, a gradual release of the pressure that had been building inside her for so long.

Silas's experience was uniquely his own. His trauma manifested not through words, but through his art. He brought a portfolio of his recent paintings to the session, each canvas a visual representation of his internal turmoil. Dr. Reed, surprisingly adept at interpreting the symbolism in his work, gently guided him through the complex imagery, helping him to unravel the layers of pain and fear that had been hidden beneath the swirling colors and chaotic brushstrokes. His paintings initially depicted scenes of overwhelming darkness, distorted figures lurking in shadowy corners, landscapes consumed by fire and tempest. As the sessions progressed, however, the paintings began to shift, slowly revealing a tentative emergence of light, of hope.

The group therapy sessions proved invaluable. Sharing their experiences with others who had endured similar trauma was both terrifying and liberating. Hearing other stories, similar in their horror and uniqueness, helped to normalize their experience, stripping away the sense of isolation that had plagued them since leaving Blackwood Manor. They learned that their reactions, their fears, their anxieties, were not unique, not signs of weakness or madness, but rather the natural consequences of a deeply traumatic event. They found comfort in the shared vulnerability, in the understanding glances that exchanged between them, in the quiet solidarity of knowing they were not alone.

Dr. Reed introduced them to various coping mechanisms: mindfulness exercises to help them manage their anxiety, EMDR therapy to process the traumatic memories, and cognitive behavioral therapy to challenge the negative thought patterns that had taken root in their minds. The process was slow and arduous, filled with setbacks and moments of profound despair. There were days when the memories of Blackwood Manor would resurface with terrifying intensity, triggering flashbacks and overwhelming waves of panic. But with each session, with each shared experience, with each act of self-reflection, they gained a renewed sense of hope.

Slowly, painstakingly, they began to rebuild their lives. The trust, fractured and shattered by the events at Blackwood Manor, began to mend. John's meticulous nature, once a source of rigidity, became a source of strength, allowing him to channel his energy into creating a safe and comforting environment for his family. Mary's nurturing spirit, once overshadowed by fear, blossomed once more, providing emotional support and unwavering love. Silas's artistry, once a conduit for his pain, became a means of healing and self-expression.

The cabin, initially a refuge, became a sanctuary. The rhythmic sounds of the nearby stream, the gentle rustling of the leaves, the comforting warmth of the fireplace, these simple things became anchors, grounding them in the present, pulling them away from the dark memories of the past. Family meals, once fraught with tension, became occasions for shared laughter and genuine connection. They celebrated small victories, acknowledging the progress they had made, and supported one another through the inevitable setbacks.

The process was far from over. The scars of Blackwood Manor would remain, a constant reminder of their ordeal. But they were learning to live with those scars, to integrate them into their narrative, to allow them to define not who they were, but what they had overcome. Their journey toward healing was a testament to their resilience, their love for one another, and the enduring human capacity for growth and recovery. The silence in the cabin was no longer fragile or tentative. It was a quiet, strong silence, the silence of peace, the silence of healing, the silence of a family slowly, painstakingly, rebuilding their lives, brick by painful brick. The darkness of Blackwood Manor still lingered in their memories, but it no longer held them captive. They were free. They were healing. They were, together, becoming whole again. The future stretched before them, uncertain yet promising, a future painted not in the shades of terror and despair, but in the vibrant hues of hope and love. The long road to recovery stretched before them, but they walked it together, hand in hand, towards a future where the memory of Blackwood Manor was no longer a source of fear, but a testament to their enduring strength.

The Weight of Secrets

The silence in the cabin, once a refuge, now felt heavy with unspoken anxieties. The weight of their shared trauma, though lessened by their progress, still pressed down on them. A new layer of complexity had settled upon their fragile peace: the agonizing question of whether or not to reveal their experience. The thought hung between them, an unspoken elephant in their newly restored sanctuary. John, ever the pragmatist, initially argued against it. "Who would believe us?" he'd said, the words harsh even to his own ears. "A haunted house? Hallucinations? They'll think we're mad."

Mary, her eyes still carrying the lingering shadows of Blackwood Manor, countered with a trembling voice, "But it happened, John. It really happened. We can't just bury it." Silas, his artistic soul more attuned to the nuances of emotion, simply nodded, his gaze fixed on a half-finished painting depicting a landscape shrouded in a disquieting mist, the colors muted, devoid of the vibrant hope that had recently begun to creep into his work.

The fear of disbelief was a palpable entity, a chilling spectre that stalked the edges of their healing. They had witnessed things that defied logic, things that shattered their understanding of reality. To recount these experiences to others, to lay bare their vulnerability, felt like inviting ridicule, judgment, and the potential for further trauma. The stigma associated with mental illness, with claims of the supernatural, hung like a dark cloud over their deliberations. Would people dismiss their story as the product of overactive imaginations fueled by stress and trauma? Would they be labeled as unstable, unreliable? The possibility was a chilling weight, threatening to unravel the carefully constructed threads of their recovering mental health.

They spent countless hours debating the ramifications, weighing the potential benefits against the overwhelming risks. The desire to share their experiences, to warn others about Blackwood Manor, was strong. They felt a responsibility to prevent other families from experiencing the same horror they endured. Yet, the fear of dismissal, of being marginalized, was an insurmountable obstacle. The mere thought of facing skeptical stares, disbelieving whispers, and the potential loss of credibility weighed heavily on them.

John, a man of unwavering logic, found himself battling with this emotional conundrum. His pragmatic mind struggled to reconcile the irrefutable evidence of their shared experience with the overwhelming probability of being dismissed as fantasists. He meticulously compiled a case file of sorts: photographs of inexplicable occurrences, audio recordings of strange noises, even Silas's paintings, which seemed to capture the essence of their ordeal. But even these tangible proofs seemed insignificant in the face of the potential skepticism of others.

Mary, usually the bedrock of their family, felt herself wavering. Her unwavering support for her sons faltered beneath the burden of the decision. The memory of the terror, the fear, the desperation, all returned, threatening to engulf her anew. She spent hours poring over old newspaper clippings, searching for any record of past incidents at Blackwood Manor, hoping to find corroborating evidence to bolster their credibility. Yet every dead end added to her despair.

Silas, usually so articulate through his art, became inexplicably withdrawn. His paintings, which had begun to show glimmers of hope, reverted to their earlier style: dark, chaotic, and fraught with a sense of impending doom. The burden of their unspoken dilemma weighed heavily on his young shoulders, manifesting as a silent, inward struggle that even Dr. Reed seemed unable to penetrate. His art, usually his escape, now reflected the deep well of uncertainty that had enveloped the family.

Their discussions stretched late into the night, fueled by anxiety and doubt. The idyllic peace of their cabin seemed to mock their internal turmoil, the gentle sounds of nature unable to mask the storm raging within their hearts. They considered various avenues: contacting the authorities, alerting the previous owners, even reaching out to paranormal investigators. Each option felt fraught with risk, laden with potential for failure and renewed trauma. The fear of being judged, of being dismissed, loomed large, stifling their efforts to find a resolution.

The weight of their unspoken secret became a heavy burden, one that threatened to fracture their newfound stability. They were bound together by this shared experience, but the decision of whether to reveal it or keep it buried threatened to tear them apart. Each family member grappled with the immense weight of the choice, their individual struggles reflecting in their actions, their silences, and their dreams. The quiet harmony of their newly established sanctuary was under siege, threatened by the haunting reality of their shared past and the uncertain future that lay ahead, a future determined by this one, excruciatingly difficult decision.

The agonizing silence continued for days, broken only by the occasional sigh, the rustling of papers, or the hushed whispers of private anxieties. The cabin, their refuge, felt less like a sanctuary and more like a pressure cooker, the unspoken tension growing with each passing hour. The shared trauma had created an unbreakable bond between them, but the possibility of revealing it, of being judged and potentially ridiculed, threatened to fracture this bond, creating a rift as deep as the ones that had opened within the walls of Blackwood Manor itself.

One evening, huddled around the fireplace, a rare silence descended, a silence heavier than any argument. It was Mary who finally broke it. Her voice, though still soft, held a newfound strength, a steely resolve that surprised even herself. "We can't live like this," she said, her eyes meeting those of her husband and son. "We have to tell someone. We have to try."

John's face showed a mixture of apprehension and reluctant agreement. He knew she was right. The weight of the secret was too heavy to bear. It was consuming them, slowly poisoning their hard-won peace. Silas, who had remained largely silent throughout the ordeal, nodded his head slightly, a flicker of determination visible in his usually downcast eyes.

They understood that there was no guarantee that anyone would believe them. They understood the risks involved. But they had also begun to realize that the risk of silence was far greater. The silence was a self-imposed prison, a cage of fear and uncertainty that prevented them from truly healing. Breaking their silence would be painful, terrifying, even potentially humiliating. But it was a necessary step on their path to recovery. It was a testament to their resilience, to their enduring belief in the truth of their shared experience. They would face the world, together, carrying the weight of their secret, not in silence, but with the quiet determination of survivors, seeking not validation, but simply the release that only truth can bring. The journey ahead would be fraught with uncertainty, but they were ready to face it, side by side, ready to share their story, ready to fight for their sanity, and ready to begin the process of truly letting go of Blackwood Manor's dark grasp. The weight of their secret remained, but now, it felt slightly lighter, carried not in isolation, but in the shared strength of a family united by a common truth.

Moving On

The decision to leave Blackwood Lane wasn't a simple matter of packing boxes and changing addresses. It was a shedding of skin, a painful and protracted process of severing ties with a place that had irrevocably altered their lives. The move to the quiet, secluded cabin had been a necessary retreat, a sanctuary where they could begin to heal, but the wounds inflicted by Blackwood Manor remained open, raw and throbbing with each passing memory. The idyllic setting, once a balm to their ravaged souls, now felt like a constant reminder of what they had escaped, the quiet whisper of the wind in the trees echoing the unsettling sounds that had haunted their nights in the old house.

The process of unpacking was agonizingly slow. Each item unearthed from the moving boxes was a trigger, a tangible link to their ordeal. John, ever the pragmatist, tackled the task with methodical efficiency, his movements precise, his expression carefully neutral, yet the tremors in his hands betrayed his underlying anxiety. He meticulously arranged their belongings, attempting to impose order on their lives, a stark contrast to the chaotic terror that had defined their time in the house on Blackwood Lane.

Mary, however, found the unpacking too painful. She left the task mostly to John, preferring to spend her time wandering the woods surrounding their cabin, seeking solace in the quiet solitude of nature. The forest felt safer than their new home, a space where the memories felt less intrusive, less vivid. She found herself drawn to the deeper parts of the woods, feeling a kinship with the ancient, silent trees, their stoic presence mirroring the calm she desperately craved. Yet, even in this seemingly peaceful environment, the shadows seemed to stretch longer, the quiet rustle of leaves sounding like whispers, the creaking branches mimicking the groans of the old house.

Silas, too, grappled with his own form of displacement. His art, once a cathartic outlet, had become a burden. He found it difficult to pick up his brush, the canvas a stark, daunting reminder of the horrors he had witnessed. The vibrant colors he had once effortlessly wielded now felt muted, lifeless, mirroring the emotional landscape that had settled upon him. His hands, once deft and sure, now shook with an uncertain hesitancy. He found himself retreating even further into himself, his silence a tangible manifestation of his internal turmoil. The hope he had briefly experienced during their time in the cabin seemed to have evaporated, replaced by a deep-seated weariness and a gnawing fear that the shadows of Blackwood Manor would forever follow them.

As the days turned into weeks, a fragile normalcy began to emerge. The immediate trauma began to fade, replaced by a low hum of anxiety, a constant undercurrent of unease. They tried to establish a routine, a sense of structure that would anchor them in their new reality. John resumed his work, though his focus remained fractured, his attention often drifting to the distant past. Mary attempted to cultivate a small vegetable garden, her hands finding comfort in the tactile process of nurturing life, yet the seeds she planted seemed to grow slower, less vibrant than they should. Silas, reluctantly, began to paint again, but his landscapes continued to be infused with a disturbing darkness, the palette subdued, the imagery unsettling.

The question of whether or not to share their story remained a heavy weight. They had decided against it for now, their decision fueled by a mixture of fear and a deep-seated exhaustion. The thought of reliving their ordeal, of facing the skeptical eyes and disbelieving whispers of others, seemed unbearable. They needed time, time to heal, time to reconcile the jarring events of Blackwood Manor with the quiet reality of their new lives.

But even as they attempted to move on, Blackwood Manor's influence lingered. John found himself checking locks and windows multiple times a night, even though their cabin was miles from any potential threat. Mary's sleep was haunted by recurring nightmares, vivid and unsettling visions of the house's shadowy corners and the unsettling whispers that had filled its empty rooms. Silas, despite his renewed efforts at painting, found his work often depicting distorted versions of their cabin, the familiar surroundings subtly altered, warped, and menacing, the comforting scenes slowly turning into haunting recreations of Blackwood Manor.

Their family dynamic, though strengthened by their shared trauma, was irrevocably altered. The experience had forged a deep bond between them, a connection based on a shared understanding of vulnerability and fear. Yet, there were subtle shifts, subtle cracks appearing in their carefully constructed facade. John's meticulous nature grew into an obsession with order and control, his anxiety manifesting in an almost oppressive need for cleanliness and predictability. Mary, though outwardly composed, remained withdrawn, her smiles strained, her eyes bearing the weight of unspoken fears. Silas's art, while a testament to his resilience, was a constant reminder of the shadows that continued to haunt them all.

The house on Blackwood Lane had not only affected their mental states but their very perceptions of reality. Their once clear distinctions between fear and imagination blurred, making it almost impossible to differentiate between reality and the haunting residue of their experience. They started to question themselves, their sanity, and their grip on reality. Every creak and whisper in their new home triggered memories of Blackwood Manor, making their present feel haunted by their past.

Their shared secret, though unspoken, still existed as a silent, ever-present force, shaping their interactions and coloring their perspectives. They found themselves constantly scanning each other's faces, searching for signs of renewed trauma or unspoken fears. Conversations were filled with subtext, layered with veiled references to their shared experience. The simple act of sharing a meal became a ritual, a silent acknowledgment of their fragile peace and the unspoken fears that lurked beneath the surface.

One evening, as they sat huddled around their fireplace, the flickering flames casting dancing shadows on the walls, Mary turned to John, her voice barely above a whisper. "Do you ever feel like… it's still with us?" she asked, her eyes wide and filled with a mixture of fear and apprehension.

John nodded slowly, his gaze fixed on the fire, a flicker of uncertainty in his eyes. "Sometimes," he admitted, "it feels like we brought a piece of Blackwood Manor with us."

Silas, who had been silently sketching in his notebook, looked up, his face pale. He nodded in agreement, the tremor in his hand betraying his unspoken fears. The shared silence that followed was heavier than any words, a testament to the lingering impact of Blackwood Manor, a haunting echo that seemed destined to forever shape their future. The move had been a necessary step, but the process of truly moving on, of escaping the house's lingering grip, had only just begun. The road ahead was long, arduous, and uncertain, but they would face it together, bound by an unbreakable chain of shared trauma and a shared determination to finally find peace. The

nightmare of Blackwood Manor might be over, but its
echoes continued to resonate, a haunting melody that would
forever shape the symphony of their lives.

A Fresh Start

The cabin, nestled deep within a stand of ancient pines, was everything Blackwood Manor was not. There were no echoing hallways, no unsettling drafts, no whispers slithering from unseen corners. It was small, rustic, and undeniably peaceful. Yet, the peace felt brittle, fragile, like a thin layer of ice over a churning, turbulent current. The move had been a desperate attempt to outrun their past, a flight from the suffocating grip of Blackwood Manor and the insidious paranoia it had instilled. But the past, they were quickly discovering, was a tenacious shadow, stubbornly clinging to them, refusing to be shaken off.

The initial relief of escaping the house gradually gave way to a different kind of unease. The silence, once a welcome respite, now felt oppressive, amplifying the whispers of their trauma. John, his hands perpetually stained with the earth from his attempts to cultivate a garden mirroring the one at Blackwood Manor (a compulsive need to recreate, to control the narrative), would often find himself staring out the window, the stillness of the forest deepening his already present anxiety. The trees, once symbols of solace for Mary, now seemed to loom, their branches like skeletal fingers reaching for them. The forest's quietude no longer brought her peace, but rather an unsettling quiet that made the silence of the cabin feel unbearable. She would often retreat to the furthest reaches of the woods, seeking a deeper silence, a refuge from her thoughts that had become a relentless tide of images from their nightmare at Blackwood Manor.

Silas found himself caught in a creative impasse. The vibrant colors of his past work seemed to mock him, a testament to a time before the darkness had settled over him. He stared at his canvases, the blank white spaces mocking his inability to create, to express the torrent of emotions that constantly roiled within him. The new environment, instead of inspiring him, seemed to drain him of his creativity. His paintings, when he did manage to produce them, were bleak landscapes populated with twisted, distorted trees – a subconscious rendering of the oppressive darkness they had escaped.

Their attempts to rebuild their lives felt like a Sisyphean task. The mundane routines – grocery shopping, cooking, cleaning – were infused with a constant undercurrent of fear. The simplest actions were fraught with anxiety. John's meticulousness, once a sign of his orderly nature, had morphed into a compulsive need for control, manifesting in an obsessive cleaning regime, checking and rechecking locks, and his inability to relax. Mary's quietude deepened, her silence punctuated by startled reactions to every unexpected sound. The forest that had once been a balm to her soul was now a constant source of apprehension, a place where the whispers of Blackwood Manor seemed to carry on the wind.

Silas, despite his efforts, found his artistic process being thwarted by the ever-present darkness. He would start paintings of the cabin, but they would invariably morph into distorted parodies of Blackwood Manor, the tranquil countryside turning into a monstrous, oppressive landscape that resembled their former home. His art became a visual manifestation of their collective trauma, a disturbing testament to the insidious nature of their shared experience.

The weight of their secret hung heavy between them, an unspoken chasm that threatened to fracture their carefully constructed unity. They were bound by their ordeal, yet the shared trauma had created a distance, a silent language of unspoken fears. Meals were eaten in a strained silence, conversations were short and stilted, punctuated by nervous laughter that failed to mask the underlying tension. Their shared glances were loaded with unspoken questions, a silent acknowledgment of the fragility of their peace.

The smallest things triggered memories: a creaking floorboard, a flickering light, the rustle of leaves in the wind. Each sound, each sensation, evoked the chilling atmosphere of Blackwood Manor. They found themselves hyper-aware of their surroundings, their senses heightened, their minds on constant alert, every sound seeming to carry the whispers of their past. Nightmares plagued them, both individually and collectively, each dream a distorted echo of their shared trauma. John would wake in a cold sweat, visions of the house's shadowy corners dancing before his eyes. Mary's dreams were filled with a suffocating sense of dread, the voices of the past seeming to beckon her back to Blackwood Manor. Silas's nights were tormented by the distorted images of the house, each nightmare a new iteration of their shared nightmare.

Their attempts at communication were often fraught with difficulty. Simple questions carried a weight of unspoken fears, the simple act of speaking their minds became an exercise in coded conversations. Their attempts to find solace in each other's company were constantly undermined by their shared sense of apprehension. The quiet moments were filled with an almost palpable tension, a reminder of the unspoken truth that hung heavy between them.

One evening, during a rare moment of shared openness, John confessed to Mary that he felt as if they had carried a piece of Blackwood Manor with them, a spectral echo of their ordeal. His words, though spoken softly, felt laden with an undercurrent of fear and resignation. He described a sensation of being watched, of being surrounded by an invisible presence, a feeling that deepened the darkness of the night, and even the daylight couldn't penetrate the palpable sense of dread. He found himself instinctively checking doors and windows, the routine actions transforming into a compulsive behavior, a tangible manifestation of his fear that could not be shaken off.

Mary, her eyes filled with tears, admitted that she, too, felt the lingering presence of their past. She spoke of an oppressive weight, a sense of being suffocated by the shadows of Blackwood Manor, a constant threat that cast a long shadow over even the brightest days. The silence that followed was heavy, a testament to the strength of their bond, but also a reminder of the depth of their trauma and the long road ahead.

As the weeks turned into months, the Millers struggled to establish a semblance of normalcy. The trauma of Blackwood Manor had irrevocably altered their lives, not just by leaving them with haunting memories and a persistent sense of unease, but by fundamentally changing their perspectives and how they interacted with each other, themselves, and the world around them. They were living in a new place, surrounded by a different environment, but the house on Blackwood Lane continued to cast a long shadow over their lives. Their fresh start was proving to be an uphill battle, the wounds of the past refusing to heal, and the weight of their shared secrets threatening to consume them. The road to recovery was long and arduous, yet the Millers, despite everything, remained bound together, their shared experience forging a bond that was both a source of comfort and a chilling reminder of the darkness they had escaped. Their new beginning was anything but simple, but they clung to the hope that, one day, the echoes of Blackwood Manor would finally fade.

Lingering Fears

The crisp autumn air did little to soothe the gnawing unease that clung to John like a second skin. He watched Silas, his son, hunched over a half-finished canvas, the vibrant colors of the paint a stark contrast to the bleakness etched on his face. The cabin, with its rough-hewn beams and crackling fireplace, should have felt like a sanctuary, a refuge from the horrors of Blackwood Manor. Instead, it served as a stark reminder of their escape, a constant, silent testament to the trauma they had endured. The forest, once a source of solace for Mary, now felt like a suffocating presence, the whispering pines seeming to echo the unseen terrors that haunted their nights.

Mary herself was a ghost of her former self. The vibrant woman John had fallen in love with had been replaced by a shadow, her eyes haunted, her laughter a distant memory. Her once bright spirit was dimmed, replaced by a pervasive anxiety that followed her like a shadow. Even the simple act of preparing a meal became a herculean task, each movement weighted down by a fear that seemed to emanate from the very walls of the cabin. The smallest sounds – the creak of a floorboard, the rustling of leaves outside – sent jolts of panic through her, plunging her back into the suffocating darkness of Blackwood Manor.

The nights were the worst. Sleep offered no escape, only a descent into a nightmarish realm where the shadows of Blackwood Manor danced and twisted, morphing into grotesque parodies of their former lives. John found himself thrashing in his sleep, his body wracked with silent screams, his mind replaying the chilling scenes of their ordeal. He would wake in a cold sweat, his heart hammering against his ribs, the image of the house's shadowy corners burned into his retinas.

Silas's nightmares were equally disturbing. His dreams were filled with a swirling vortex of distorted images – the twisted trees, the echoing hallways, the unsettling whispers – all morphing into a terrifying landscape that mirrored the dark recesses of his mind. His paintings, once filled with vibrant life, had become a grotesque reflection of his inner turmoil, dark and twisted landscapes populated by menacing figures that seemed to embody their shared nightmare. He would wake up gasping for air, his body trembling, the images of his dreams clinging to him like a shroud.

The silence in the cabin was as oppressive as the sounds had been in the Manor. The family existed in a state of perpetual unease, their shared trauma creating an invisible barrier between them. Meals were eaten in a strained silence, punctuated only by the clatter of cutlery and the occasional forced chuckle. Conversations were stilted and short, each word measured and cautious, a testament to the unspoken fears that hung heavy in the air. Their attempts at connection were fragile, often disrupted by sudden bursts of anxiety or the distant echo of a forgotten sound.

One evening, as the sun cast long shadows across the cabin floor, John broke the silence. He spoke of the feeling of being watched, a constant, unsettling presence that seemed to permeate every corner of their new home. He described a subtle chill that accompanied this feeling, a sense of being observed by unseen eyes, a constant presence that chilled him to the bone, even when the sun blazed down. He'd find himself obsessively checking doors and windows, a compulsion he couldn't seem to shake, the metallic clang of the locks a small comfort in the face of this overwhelming fear.

Mary, her voice barely a whisper, admitted to similar sensations. She described the lingering scent of decay, a phantom smell that clung to the air, a lingering reminder of the house's unsettling history. She would often find herself paralyzed by a sudden wave of anxiety, the darkness of Blackwood Manor momentarily eclipsing the light of their new surroundings. The scent of decay, faintly sweet, yet undeniably foul, was something she couldn't escape, even in the vast, open spaces surrounding the cabin.

Silas, usually reserved, spoke of the recurring images that plagued his dreams, the twisted trees and shadowy figures that seemed to mock their escape. He spoke of a constant pressure in his chest, a tightness that mirrored the suffocating dread he felt during their ordeal at Blackwood Manor. His art, he confessed, was his way of processing the trauma, a desperate attempt to exorcise the demons that continued to haunt him. Each painting was a battle, a struggle against the dark forces that seemed determined to consume him.

The weight of their collective fear was palpable, a heavy blanket that stifled their hope and threatened to consume them. They had escaped Blackwood Manor, but the house, with its dark secrets and haunting memories, had followed them into their new sanctuary. Their attempts at a new beginning had failed to erase the trauma they had endured, its specter clinging to them, a silent reminder of their ordeal.

Days bled into weeks, weeks into months, and the family's struggle continued. John's compulsive need for control intensified. He spent hours meticulously cleaning and organizing, his actions driven by a desperate need to regain a sense of order in a world that had become chaotically unstable. He would check and re-check locks, ensuring the safety of his family, a behavior that verged on obsessive, leaving him worn and exhausted. The weight of his anxiety was manifest in the deep lines around his eyes, the relentless strain on his face. His attempts to create order in the physical world, were a hopeless effort to regain control over the emotional chaos that gripped him.

Mary's anxiety manifested in a different way. She retreated further into herself, her silence deepening, her responses becoming increasingly erratic. The quiet solace she had once sought in the woods was now replaced by a sense of apprehension, the rustling leaves and creaking branches seeming to carry the whispers of their past. She found herself constantly jumping at sudden sounds, her heart racing with an irrational fear. Her once gentle nature became guarded, her eyes always scanning her surroundings, searching for potential threats that never materialized.

Silas, consumed by his art, became increasingly isolated. His paintings, dark and disturbing, were a testament to the darkness that continued to consume him. The vibrant colors of his earlier work were replaced by a palette of grays and blacks, reflecting the bleakness that had settled over his soul. His art had become a ritual, an attempt to exorcise his demons through the act of creation. However, the more he painted, the more intense his nightmares became. He felt that he was trapped in a cycle, a perpetual state of artistic and emotional turmoil.

They tried to communicate, but their attempts were often fraught with misunderstandings and unspoken fears. Simple questions carried the weight of unspoken anxieties. Their shared glances were loaded with apprehension, a silent acknowledgement of the fragility of their hope. Even the most mundane conversations were filled with an underlying current of tension. Their attempts at casual conversation often devolved into uneasy silences, broken only by the occasional nervous laughter.

One night, under a sky filled with indifferent stars, John confessed his fear that their past would always haunt them. The trauma of Blackwood Manor, he said, was etched into their souls, an indelible mark that would forever alter their lives. He spoke of the house as an entity, a malevolent presence that continued to exert its influence, even from a distance.

Mary, her eyes brimming with tears, nodded in agreement. She admitted to feeling a constant sense of dread, a pervasive fear that was impossible to ignore. The cabin, despite its rustic charm, was not a sanctuary but a prison of memories.

Silas, listening in silence, confessed that he feared they would never truly escape the past, that the shadow of Blackwood Manor would always loom large over their lives. Their shared confession was a heavy weight on the silence that followed. It was a brutal acknowledgment of their shared trauma, of the invisible chains that bound them together and the scars that had been left on their psyches.

Their new beginning was a painful lie. The escape had been an illusion. Blackwood Manor, with its insidious tendrils, had infiltrated their lives, their thoughts, their very beings. Their attempts to rebuild their lives were overshadowed by the specter of their past, a grim reminder of the horrors they had witnessed and the trauma they had endured. The road to recovery was long and winding, filled with obstacles that seemed insurmountable, and the path ahead was uncertain. Yet, despite the lingering fears and the ever-present shadow of Blackwood Manor, the Millers remained bound together, their shared experience forging a bond that was as fragile as it was unbreakable. Their journey towards healing was just beginning.

Family Dynamics

The shared confession under the indifferent stars became a turning point, a fragile bridge built across the chasm of their unspoken fears. The weight of their collective trauma, once a suffocating burden, began to slowly transform into a shared understanding, a bond forged in the crucible of their ordeal. They started to talk, not just about their fears, but about the small, everyday things that had once brought them joy. Mary, hesitant at first, shared a memory of a family picnic, a seemingly insignificant detail, yet it brought a flicker of warmth to their conversation, a reminder of simpler times before Blackwood Manor had cast its long shadow.

Silas, inspired by this shared reminiscence, brought out a sketchbook, his fingers tracing the lines of a half-finished drawing – a portrait of his mother, her smile captured in a way that hinted at the woman he remembered before the darkness descended. It wasn't a perfect representation, the lines a little shaky, the colors subdued, but the intent was clear: an attempt to recapture the light that had been dimmed by their trauma. The act of creating, once a torturous process, now felt like a form of healing, a way to express the emotions he had buried deep within.

John, observing his son's quiet concentration, felt a pang of remorse. His own obsessive need for control had driven a wedge between them, creating a distance that he now desperately sought to bridge. He reached out, his hand gently resting on Silas' shoulder, a gesture of unspoken apology and support. The simple touch, devoid of words, spoke volumes, bridging the gap that had formed between father and son.

As the days turned into weeks, a subtle shift occurred in their family dynamic. The heavy silence that had once permeated the cabin began to dissipate, replaced by a hesitant, tentative communication. They started sharing their fears, not in a frantic rush to uncover every dark secret, but in a slow, deliberate process of acknowledging and processing their shared trauma. They learned to listen, truly listen, to one another, without judgment or interruption, allowing their unspoken fears and anxieties to surface gradually, like bubbles gently rising to the surface of a calm pond.

Their shared meals, once fraught with tension and strained silences, became opportunities for genuine connection. They shared stories, not just about their ordeal at Blackwood Manor, but also about their lives before the darkness descended—memories of holidays, laughter, shared triumphs, and failures. These seemingly simple stories served as anchors in the storm of their trauma, reminders of the resilient bonds that connected them as a family. The clatter of cutlery was no longer a jarring sound, but rather a gentle rhythm in the symphony of their recovering family life.

Mary, initially withdrawn and hesitant, began to rediscover her love of gardening. The surrounding woodland, once a source of fear, now became a source of comfort and solace. The act of tending to the earth, nurturing life from the soil, seemed to soothe her troubled spirit. The fresh scent of soil and blooming flowers replaced the haunting smell of decay that had clung to her like a phantom.

Silas's art, though still bearing the mark of his trauma, began to evolve. The darkness remained, but it was now interwoven with threads of light, hints of hope, and the promise of healing. His paintings became a journey, a visual representation of their collective struggle, documenting their transformation from victims to survivors. Each brushstroke was an act of catharsis, a process of healing.

John, recognizing the importance of self-care, finally sought professional help. Therapy proved to be a powerful tool, giving him the space to process his trauma and to address his obsessive tendencies. He learned to manage his anxiety, to let go of his need for total control, and to embrace the inherent uncertainty of life. He realised the futile nature of his control-driven behaviour. The relief was immense, and his interactions with his wife and son were no longer overshadowed by his anxiety.

The family's journey was not without its setbacks. There were days when the darkness threatened to engulf them once more, when the memories of Blackwood Manor resurfaced with vivid intensity, triggering waves of fear and anxiety. There were arguments, misunderstandings, and moments of deep despair. But they learned to navigate these difficult moments together, drawing strength from their shared experience and from their growing understanding of one another's struggles.

They discovered that their resilience lay not in suppressing their trauma but in acknowledging and confronting it together. They developed new rituals, new ways of communicating, and new strategies for coping with their anxieties. Their communication was now underpinned by empathy, patience, and a deep understanding of their shared vulnerability. Their shared trauma had not only damaged their individual psyches but had profoundly altered the dynamics within their family. However, they were actively striving to repair that damage, to reconstruct their family dynamic from the ashes of their ordeal.

Their new beginnings were not instantaneous, not magical, and certainly not devoid of pain. The scars of Blackwood Manor would remain, etched into their memories and shaping their perspectives for years to come. But amidst the lingering fears and the persistent shadows of the past, a resilient hope had taken root. Their bond, strengthened by shared adversity, now stood as a testament to their enduring strength, their capacity for healing, and their unbreakable family unit. They had escaped the physical confines of Blackwood Manor, but more importantly, they were collectively escaping the psychological prison of their trauma. Their journey was far from over, but the path ahead, though uncertain, was now paved with the shared determination to rebuild their lives, stronger and more resilient than before. The scars remained, a permanent reminder, but they were no longer the dominant feature of their existence. The darkness was still present, a lurking shadow, but it no longer controlled their lives. They were finding their light, collectively and individually. Their shared journey towards healing was a testament to the power of family, the enduring strength of the human spirit, and the transformative power of forgiveness and understanding. The wounds remained, but they were beginning to heal. The road ahead was not without pitfalls, but their steps were surer, their gazes more forward-looking. Their new beginnings were slowly becoming reality.

Healing Process

The initial weeks after leaving Blackwood Manor were a blur of fragmented memories and lingering anxieties. The silence in their rented cottage, a stark contrast to the oppressive quiet of the old house, felt almost deafening. It was a silence pregnant with unspoken fears, a constant reminder of the horrors they had endured. Mary found herself repeatedly checking the locks, her hands trembling, even though there was no one to fear. Silas, despite the relative safety of their new surroundings, continued to experience vivid nightmares, his sleep punctuated by screams and sudden awakenings. John, despite the therapeutic progress, still wrestled with his obsessive need for control, finding solace only in meticulously organizing their belongings and planning their days down to the minute.

Therapy became a crucial element in their healing process. Individual sessions allowed each family member to confront their trauma in a safe and controlled environment. Mary, under the guidance of her therapist, began to unpack the years of suppressed emotions, revealing the deep-seated anxieties that Blackwood Manor had brought to the surface. The therapist helped her understand that her fears weren't irrational, but rather a natural response to the terrifying experiences they had faced. Cognitive Behavioral Therapy (CBT) proved particularly effective in helping her reframe her negative thought patterns and develop coping mechanisms for managing her anxiety. She learned to identify her triggers and to develop strategies for managing her panic attacks, replacing her fear-based responses with more rational and healthy reactions. Slowly, painstakingly, she began to reclaim her sense of self, her identity no longer defined by the horrors of Blackwood Manor.

Silas's therapy focused on his artistic expression as a means of processing his trauma. He worked with an art therapist, who helped him translate his nightmares and anxieties into tangible forms, creating a visual narrative of his journey through darkness and into the light. His initial paintings were dark and disturbing, reflecting the intensity of his experiences. But as the therapy progressed, so did his art. The colors became brighter, the strokes more fluid, the imagery less nightmarish. His art became a tangible representation of his healing process, a testament to his resilience and capacity for growth. The sessions weren't just about expressing the trauma, but also about finding beauty and hope in the midst of the darkness, about learning to see the light even in the deepest shadows. He learned to channel his fears into his creative work, turning pain into power and darkness into art. His sketchbook became his diary, a visual chronicle of his emotions, both dark and hopeful. The act of creation helped him to process his trauma in a healthy way and to find solace in his creativity.

John's therapy focused on addressing his obsessive-compulsive tendencies and his need for control. He learned to identify the roots of his anxiety and to develop healthier coping mechanisms. The therapist helped him understand that his need for control stemmed from a deep-seated fear of losing his family, a fear that had been amplified by their experience at Blackwood Manor. Through exposure therapy and relaxation techniques, he learned to gradually confront his fears and to accept the inherent uncertainty of life. He practiced mindfulness exercises, learning to live in the present moment rather than constantly worrying about the future. The process was arduous, requiring immense patience and self-awareness, but it yielded significant results. He learned to relinquish his obsessive need for control, replacing it with a more balanced approach to life, one that valued flexibility and adaptation. He started to trust in the inherent strength of his family and his ability to cope with life's unpredictability.

Their family therapy sessions were equally crucial. They learned to communicate openly and honestly with one another, sharing their fears, anxieties, and vulnerabilities without judgment or criticism. They practiced active listening, developing empathy and understanding for each other's struggles. The therapist guided them in identifying unhealthy family dynamics and in developing healthier communication patterns. They learned to acknowledge and validate each other's emotions, creating a space for open and honest dialogue. Family meals, once fraught with tension, became opportunities for genuine connection and shared laughter. They began to rebuild their family unit, forging a stronger, more resilient bond based on trust, mutual respect, and unwavering support. They rebuilt their shared foundation, strengthening it with a renewed sense of communication and mutual support.

The healing process was far from linear. There were setbacks, relapses, and moments of deep despair. The memories of Blackwood Manor continued to haunt them, triggering waves of anxiety and fear. There were arguments, misunderstandings, and tears. But they learned to navigate these difficult moments together, drawing strength from their shared experience and from their growing understanding of one another. They had learned the importance of patience and the value of supporting each other during moments of vulnerability. They celebrated their small victories and acknowledged their setbacks without succumbing to self-recrimination.

As time passed, the darkness began to recede, replaced by a cautious optimism. Mary's garden, once neglected, flourished, her green thumb a testament to her renewed sense of self. Silas's art, while still bearing the mark of his trauma, reflected a growing sense of hope and resilience. His paintings, no longer dominated by dark shadows, showcased vibrant colors and uplifting imagery. John's obsession with control diminished, replaced by a quiet acceptance of life's uncertainties. His days were no longer defined by meticulous schedules and rigid routines; spontaneity and flexibility found a place in his life. He learned to appreciate the beauty of the unpredictable and to embrace the impermanence of things.

Their new beginnings were not a sudden transformation but a gradual, painstaking process of healing and growth. The scars of Blackwood Manor remained, etched into their memories, but they no longer defined their lives. They had learned to live with the shadows of the past, incorporating them into their narrative without allowing them to dictate their future. They had found a new equilibrium, a new normalcy, forged in the crucible of their shared trauma. Their family unit, strengthened by adversity, stood as a testament to the resilience of the human spirit and the enduring power of love and forgiveness. They were survivors, not just of Blackwood Manor, but of their own internal battles, their own demons. Their journey continued, but the future, although uncertain, held the promise of lasting peace and happiness. The scars remained, but they were fading, replaced by the vibrant colors of a new life, a life built on the foundations of shared trauma, resilience, and unwavering love. They were healing, together.

Acceptance

The cottage, nestled amongst rolling hills far from the oppressive shadows of Blackwood Lane, offered a fragile peace. The sun streamed through the windows, painting warm stripes across the worn wooden floorboards, a stark contrast to the perpetual gloom they'd endured. Yet, the sun's warmth couldn't entirely erase the lingering chill that clung to them, a residual effect of the darkness they'd escaped. Acceptance, they discovered, wasn't a sudden switch flipped on, but a slow, gradual thawing of frozen hearts, a painstaking process of piecing shattered selves back together.

Mary, her hands still trembling slightly as she watered her burgeoning herb garden, felt the grip of anxiety loosen its hold. The garden, a small testament to her resilience, bloomed with vibrant life, reflecting the slow but steady blossoming within her. The meticulous arrangement of herbs, each carefully placed in its designated spot, was a far cry from the obsessive need for order that had consumed John. She found solace in the rhythm of tending to the plants, the cycle of growth and decay mirroring her own journey through darkness and into the light. The soil, rich and fertile, felt grounding, anchoring her in the present moment, preventing her mind from wandering back to the echoing whispers of Blackwood Manor. She found herself humming as she worked, a simple melody that expressed a quiet joy, a newfound appreciation for the simple beauty of life. Her laughter, once muted by fear, now rang clear and bright, a sound that echoed through the cottage and filled it with life. She still had moments of apprehension, fleeting shadows that momentarily clouded her mind, but they no longer held the power to overwhelm her. She had learned to recognize these shadows for what they were - fleeting remnants of a past she was actively leaving behind.

Silas, his canvases now awash with vibrant colors and hopeful imagery, found his art evolving into a celebration of life. The dark hues that had once dominated his work, reflecting the shadows of his nightmares, were gradually replaced by sun-drenched landscapes, vibrant portraits filled with light, and abstract expressions of newfound joy. He painted the cottage, capturing the warm light that streamed through the windows, the lush green hills surrounding their sanctuary, and the delicate wildflowers that sprung up between the stones. He painted his family, their faces reflecting a quiet contentment that had been absent for so long. His art became a chronicle of their healing, a visual testament to their journey from despair to hope. He still felt the lingering effects of his trauma, the occasional nightmare still jolted him from sleep, but his art became his refuge, his means of transforming darkness into light, fear into strength. The act of creation was therapeutic, a channel for his emotions, allowing him to process his trauma in a way that words couldn't capture. He now understood that his art was not just a representation of his past, but a blueprint for his future, a vibrant expression of hope and resilience.

John, freed from the rigid shackles of his obsessive-compulsive disorder, found himself embracing the gentle chaos of life. His days were no longer dictated by meticulously planned schedules and rigid routines. While order still provided him comfort, he now understood that a life lived too tightly controlled could suffocate the soul. He discovered the joy of spontaneity, the thrill of unplanned adventures, and the beauty of embracing life's unpredictable nature. He learned to trust his family's innate resilience, understanding that their bond was stronger than any external force. His need for control had been rooted in his fear of losing them, but through therapy he realized that true security lay not in rigid structure, but in the strength of their shared love. He learned to delegate, to trust, and to let go of the reins he'd once held so tightly. He still maintained a degree of organization, finding solace in the predictability of certain aspects of his life, but he now allowed for flexibility, appreciating the subtle beauty of the unpredictable. He discovered the joy of simply "being," free from the overwhelming pressure of maintaining constant control.

Their family dinners, once tense affairs punctuated by strained silences and unspoken anxieties, were now filled with laughter, shared stories, and genuine connection. They talked openly about their experiences, not dwelling on the darkness, but acknowledging it as a part of their shared journey. They celebrated their milestones, both big and small, and they supported each other through setbacks, embracing vulnerability without judgment. The trauma they'd endured had forged a bond between them that was unbreakable, a testament to their resilience and their unwavering love. They realized that their shared experience had not broken them but had strengthened their connections in unexpected ways. The past was acknowledged but not allowed to define their present or dictate their future. They were a family reborn, forged in the crucible of adversity.

The healing wasn't always smooth; there were moments of regression, times when the memories of Blackwood Manor threatened to overwhelm them. But they had learned to navigate these difficult moments together, offering each other support, understanding, and unwavering love. Their therapist's words resonated with them: "The past is a part of your story, but it doesn't have to be the ending." They embraced this truth, recognizing that their experiences at Blackwood Lane had shaped them, but hadn't broken them.

They had emerged stronger, more resilient, and deeply connected.

Their new life wasn't a blissful escape from their past, but a conscious choice to move forward, to build a future based on healing, forgiveness, and unwavering love. They carried the scars of Blackwood Manor within them, subtle reminders of the darkness they'd faced, but these scars were fading, replaced by the vibrant colors of a life rebuilt, a life filled with love, laughter, and a quiet sense of peace. They had found a new normalcy, a new equilibrium, a life forged in the crucible of trauma, yet brimming with hope and the promise of lasting happiness. They had faced the darkness and emerged into the light, together. The future was uncertain, but it held the promise of continued healing and growth, a testament to their resilience and the enduring strength of their family bond. They had learned to accept the past, not as a defining factor, but as a stepping stone on their path towards a brighter, more hopeful future. Their journey was far from over, but they were walking towards the horizon, hand in hand, together.

Recurring Visions

The cottage's tranquility, a balm against the scars of Blackwood Lane, proved a deceptive shield. While the Miller family found solace in their new life, a subtle unease persisted, a disquiet that couldn't be attributed to lingering trauma alone. It began subtly, with fleeting images flashing across Emily's mind – a glimpse of the shadowed hallway, the unsettling curve of the staircase, a chilling reflection in a dusty mirror. These weren't simple memories; they were vivid, visceral visions, replete with the oppressive atmosphere of the house, the feeling of unseen eyes watching, the chilling whisper of unseen voices.

At first, Emily dismissed them as residual stress, the lingering effects of their ordeal. She'd confided in her therapist about the occasional night terrors, the unsettling dreams filled with shadowy figures and the ever-present sense of being watched, but these daytime visions felt different, more insidious, clinging to the edges of her consciousness, disrupting the fragile peace she'd worked so hard to achieve. They weren't confined to moments of stress or fatigue; they appeared seemingly at random, startling her mid-conversation, interrupting her work, even intruding upon the moments of shared laughter with her family.

The visions were fragmented, disjointed glimpses rather than coherent narratives. One moment, she'd see Silas, his face pale and strained, standing at the foot of the Blackwood Manor stairs, his eyes wide with terror. The next, she'd be back in the kitchen, her hands slick with unseen blood, a knife clutched tightly in her grasp. She'd then see John, his face contorted in a silent scream, trapped within the attic's suffocating darkness. These fragmented scenes were never the same, always shifting, always just out of grasp, like trying to catch smoke. She'd struggle to recall the specific details, the sharp edges of the images blurring into an unsettling fog, leaving only a chilling residue of fear and confusion. The recurring nature of these visions, their unpredictable emergence, gnawed at her sanity. They were a constant, low-level hum of unease, a dissonant chord in the otherwise harmonious melody of her new life.

Mary noticed the subtle shifts in Emily's demeanor. The vibrant energy that had blossomed in the cottage began to dim, replaced by a haunted look in her eyes. The cheerful hum that once accompanied her gardening was replaced by quiet introspection, her laughter less frequent, her movements more hesitant. Mary sensed a deepening anxiety, a subtle withdrawal, that went beyond the lingering trauma of Blackwood Lane. There was a new dimension to her fear, something beyond the house itself, something more personal, more menacing.

John, attuned to the subtle shifts in his daughter's emotional state, initially dismissed Emily's increasingly erratic behavior as a natural part of the healing process. He understood the power of trauma to linger, to manifest in unpredictable ways. However, the intensity of her visions, the sheer persistence of these fragmented images, was starting to alarm him. He saw the fear in her eyes, the subtle tremors in her hands, and his rational mind couldn't entirely dismiss the possibility that something more sinister was at play. His obsessive need for order had been replaced with a more measured approach, a willingness to acknowledge and accept the uncertainties of life, yet this new uncertainty, this mysterious threat to his daughter's well-being, stirred a deep unease within him. He found himself unconsciously reverting to old habits, meticulously checking doors and windows, his sense of security once again threatened by forces he couldn't comprehend.

Silas, deeply connected to Emily through his artistic expression, also noticed a change in her art. The vibrant colors, the hopeful imagery that had marked her recent work, had begun to fade, replaced by a darker palette, more muted tones, and disturbing symbolism. Her paintings, once a testament to her healing journey, now depicted shadowy figures lurking in corners, distorted faces peering from behind trees, and unsettling scenes of intense fear and isolation. He saw the reflection of her visions in her art, the fragmented glimpses of Blackwood Manor manifesting as cryptic symbols and unsettling imagery. The vibrant hues that had once represented her healing were being slowly consumed by a growing darkness, a darkness that mirrored the shadows creeping into her mind.

Their therapist, Dr. Albright, a woman known for her calm demeanor and insightful understanding of the human psyche, was initially skeptical. She attributed the visions to post-traumatic stress, a normal, albeit challenging, phase in the recovery process. However, as Emily's descriptions became more detailed, more unsettling, even more vivid, even Dr. Albright began to acknowledge a potential element beyond simple trauma. The specificity of the visions, the recurring elements, the emotional intensity they evoked - all pointed towards a possible deeper, more insidious threat, a threat that refused to be confined to the past.

The visions became more frequent, more intense. Emily began to experience them in public places, her body freezing mid-sentence as a terrifying flash of Blackwood Manor would momentarily engulf her. The line between reality and delusion started to blur, the fear intensifying with each vision. Her once bright eyes now held a haunted expression, a constant look of fear that mirrored the disquiet growing within her family. The quiet contentment of their cottage life was fading, replaced by a creeping dread, a constant low hum of anxiety that permeated every aspect of their lives. Their shared sense of peace was fractured, the shared healing process suddenly threatened by this new, unseen enemy.

One evening, during a family dinner, Emily suddenly froze, her eyes wide with terror. The room seemed to fall silent as the vision engulfed her, her face contorted in a silent scream. She saw herself standing in the Blackwood Manor kitchen, the knife dripping blood, John's lifeless body sprawled on the floor. The image was horrifically realistic, the smell of blood and the chilling silence of the room seeming to invade their present reality. The vision faded as quickly as it had arrived, leaving Emily trembling and gasping for air. The shared trauma of Blackwood Manor, the fragile peace they'd managed to cultivate, seemed to shatter in that instant, the unseen threat suddenly and terrifyingly real.

The family, united in their love and their shared past, now faced a new challenge, a more subtle, more insidious threat than the house itself. The darkness they'd escaped still lingered, clinging to Emily, poisoning the fragile equilibrium they'd managed to achieve. The question haunted them: was it the house, the past, or something else entirely? The answer was elusive, but the feeling of being watched, of being threatened, was now undeniable. Their new life, once a sanctuary of healing, was once again under siege, and this time, the enemy was invisible, intangible, and terrifyingly close. The idyllic cottage, once their safe haven, was becoming a refuge under siege, the idyllic picture cracking and revealing an unsettling darkness beneath the surface.

A Shadowy Presence

The unsettling feeling wasn't confined to Emily. John, a man who prided himself on his rationality, found himself increasingly on edge. He'd always been meticulous, but now his attention to detail bordered on obsession. He double-checked locks, examined every shadow, and listened for any unusual sounds, his ears straining for the whispers that seemed to dance just beyond the threshold of hearing. The quiet cottage, once a haven of peace, now felt like a stage set for an unseen play, its stillness pregnant with unspoken menace.

Mary, ever the pragmatist, initially dismissed the growing unease as a collective anxiety, a lingering effect of their traumatic experience. But the pervasive feeling of being watched, the subtle shifts in the atmosphere, were too persistent to ignore. Objects seemed to move inexplicably, doors creaked open in the dead of night, and a chill permeated the air, even on the warmest days. She found herself scrutinizing the faces of her family, searching for signs of shared paranoia, or perhaps, a deeper unspoken fear. The shared trauma, she realized, had left them vulnerable, their senses heightened to a point where even the slightest anomaly felt like a potential threat.

Even Silas, the youngest, felt the shift. His artistic expression, once a vibrant outlet for his emotions, became increasingly dark and disturbing. His sketches, once filled with playful imagery and bright colors, now featured shadowy figures, haunted landscapes, and a recurring motif of a looming, unseen presence. He would often find himself sketching the same shadowy form, a figure that shifted and changed with each attempt, yet remained undeniably unsettling. He couldn't explain it, this sudden shift in his artistic vision; it felt as if an unseen hand were guiding his pencil, imposing a darker narrative on his canvas.

The most alarming aspect was the lack of any concrete evidence. There were no physical manifestations, no obvious signs of intrusion. It was the subtle shifts, the unseen movements, the palpable sense of being watched that truly unsettled them. This was not the physical terror of Blackwood Lane; this was a psychological siege, a slow, insidious erosion of their peace. It was as if the darkness they had escaped had somehow followed them, clinging to their shadows, seeping into the very fabric of their new life.

One evening, John woke to a sound—a soft scratching at the window. He froze, his heart pounding in his chest. He slowly approached the window, his hand trembling as he reached for the curtain. When he pulled it back, he saw nothing but the inky blackness of the night. But the feeling persisted, the scratching replaced by a low, almost imperceptible hum, a vibration that seemed to emanate from the walls themselves. He felt a prickling sensation on his skin, a sense of unease so profound it was almost physical. He tried to rationalize it, telling himself it was the wind, a branch scraping against the glass. But the feeling lingered, a cold dread that settled deep in his bones.

The following day, Mary discovered a small, antique music box hidden in the attic. It was intricately carved, made of dark, polished wood, and looked centuries old. When she wound it up, a haunting melody filled the room, a melody that seemed both familiar and strangely alien. The tune, melancholic and slightly discordant, evoked a feeling of profound sadness and unease. It was a melody that resonated with the unsettling atmosphere of the cottage, amplifying the sense of dread that had begun to permeate their lives. The music box became a chilling symbol of their predicament, a constant reminder of the unseen forces at play.

Emily's visions became more frequent, more vivid, more terrifying. She saw herself trapped in Blackwood Manor, the shadowy figures closing in, the sense of suffocation overwhelming. She would wake up screaming, drenched in sweat, her body trembling uncontrollably. During the day, she'd see glimpses of shadowy figures from the corner of her eye, fleeting visions that were difficult to articulate, yet impossible to ignore. The shadows seemed to follow her, lurking just beyond the periphery of her vision, their presence a constant reminder of the unseen threat that loomed over them.

One afternoon, while gardening, Emily felt a sudden icy breath on her neck. She spun around, her heart pounding, but found nothing. The sun shone brightly, the birds sang merrily, yet the chilling sensation remained, a phantom touch that whispered of something unseen, something malevolent. This wasn't the lingering trauma of Blackwood Lane; this was something new, something more insidious, more personal.

Dr. Albright, increasingly concerned, suggested a series of tests to rule out any underlying medical conditions. She also recommended a change of environment, suggesting a temporary move to a different location to see if the symptoms persisted. However, even as they explored these possibilities, a nagging feeling remained: the unsettling atmosphere, the palpable sense of being watched, persisted regardless of time or location. It wasn't just the house, it was something more.

The family decided to investigate their cottage's history. They unearthed old records, dusty photographs, and faded newspaper clippings that hinted at a darker past, a series of unexplained occurrences that mirrored their own experiences. They discovered tales of vanished residents, inexplicable noises, and a persistent sense of unease that had plagued the cottage for generations. The more they learned, the more convinced they became that they weren't dealing with mere coincidence; they were facing something that had been waiting for them, something that seemed to be tied to their family, their past, and their connection to Blackwood Manor.

Their research revealed a series of unsolved disappearances linked to the cottage, stretching back over a century. The accounts bore an uncanny resemblance to their own experiences – objects moving inexplicably, whispers echoing through empty rooms, and a persistent sense of being watched. The chilling similarities were unsettling, pointing toward a sinister pattern, a dark legacy that had followed them from Blackwood Manor to their seemingly idyllic retreat. Each new detail served to deepen their fear, confirming the presence of a shadowy entity that defied logic, reason, and explanation.

The constant feeling of being observed amplified their existing anxieties, driving wedges between them. Suspicions began to fester, fueling the already simmering tensions. The once-strong familial bond started to fray under the relentless pressure of fear and uncertainty. John's rational approach became increasingly strained, his patience wearing thin under the weight of the unseen threat. Mary's pragmatism began to crumble, replaced by a growing fear that surpassed any logical explanation. Emily, burdened by the visions, retreated further into herself, her once-vibrant spirit dimmed by the persistent shadows that clung to her.

Even Silas, usually the calmest of the family, felt the strain. His art, a reflection of his inner turmoil, grew increasingly dark, the shadowy figures becoming more defined, more menacing. His sketches became a visual diary of their torment, a haunting depiction of their descent into fear and paranoia. The once-united family, their shared trauma forging a bond of resilience, was fracturing under the relentless pressure of this new, unseen enemy.

One night, during a particularly intense period of unsettling occurrences, Emily's visions reached a horrifying climax. She saw herself, bathed in the eerie glow of moonlight, standing over the lifeless bodies of her family, the knife from Blackwood Manor clutched tightly in her hand. The vision was so vivid, so realistic, that the line between reality and illusion blurred completely. She screamed, waking up in a cold sweat, convinced that she was somehow responsible for the unseen terror that plagued them.

The family, shaken to their core, found themselves questioning not only the house but also each other. The fear of the unseen threat was amplified by the burgeoning mistrust, the seeds of doubt planted by the ever-present shadows. Their sanctuary was no longer a place of healing but a battleground, where the enemy was invisible, the threat constant, and the bonds of family teetering on the brink of collapse. Their shared past, once a source of strength, had become a burden, a dark heritage that threatened to consume them all. The fight for survival, once focused on escaping Blackwood Manor, had shifted to a desperate struggle against a foe far more insidious and terrifying – the insidious shadow that haunted their minds and threatened to tear their family apart.

Growing Unease

The unsettling events continued, escalating in both frequency and intensity. What had begun as subtle anomalies – a flickering light, a misplaced object – now manifested as full-blown disturbances. Doors slammed shut with violent force, leaving them echoing in the sudden, chilling silence. Footsteps echoed from empty rooms, and whispers, once faint and elusive, now seemed to carry the weight of sinister secrets. The previously comforting sounds of the cottage—the creak of the floorboards, the gentle sigh of the wind through the trees—were now infused with a malevolent undertone, each sound laced with a foreboding that sent shivers down their spines.

John, despite his attempts at rational explanation, found his meticulously ordered world crumbling. Sleep became a luxury, replaced by restless nights filled with vivid nightmares. He'd wake up in a cold sweat, his heart pounding, the images of shadowy figures clinging to the edges of his consciousness. His usually sharp mind felt clouded, his logic failing him under the weight of the unseen terror. He started carrying a heavy flashlight, its beam cutting through the darkness, a feeble attempt to dispel the fear that gnawed at his insides. He found himself checking the locks multiple times a night, his actions driven not by logic but by a primal, desperate need for security.

Mary, once the family's pillar of strength, found her pragmatism failing her. The rational explanations she'd offered to her family and herself no longer held any sway. The sheer persistence of the unsettling occurrences, the cumulative effect of the whispers, the chilling atmosphere, had worn her down. She started experiencing unsettling physical symptoms: sleepless nights plagued by anxiety, debilitating headaches, and a pervasive sense of dread that clung to her like a shroud. She found herself retreating into herself, her usually bright eyes clouded by a weary exhaustion. The weight of their shared trauma and the ever-present unease threatened to consume her completely.

Even Silas, despite his young age, seemed to understand the gravity of their situation. His artistic output, initially a way of processing his experiences, became a frightening depiction of their present torment. His drawings became darker, more disturbing, each sketch filled with grotesque imagery and a palpable sense of impending doom. He started sketching not only shadowy figures but also disturbing self-portraits, his eyes wide with an unsettling fear, his mouth twisted into a silent scream. The disturbing self-portraits hung like a dark prophecy in their home, adding to the already pervasive sense of dread.

Emily's visions, once sporadic and easily dismissed as lingering effects of their trauma, intensified. They were no longer fleeting glimpses but full-blown, horrifying experiences that left her emotionally and physically drained. She saw herself trapped in a nightmarish landscape, the shadowy figures surrounding her, their whispers filling her ears with promises of destruction. These visions were so vivid, so real, that she'd wake up screaming, her body convulsing with terror. She began to question her own sanity, wondering if she was the source of their troubles, a harbinger of their doom.

The family's attempts to find a rational explanation for their experiences intensified. They scoured historical records, delving deeper into the cottage's history. They discovered fragmented tales of previous residents, stories of unexplained disappearances, and unsettling accounts of unusual happenings. The more they learned, the more certain they became that their experiences weren't isolated incidents; they were part of a sinister pattern, a dark legacy tied to the very fabric of their new home.

They discovered a series of newspaper clippings from the early 20th century detailing the mysterious disappearance of a family living in the cottage. The descriptions of their final days echoed their own experiences – inexplicable noises, objects moving on their own, and a palpable sense of being watched. The unnerving similarities sparked a chill down their spines, solidifying their belief that they were not alone and that the unseen threat was more than a mere coincidence.

Their research also revealed a local legend, a whispered tale about a malevolent entity that had haunted the cottage for generations, preying on the minds of its inhabitants, twisting their perceptions and driving them to madness. This legend, initially dismissed as folklore, now held a chilling relevance, casting a dark shadow over their reality. The tales of the entity's power over the minds of its victims fed into their growing fear and paranoia.

The increased awareness of their predicament further eroded their once-strong familial bonds. Suspicion and distrust started to creep into their interactions. John, despite his desperate attempts at maintaining a facade of rationality, became increasingly short-tempered and irritable. His normally calm demeanor was replaced by fits of rage, often directed at his family members, born out of a misplaced frustration and deep-seated fear. Mary's attempts to maintain order and provide comfort were undermined by her own growing anxiety and inability to comprehend the unseen threat.

Emily, consumed by her terrifying visions, withdrew further into herself, becoming emotionally distant and withdrawn. The vibrant young woman they once knew was now replaced by a shell of her former self, her eyes haunted by shadows only she could see. Silas, observing the disintegration of his family, started to isolate himself, his sketches becoming increasingly darker and more ominous.

The sense of isolation was profound. Their friends and neighbors, initially sympathetic, started to distance themselves, unable to fully comprehend their experiences and increasingly concerned about their well-being. The once vibrant and welcoming family was becoming a recluse, retreating further into the darkness that surrounded their home. The fear wasn't just confined to the walls of their cottage; it now extended to the community around them, isolating them even further.

One night, as a storm raged outside, the family huddled together in the living room, the flickering candlelight casting dancing shadows on the walls. The wind howled like a banshee, rattling the windows and doors, amplifying their already heightened sense of anxiety. Suddenly, the lights flickered and died, plunging them into absolute darkness. A bloodcurdling scream echoed through the cottage, followed by the sound of shattering glass and the frantic scramble of footsteps. In the darkness, fear consumed them, fueling the existing tensions and amplifying the suspicions they held against each other. The storm outside mirrored the chaos and turmoil that had become their reality, a tempest in their lives that promised to leave nothing untouched. Their fight for survival was no longer just against the unseen threat; it was against their own fears, their doubts, and the insidious erosion of their familial bonds, a battle that seemed destined to tear them apart. The unseen threat had not only infiltrated their home but had also wormed its way into their hearts and minds, threatening to destroy everything they held dear.

The Return

The scream, sharp and piercing, had ripped through the suffocating silence of the power outage, leaving a chilling echo in its wake. It was Emily's voice, a sound so filled with terror that it sent a fresh wave of icy dread through John, Mary, and Silas. The shattering of glass followed, the sound sharp and brittle against the relentless drumming of the rain against the windows. In the darkness, punctuated only by the erratic flashes of lightning, a primal fear gripped them, a cold hand squeezing their hearts. John fumbled for his flashlight, its beam cutting a shaky swathe through the oppressive blackness, revealing shards of glass scattered across the floor and the overturned remnants of a lamp.

The storm raged outside, mirroring the tempest within their home. The wind howled, a mournful wail that seemed to feed on their fear, whipping around the house like a vengeful spirit. In the flickering light of the flashlight, John saw Mary clutching Silas, her face pale and etched with terror. Emily was nowhere in sight.

"Emily!" John shouted, his voice barely audible above the storm's fury. His voice trembled with a mixture of fear and anger. He felt a surge of irrational guilt, a wave of responsibility crashing over him. He should have been more vigilant, more protective. He should have seen this coming.

They searched frantically, their movements clumsy and panicked in the darkness. Each creak of the floorboards, each gust of wind, sent a fresh jolt of adrenaline through their veins. The house seemed to breathe around them, its familiar contours warped and distorted in the darkness, transforming into a menacing labyrinth of shadows and fear.

Finally, John found her in the hallway, huddled against the wall, her body shaking uncontrollably. She was clutching a small, antique music box, its intricate carvings barely visible in the dim light. Her eyes were wide and unfocused, her breath coming in ragged gasps.

"The music… it called to me," she whispered, her voice barely a breath. "It… it was playing… and I had to follow."

The music box. It was one of the items they had found during their research into the house's history, a relic from one of the previous occupants, a family whose fate eerily mirrored their own. Its discovery had already stirred unsettling feelings within them, a premonition of impending doom. Now, here it was again, central to this latest terrifying event. The implications were chilling.

John carefully took the music box from her trembling hands. As he did, he noticed a small, almost imperceptible scratch on its surface, a minute imperfection that had been unseen before. As he examined it more closely, he realized the scratch formed a sequence of symbols, ancient-looking runes etched deep into the wood. His blood ran cold. This was not just a random artifact; it was a key, a piece of a puzzle that was far more sinister than they could have ever imagined.

The following days were a blur of anxiety and fear. They contacted a local historian specializing in arcane symbols, a woman with a reputation for deciphering ancient languages and texts. Dr. Evelyn Reed, a woman as enigmatic as the symbols themselves, agreed to examine the music box. Her assessment was chilling. The runes, she explained, were a form of ancient sigil, a powerful invocation to a malevolent entity—the very entity whispered about in the local legends they had dismissed earlier as folklore.

The sigil, she explained, wasn't just a representation; it was a conduit, a gateway through which the entity could exert its influence. The music box, far from being a mere antique, was a powerful instrument, deliberately crafted to amplify the entity's power and extend its reach. The disturbances they had been experiencing weren't random; they were orchestrated, deliberately summoned by those who had come before them. They had opened a door, and the entity was using them to remain in this world.

The revelation hit them like a physical blow, a crushing weight of despair and dread. Their initial fear was compounded by a chilling understanding: they were not just victims of a haunted house; they were pawns in a sinister game, manipulated by forces far older and more powerful than themselves. Their idyllic suburban life had become a battleground for an ancient evil, a struggle for survival against a foe they barely understood.

Dr. Reed suggested a way to break the connection, a ritual to banish the entity back to where it belonged. But it was dangerous, a gamble with potentially catastrophic consequences. It involved a complex series of steps, requiring precise actions and a profound understanding of the entity's nature. Failure would not only leave them vulnerable to the entity's wrath but also could unleash a far greater evil upon the world. The stakes were impossibly high.

The family, their bonds tested and strained to the breaking point, huddled together, their faces reflecting the flickering candlelight. The weight of their shared fear, their mutual responsibility, was almost palpable. The initial shock of the revelation was slowly giving way to a grim determination. They were facing the ultimate test, a choice between surrendering to their fear and fighting for their lives, for their sanity, and for the future they had so desperately tried to create.

The ritual required them to work together, their individual strengths combining to counter the entity's influence. John, despite his internal conflict and the lingering doubts gnawing at him, relied on his innate logic and meticulous approach to navigate the complex steps of the ritual. Mary, her earlier pragmatism slowly re-emerging through her fear, took charge of the practical aspects, organizing and coordinating their actions. Even Silas, his artistic talents finding a new and unexpected purpose, crafted the necessary tools for the ritual, his youthful energy strangely fueling their determination.

Emily, though still haunted by her visions, found a newfound strength. She understood the music box, the entity's influence over it, better than anyone else. Her visions, now viewed as a disturbing gift, provided glimpses into the entity's tactics, revealing its weaknesses and potential vulnerabilities. Her terrifying experiences, far from paralyzing her, empowered her, transforming her from a terrified victim into an active participant in the fight for survival.

The ritual itself was as terrifying as it was complex. The night was filled with a cacophony of unsettling sounds—whispers, guttural growls, and the chilling echo of laughter from the depths of the house. The air crackled with unseen energy, and the very foundations of the cottage seemed to tremble. The shadows in their eyes were a combination of fear and determination, a testament to their resolve in confronting a force beyond their comprehension.

The climax of the ritual was agonizingly slow and tense. The air was charged with an almost palpable energy, and the very essence of reality seemed to shimmer and bend. John's meticulousness, Mary's pragmatism, Silas's artistic skill, and Emily's disturbing visions were their weapons against an ancient evil. Their collective effort seemed like a tiny spark against a consuming inferno, but it was their only hope.

As the final rune was etched, a wave of chilling energy washed over them. The house groaned and shuddered, as if under a tremendous strain. The entity's presence, so potent before, began to recede, its power dwindling under the assault of their combined efforts. The unseen threat, once so pervasive, began to retreat, its influence weakening with each passing moment.

The dawn broke, painting the sky in hues of pale pink and soft gold, bringing a fragile sense of peace after the night's terrifying ordeal. The storm had subsided, leaving behind an eerie stillness. The house, battered but not broken, seemed to breathe a sigh of relief, casting off the shadows that had clung to it for so long. The Millers, exhausted but alive, stood together, the survivors of a harrowing ordeal, their bonds forged stronger in the crucible of their shared struggle.

But the ordeal wasn't entirely over. While the immediate threat seemed to have receded, the memory of the unseen threat would forever be etched into their memories. They had faced their fears, faced their own vulnerabilities, and ultimately faced the malevolent force that had invaded their lives. They had survived. But the scars remained, a constant reminder of the fragility of their sanity and the insidious darkness that lurks just beneath the surface of the seemingly perfect world they had once known. Blackwood Lane, once the symbol of their dreams, now stood as a stark reminder of their harrowing confrontation with the past, a battle won, but a victory hard-earned and bought at a heavy price. The unseen threat may have been banished, but its presence still lingers, lurking at the periphery of their lives, a haunting reminder of what they had endured and the darkness they had faced. The family, bound together by trauma and shared struggle, must now face the daunting task of healing and rebuilding, forever changed by the ordeal on Blackwood Lane.

Reckoning

The fragile peace of the dawn was a deceptive calm. The storm had passed, but the tempest within the Miller family raged on. The banishing of the entity, while a victory of sorts, had laid bare the deeper fissures within their relationships, wounds far older and more insidious than the ancient evil they had just confronted. The house, though seemingly cleansed, felt different, heavy with the residue of fear and the weight of unspoken accusations.

John, ever the pragmatist, focused on the immediate aftermath – securing the house, contacting the authorities (though what could he possibly tell them?), and tending to the family's physical wounds. But beneath his outward calm, a deep unease gnawed at him. The ritual had worked, or so it seemed, but it had also exposed a truth he'd been unwilling to face: his own failings as a husband and father. He'd been too absorbed in his work, too focused on the material aspects of their "perfect" life, neglecting the emotional needs of his family. The house had mirrored their internal chaos, amplifying their existing vulnerabilities.

Mary, though outwardly supportive, was consumed by a simmering resentment. She felt betrayed, not only by the house and its dark history, but by John's obliviousness to the cracks that had been developing in their marriage for years. The crisis had brought these issues into sharp relief, and the unspoken accusations hung heavy in the air. The shared trauma had forged a bond, but it was a bond tempered with bitterness and a growing sense of distrust.

Silas, the youngest, bore the burden of his own silent anxieties. While his artistic talents had proven instrumental in the ritual, he felt overwhelmed by the weight of responsibility he'd shouldered, the unseen pressure of being the one to provide a tangible solution to their predicament. His youthful idealism had been shattered, replaced by a haunting awareness of the darkness that lurked beneath the surface of the world. He struggled to reconcile the idyllic image of his family with the terrifying reality they had faced.

Emily, though seemingly liberated from the entity's influence, was left with the chilling echoes of her visions, the fragmented images of a past she never knew, yet felt intimately connected to. The music box, the ancient runes, the whispers from the empty rooms – these fragments of the past were indelibly etched in her memory, a constant reminder of the darkness that had threatened to consume them. She carried the weight of a knowledge too heavy for her years, an understanding of the malevolent forces at work that set her apart from her family.

The days that followed were a blur of forced normalcy, a fragile attempt to reclaim a semblance of their former lives. But the shadows lingered. The quiet moments were filled with unspoken tension, the shared silences heavy with the weight of their ordeal. Meals were eaten in strained silence, the familiar sounds of their home now punctuated by the constant hum of unspoken anxieties. The air was thick with the unacknowledged truth of their fractures and the underlying reality of their individual struggles.

John attempted to re-establish a sense of normalcy, pushing himself relentlessly into his work, trying to regain control, to fix what felt irreparably broken. But his attempts only served to exacerbate the existing tensions. His distance, interpreted as indifference, fueled Mary's anger. His need to fix things, to restore order, only emphasized the disorder within their family structure, reminding them of the wounds that had been laid bare.

Mary retreated into herself, her pragmatism overwhelmed by a wave of despair. She started revisiting past hurts, old resentments re-surfacing. She was struggling with her feelings of insecurity, a feeling of being ignored in the past, now exacerbated by John's attempts to manage everything alone. She felt a lack of appreciation for her contributions, her feelings of inadequacy creeping up, threatening to destabilize her sense of self.

Silas withdrew into his art, seeking refuge in the familiar comfort of creativity. But even his art reflected the darkness that had entered their lives, the vibrant colors and playful forms replaced by stark lines, brooding shadows, and unsettling imagery. He felt the pressure of being the family's 'savior', the one who had helped resolve their crisis, but his actions now amplified his underlying fears and anxieties.

Emily, burdened by her visions, found herself increasingly isolated, her fragmented glimpses of the past becoming more frequent and intense. She struggled to reconcile her experiences with the reality of her present, the line between past and present blurring dangerously. The shared trauma had made her older and more insightful.

The need to confront their pasts became unavoidable. They began individual therapy, each grappling with their own demons, their individual struggles brought into focus. John confronted his neglect, the years he'd lost in the pursuit of a life he no longer recognized, a life that had almost destroyed his family. Mary explored her feelings of inadequacy and resentment, her past struggles and unhealed wounds laid bare. Silas confronted his fears and the pressure he'd placed upon himself to be the solution to his family's problems.

Emily processed the terrifying insights provided by her visions, separating the past from the present and coming to terms with her experiences.

As they delved deeper into their individual psyches, they gradually began to understand the interconnectedness of their struggles, how their individual issues had combined to create the perfect storm that had been unleashed in Blackwood Lane. The house had acted as a catalyst, but the deeper issues, the resentments, the unspoken anxieties, were their own making.

The family therapy sessions became a space for honest confrontation, a crucible where old wounds were examined and new understanding slowly began to emerge. They began to communicate their feelings, to address their unspoken resentments and anxieties. The shared trauma, initially a source of division, slowly began to forge a deeper, more honest connection between them. The wounds were still raw, the scars visible, but a fragile hope began to take root, nurtured by their shared struggle and their newfound commitment to understanding and healing.

The house on Blackwood Lane remained. It stood as a stark reminder of their ordeal, a constant presence in their lives. But it was no longer a symbol of fear. It was a testament to their resilience, a marker of the darkness they had confronted and the bonds they had forged in the crucible of their shared struggle. The unseen threat had been banished, but the real work, the work of healing and rebuilding their family, had only just begun. Their journey toward recovery was long and arduous, but as they walked hand-in-hand, they faced it with a newfound strength, their collective resilience born from the fires of adversity, the hope for a future strengthened by the shadows of the past. The scars remained, a reminder of the unseen threat and the fragility of their minds, but they also bore witness to their resilience and the love that bound them together. Their shared struggle had not only forged a stronger family but also a collective strength that would forever sustain them against future storms.

Unraveling the Past

The dusty attic yielded its secrets reluctantly. Sifting through cobweb-draped trunks and forgotten relics, Silas unearthed a leather-bound journal, its pages brittle with age. The spidery script within spoke of a clandestine society, a sect worshipping ancient entities, their rituals steeped in pagan mysticism and shadowed by chilling sacrifice. The journal detailed the construction of the house on Blackwood Lane, not as a simple dwelling, but as a nexus of power, a conduit for channeling forbidden energies. It described the community that existed before the Millers, the community that lived and died around this nexus of power. The cult's rituals had intertwined with their lives for centuries.

The chilling realization dawned on them slowly, a creeping dread that seeped into their bones. The names in the journal – names etched into the house's woodwork, whispered in Emily's visions – were their own ancestors, their family lineage inextricably linked to the cult's dark history. The entity they had banished wasn't just a malevolent spirit; it was a manifestation of their own ancestral sins, a karmic retribution for the darkness that had flowed through their bloodline for generations.

John, initially resistant to this revelation, found himself grappling with a heritage he never knew existed. The man of logic and reason was forced to confront the supernatural, the reality of a past he'd never considered. The perfect life he so meticulously crafted was revealed to be a fragile construct, built on a foundation of buried secrets and ancestral guilt. This new understanding fueled his feelings of inadequacy as a husband and father, a weight heavier than any material success he had achieved. He realized how his pursuit of perfection had blinded him to the deeper, more insidious threats that had lurked in his family's history. His efforts to create a perfect family had left a void, unable to meet the standards he had set.

Mary, burdened by her own ancestral connections, found a chilling echo of her own struggles within the journal's pages. The women described within, bound to the house and the cult's rituals, echoed her own feelings of entrapment, her own struggle for autonomy within the confines of a patriarchal society, a history repeated throughout her family. The weight of their past suffocated her. She felt a profound connection to these women, their shared suffering, their unheard voices crying out through time. This discovery heightened her feelings of inadequacy, reinforcing the resentments she carried, not just against John, but against a lineage that had held women captive for generations. The trauma felt generational, passed down like a cursed inheritance.

Silas, already burdened by his role in the banishing ritual, felt the added pressure of carrying the weight of his family's dark history. The journal's revelations added a layer of ancestral guilt to his personal anxieties. The artistic talent that had previously been a source of comfort now became a vehicle for expressing his feelings of overwhelming responsibility. His art evolved into a darker, more introspective exploration of his family's legacy, his paintings depicting the cycle of suffering and the struggle for redemption that spanned generations. He wondered if the family's actions were predetermined, woven into the fabric of their heritage, or if there was a chance to break free.

Emily, with her uncanny ability to tap into the house's history, found the journal's details mirroring her fragmented visions. The images that had haunted her – ritualistic sacrifices, whispered prayers, faces twisted in agony – found clarity in the journal's chilling narrative. The journal was a validation of her experiences, but it also amplified the fear and confusion she felt. She found solace in her visions, not just the terrible images but also the glimpses of hope that were woven throughout the images, whispers of rebellion and resistance against the cult's dark influence. The ancient runes, previously enigmatic symbols, now held a grim significance, revealing the names of her ancestors who defied the cult and paid a terrible price for it. This realization, while disturbing, was also empowering. She could see a pattern of resistance within the history of her family, a flicker of hope amongst the darkness.

The family decided to consult Dr. Albright, a historian specializing in esoteric cults and forgotten sects. Dr. Albright, initially skeptical, became captivated by the journal's contents. He confirmed the cult's existence, revealing details of its long-standing influence on Blackwood Lane, tracing their involvement back to the early settlers of the region. He corroborated Silas's findings and pieced together the fragments of Emily's visions, creating a timeline of the cult's activities, their ritualistic practices, and the horrifying sacrifices they made. He also uncovered details of the resistance, the ancestors who fought against the dark forces of the cult, their acts of defiance echoing through history.

Dr. Albright's research revealed that the house wasn't simply built on sacred ground; it was designed as a physical embodiment of the cult's power, its architecture mirroring their intricate rituals. The layout of the rooms, the placement of windows and doorways, even the seemingly insignificant details like the placement of the fireplace and staircase, all contributed to the house's malevolent aura and reinforced the cult's influence. He explained that the rituals performed within the house amplified its power, creating a space where the cult's influence grew stronger with each generation, creating a legacy that affected the Millers.

The weight of their ancestral legacy pressed down on the Millers, a suffocating blanket of darkness. They were not just victims of a haunted house; they were inheritors of a cursed lineage, bound by generations of secrets and transgressions. Their family therapy sessions took on a new intensity, each member grappling not only with their personal struggles but also with the weight of their family's dark history. They had to confront their past and the consequences of their ancestors' actions, acknowledging the role that their heritage played in their ordeal.

John grappled with the paternal sins of generations past, realizing that his own neglect stemmed from a deep-seated fear, a fear that echoed the anxieties and traumas his ancestors had carried. Mary found solace in discovering a legacy of resistance and rebellion, a lineage of women who defied the cult, giving her a sense of strength and purpose. Silas used his art to reconcile the dark history of his family with the possibility of redemption, the struggle against the darkness mirrored in the vibrant colors and dynamic brushstrokes of his paintings. Emily, no longer a mere observer, became an active participant in their journey of healing, her visions providing critical insights and guidance, leading them toward understanding the secrets of the past.

Their journey became not just a struggle for survival but a quest for redemption, a fight to break free from the chains of their ancestral legacy. They worked together, supporting each other as they delved into their past and faced the darkest aspects of their family history. The house on Blackwood Lane remained, a permanent reminder of the events that had transpired, yet it was no longer a source of fear. It was a symbol of their collective strength and determination, a testament to their resilience in the face of overwhelming odds. The Millers chose to confront the darkness head-on, not just for themselves, but for their ancestors, and in doing so, they began to forge a new future, free from the clutches of their haunted past. The scars of their ordeal remained, but they were now badges of honor, testaments to the strength they had found within themselves, within their family, and within the echoes of those who had come before them. The fight for redemption was far from over, but they stood together, facing the darkness with a newfound hope, a legacy forged not in fear, but in resilience and love.

Confronting the Cult

Armed with Dr. Albright's research and a newfound understanding of their ancestral burden, the Millers embarked on a perilous confrontation with the lingering vestiges of the Blackwood Lane cult. The historian had provided them with more than just historical data; he'd given them a roadmap, a blueprint of the cult's rituals and the locations within the house where their power was most concentrated. He'd also highlighted the subtle symbols – carvings, markings, and even the arrangement of furniture – that served as markers for the cult's activities. These weren't just decorations; they were conduits of energy, focal points for the channeling of malevolent forces.

Their first target was the cellar, the heart of the house, where the cult's most potent rituals had taken place. Descending the creaking stairs, the Millers felt a palpable shift in the atmosphere; the air grew heavy, thick with an oppressive energy that seemed to press down on them. John, armed with a heavy oak mallet – a somewhat futile weapon against centuries of entrenched malevolence – led the way, his resolve a thin shield against the encroaching dread. Mary, clutching a small, intricately carved wooden box recovered from the attic – a relic of a past rebellion against the cult – followed closely behind. Silas, his face pale but determined, carried a large canvas and brushes, intending to document their confrontation, to visually capture the final chapter of their family's ordeal. Emily, her eyes wide with a mix of apprehension and an unsettling calm, trailed behind, her presence a strange mixture of vulnerability and unexpected strength. She seemed to sense the movements of unseen energies, her whispers of warnings guiding them through the labyrinthine corridors of the cellar.

The cellar was a claustrophobic space, dimly lit by flickering candles, the air thick with the smell of damp earth and something else, something ancient and unsettlingly acrid. The walls were lined with shelves filled with dusty jars and strange artifacts – remnants of the cult's practices. Emily pointed to a series of symbols etched into the stone floor, a complex pattern that Dr. Albright had identified as a summoning sigil. It was here, she sensed, that the cult had conducted their most potent rituals. Silas began to sketch the symbols, his movements precise and steady, his brushstrokes capturing the sinister beauty of the markings.

As they ventured deeper into the cellar, they encountered a hidden chamber, concealed behind a false wall. Inside, they found a collection of ancient texts, their pages filled with chilling descriptions of the cult's rituals and beliefs. The texts detailed the methods by which the cult drew power from the land, how they manipulated the energies of the house to achieve their sinister goals. Mary, her fingers tracing the faded script, felt a surge of anger, a righteous fury against the generations of oppression described within the pages.

The final confrontation took place in the center of the chamber. The air crackled with unseen energy, the candles flickering wildly, their flames dancing in a macabre ballet. A low humming sound filled the chamber, growing steadily louder, more intense. Emily, her vision sharpened, saw swirling mists forming in the center of the room, coalescing into a shadowy figure, its form shifting and changing, its features obscured by darkness. This was the manifestation of the entity they had been battling, the embodiment of their ancestral sins, the culmination of generations of darkness.

The fight was not one of brute force but of will, of spiritual resistance. John, though armed with the mallet, found his weapon useless against the intangible force. Mary, however, found her strength in the wooden box, its intricate carvings seemingly resonating with an opposing energy. She opened the box, revealing a collection of small, intricately carved stones, each imbued with a protective energy. As she tossed the stones into the swirling mists, a counter-energy emanated from them, pushing back against the darkness, weakening the entity's hold.

Silas, meanwhile, continued to paint, his brushstrokes becoming more frantic, his colors more vivid, his art a form of counter-magic, a visual representation of their resistance. His canvases became a battlefield, a clash of light and shadow, of hope and despair. Emily, acting as a conduit, channeled her visions, focusing her energy towards the stones, guiding the counter-energy, her presence bolstering their efforts.

The confrontation was a test not only of their physical and spiritual strength but also of their family bond. They faced the darkness not as individuals but as a united front, their shared history, their shared trauma, forging an unbreakable bond. The swirling mists began to recede, the humming sound fading, the oppressive energy dissipating. The entity, weakened by their combined efforts, eventually dissipated, leaving behind only a lingering sense of unease.

Exhausted but triumphant, the Millers emerged from the cellar, the weight of generations lifted from their shoulders. The house, once a symbol of their terror, now held a different significance. It was a testament to their resilience, to their ability to overcome the darkness that had haunted them for so long. They had faced the darkness, not only within the house but within themselves, and emerged stronger, their family bond forged anew in the crucible of their shared ordeal. The scars remained, but they were now reminders of their strength, their courage, and their unwavering love. The fight for redemption was over, for now. The future remained uncertain, but it was a future they would face together, as a family. The house on Blackwood Lane remained, a constant reminder, yet no longer a source of terror, but a testament to their courage. The Millers had faced the darkness, and they had won. Their family, tested by unimaginable horrors, had not only survived but thrived. The past was behind them, a shadow they'd emerged from, stronger and more united than ever before. Their shared trauma had become their shared strength. They had confronted the cult, and they had won. And in that victory, they found peace. The house remained, but it was just a house now.

The Final Battle

The air in the cellar hung thick and heavy, a miasma of fear and ancient dread. The humming that had begun subtly in the hidden chamber now resonated through their bones, a physical vibration that threatened to shatter their resolve. The shadowy figure, the embodiment of the Blackwood Lane cult's malevolent energy, had solidified, its form less amorphous, more defined. It was tall and gaunt, draped in tattered robes that seemed to shift and writhe like living things. Its face remained obscured, a void of impenetrable darkness, yet its presence exuded an overwhelming sense of malice, of centuries of accumulated wickedness.

John, his oak mallet feeling ludicrously inadequate, stepped forward, his heart hammering against his ribs. He'd faced down raging bulls in his younger years, wrestled with business rivals, but this…this was different. This was a battle against something primal, something beyond his comprehension. He swung the mallet, the wood whistling through the air, but the blow passed harmlessly through the entity, the shadowy figure merely flickering before reforming itself.

Mary, clutching the box of carved stones, knew brute force wouldn't work. Dr. Albright's research had spoken of a counter-energy, a resonant frequency that could disrupt the cult's power. She focused her mind, channeling her anger, her grief, her determination into the stones. She began to chant an ancient rhyme, a forgotten incantation she'd gleaned from the tattered texts, her voice low and resonant, a counterpoint to the ominous humming that filled the chamber.

As she chanted, the stones in her hand glowed faintly, pulsing with a warm, ethereal light. She flung the first stone, aiming for the heart of the shadowy figure. It passed straight through, striking something unseen yet palpable, causing the entity to recoil momentarily, a ripple of distortion across its insubstantial form. This was it. This was their chance.

Silas, his brushstrokes frantic, captured the scene on canvas with terrifying accuracy. He wasn't just painting; he was fighting too, imbuing his art with his own will, channeling his fear, his rage, his hope into every stroke of the brush. The colors were violent, clashing – deep crimson, searing gold, and a ghostly, ethereal white. He saw the strokes on the canvas as a physical representation of the battle, each brushstroke pushing back against the darkness. His painting became a conduit for his energy, a symbolic counterattack against the oppressive forces surrounding them.

Emily, her eyes closed, stood at the edge of the chamber, her face pale but serene. She wasn't fighting physically; her role was more subtle, more crucial. She acted as an anchor, a grounding force, drawing strength from the earth, channeling the raw energy of the house itself – not the dark energy the cult used, but the inherent power of the land, the resilience of nature. Her whispers, barely audible above the humming, were words of power, words of protection, words that held the family together. She felt the shift in energy, the ebb and flow of the battle reflected in her very being.

The battle intensified. The shadowy figure lunged, its insubstantial form attempting to engulf them, a wave of cold, suffocating darkness washing over them. John fought back with renewed vigor, his blows growing more desperate, yet still futile against the creature's spectral form. Mary continued to chant, flinging stones into the swirling mists, each one weakening the entity, each one chipping away at its power. Silas painted relentlessly, each stroke a prayer, a battle cry, a declaration of defiance.

Then, suddenly, a change. Mary's chants grew stronger, more resonant. The stones she hurled emitted a blinding light, and a powerful surge of energy rippled outward, shattering the oppressive silence. Silas's painting erupted in a burst of light, a blinding flash of white that seemed to sear the darkness away. Emily cried out, a sound of power, of release, and the house seemed to groan, as if exhaling a long-held breath.

The shadowy figure began to shrink, to disintegrate, its form dissolving into swirling mists, the humming fading to a whisper, then silence. The oppressive weight lifted, the air clearing, the atmosphere becoming noticeably lighter, free from the miasma of malice. The final remnants of the entity vanished, leaving behind an almost unbearable stillness.

The Millers stood, exhausted but unbroken, their bodies trembling, their minds reeling from the intensity of the battle. They looked at each other, their faces etched with exhaustion, but also relief, a profound sense of shared accomplishment. Their family, bound together by a shared trauma, had faced the ultimate darkness and emerged victorious. The victory was not just against the cult; it was a victory over their own fears, their doubts, their internal struggles.

They had faced the darkness within the house and the darkness within themselves, and they had overcome both. They had saved themselves. They had saved each other. They left the cellar, the steps feeling easier under their feet, their backs straighter. The house felt different; it had breathed, and in its exhalation, it had released its grip.

The remaining cult members, having lost their primary conduit of power, were significantly weaker. They were scattered, their organization shattered. The police investigation, spurred by Dr. Albright's research and the Millers' testimony, netted several arrests, but some escaped. The threat was not entirely gone, yet the core of the darkness that had plagued the family and the house had been eradicated.

In the aftermath, the Millers chose to stay. The house on Blackwood Lane was no longer a place of terror but a testament to their resilience, their strength, and their unwavering love for one another. The scars remained, both visible and unseen, but they were badges of honor, reminders of their harrowing ordeal, and a symbol of their ultimate triumph. The house became a quiet reminder of their shared victory, a space of healing, a space where they could rebuild and forge a new chapter in their lives. The future remained uncertain, filled with the lingering specter of the past, but they would face it together, stronger, more resilient, more united than ever before. They had faced the darkness, and they had won. They were a family, forever bound together by their shared ordeal, and their shared victory. The haunting whispers of Blackwood Lane were finally silenced, replaced by the quiet murmur of their renewed hope.

Unexpected Alliances

The chilling silence that followed the dissipation of the shadowy entity felt heavier than the oppressive presence it had replaced. A profound exhaustion settled over the Millers, a bone-deep weariness that went beyond physical fatigue. They stood in the damp cellar, the air thick with the lingering scent of decay and the faint, metallic tang of blood – a silent testament to their harrowing ordeal. John, his hands still clutching the useless mallet, looked at his family, his gaze lingering on each of their faces, etched with exhaustion and the stark reality of their near-death experience.

Mary, her breath coming in ragged gasps, carefully gathered the remaining carved stones. The ethereal glow had faded, leaving them cold and inert in her palm. The ancient incantation, once a potent weapon, now felt like a distant memory, a forgotten spell uttered in a dream. She felt the lingering tremor in her hands, a physical manifestation of the raw energy she had unleashed.

Silas, his hands trembling, carefully lowered his brush, the paint still wet on the canvas. The painting, a chaotic masterpiece of clashing colors and violent strokes, stood as a stark visual representation of their struggle. The vibrant hues, once symbols of their fight, now seemed to mock their exhaustion. He felt a strange detachment, a sense of watching himself from afar, as if he were observing a scene from a distant, terrifying dream.

Emily, her eyes still closed, remained anchored to the earth, drawing strength from the land. She felt the lingering vibrations of the battle, the echoes of the struggle resonating deep within her core. The raw energy she had channeled still flowed through her, a quiet hum of power that pulsed beneath her skin. She opened her eyes slowly, her gaze focusing on the faces of her family. A shared understanding passed between them, a silent acknowledgment of their shared trauma and the profound bond that had been forged in the crucible of fear.

Their victory, however hard-won, was incomplete. The remnants of the Blackwood Lane cult still existed, scattered and weakened but not destroyed. The police investigation, though promising, was hampered by the cult's secrecy and the cryptic nature of their rituals. Dr. Albright, a lifeline in their darkest hours, had provided invaluable assistance but even he couldn't completely unravel the centuries-old secrets embedded in the house and its dark history. A deeper, more insidious threat lurked, unseen, its tendrils reaching into the shadows.

It was then that an unexpected alliance emerged. Detective Harding, the lead investigator on the Blackwood Lane case, a man initially skeptical of the Millers' accounts, had witnessed the aftermath of their battle in the cellar. He had seen the evidence – the shattered remnants of the shadowy figure, the glowing stones, the painting that somehow seemed to mirror the events with unnerving accuracy. His skepticism had been replaced by a reluctant, grudging respect, a recognition of something beyond his understanding.

Harding, burdened by the weight of unsolved cases and the frustration of dealing with a cult that seemed to defy logic, saw a chance to finally crack the case. He saw the Millers not as victims but as key witnesses, and more importantly, as allies. His initial approach had been one of detached professionalism, but after the events in the cellar, his perspective shifted. He proposed an alliance, a collaboration between the police and the Millers, a shared effort to dismantle the cult once and for all. The offer, initially met with hesitation and suspicion, was ultimately accepted.

This unexpected alliance expanded beyond Detective Harding. Dr. Albright, recognizing the magnitude of the threat, went beyond the academic realm. He actively engaged in the investigation, his knowledge of occult history and symbolism proving invaluable. He became a key advisor to Harding, providing insights into the cult's rituals, their history, and their remaining members. His deep understanding of the cult's methods provided a crucial advantage in unraveling their complex network of operations.

Their collaboration led to unexpected breakthroughs. Dr. Albright's research uncovered a hidden network of safe houses utilized by the cult. These locations were scattered throughout the region, each carefully concealed and shrouded in secrecy. The Millers' firsthand experience of the cult's rituals provided invaluable intel, enabling the police to anticipate the cult's actions and anticipate their next moves.

Harding's investigation also unearthed the cult's financial network, a complex web of shell corporations and offshore accounts. Tracing the flow of funds led to the arrest of several key figures within the cult's leadership, dismantling their financial infrastructure. This financial disruption significantly weakened the cult, stripping them of their resources and reducing their operational capacity. The collaboration between the Millers, Dr. Albright, and Detective Harding became a finely-tuned instrument of justice, each element complementing the other.

The final confrontation took place not in the confines of Blackwood Lane but in a secluded forest clearing, a remote location where the remaining cult members had gathered for a desperate attempt to regain their strength and revive their rituals. The police, armed with information gleaned from the Millers and Dr. Albright, executed a coordinated raid, arresting several key figures, including the cult's enigmatic leader, a shadowy figure who had remained elusive throughout the investigation.

The raid was fraught with danger, a harrowing clash between law enforcement and the remnants of a desperate cult. The Millers, though initially hesitant to become directly involved, found themselves drawn into the heart of the conflict. Their unique understanding of the cult's rituals and their ability to sense the cult's energy proved crucial during the confrontation.

Mary, using her newfound understanding of the carved stones, channeled their residual power to disrupt the cult's rituals, throwing the cultists into disarray. Silas, armed with his artistic intuition, used his paintings as a conduit to express and project their collective energy, creating a disruptive force that intensified the effects of Mary's actions. Emily, acting as the anchor, grounded the family's collective power to the earth, strengthening their resistance and enhancing their effectiveness. John, though his strength lay in physical courage, played a crucial role in ensuring their strategic safety.

The final battle was a desperate, chaotic struggle; a clash of wills, a battle for control over the lingering energy tied to Blackwood Lane. The cultists fought back with wild desperation, fueled by their dwindling power and fading hope. The outcome was a hard-fought victory, achieved through the unexpected collaboration of the Miller family,

Detective Harding, and Dr. Albright. Their united front, their shared understanding, and their collective strength, shattered the remnants of the Blackwood Lane cult, dismantling the organization from within.

In the aftermath, the Millers stood amidst the chaos, physically and emotionally exhausted, their shared victory a heavy weight on their shoulders. They had faced unspeakable horrors, stared into the abyss, and emerged victorious, forever bound together by their shared ordeal. The house on Blackwood Lane remained, a silent testament to their resilience and their shared triumph. The scars remained, both visible and unseen, but they were badges of honor, reminders of their harrowing journey and the strength they had discovered within themselves. The whispers of Blackwood Lane were finally silenced, replaced by the quiet murmur of a renewed hope. They had saved themselves, saved each other, and saved their community from a darkness that threatened to consume them all. The unexpected alliances forged in the face of unimaginable horror had proven that even in the darkest of times, unity and collaboration could conquer all.

Sacrifice II

The clearing was silent, save for the crackling of the dying embers of a bonfire and the rustling of leaves in the late autumn wind. The air hung heavy with the scent of woodsmoke and damp earth, a stark contrast to the cloying, metallic scent that had permeated their cellar. The remnants of the Blackwood Lane cult huddled around the fire, their faces gaunt and drawn, their eyes reflecting the flickering flames. They were a defeated army, their power diminished, their numbers thinned, but their desperation remained, a palpable energy that pulsed in the air.

Mary, her gaze fixed on the cultists, felt a familiar tremor in her hands. The carved stones, now cleansed of the malevolent energy they once held, rested warm in her pocket. The power they had wielded in the cellar, however, felt diminished, muted, a mere echo of its former intensity. She knew that another sacrifice was needed, a final offering to secure their victory, to ensure the complete eradication of the cult's influence.

The realization struck her with the force of a physical blow. It wasn't a sacrifice of blood, not this time. This sacrifice would be of something far more precious, far more personal. It would be a sacrifice of their shared trauma, of the collective pain that bound them together. It was a sacrifice of their fear, their lingering doubts, their unspoken anxieties – the very things that had fueled the cult's power over them.

She looked at her family. John, his jaw tight with resolve, stood beside her, his hand resting reassuringly on her arm. Silas, his eyes filled with a haunted intensity, clutched his paintbrush as if it were a weapon. Emily, her gaze steady and clear, stood rooted to the ground, her connection to the earth palpable. They had faced unimaginable horror, but their shared resilience, their shared pain, had forged an unbreakable bond between them. This was the strength they would offer as their sacrifice.

Silas, understanding the unspoken message passing between them, began to paint. Not the chaotic, violent strokes of their previous battle, but something different, something deliberate. His brush moved with a quiet grace, creating a canvas that depicted not their struggle, but their shared strength, their resilience, their unbreakable connection as a family. It was a portrait of unity, a testament to their courage, a visual representation of their inner strength.

As he painted, the air around them shifted, the energy in the clearing altered. The cultists, sensing the change, stirred uneasily, their whispers growing louder, more frantic. They could feel their power waning, their control slipping away. Silas' painting was not just a work of art; it was a weapon, a projection of their shared willpower, a beacon of hope that pierced the darkness surrounding them.

Emily, meanwhile, anchored herself to the earth, channeling the energy of the land, drawing strength from the ancient wisdom of the forest. She felt the power of the land flowing through her, strengthening her family, amplifying their resolve. She felt the tremors of their sacrifice rippling outward, affecting the cultists, weakening their resolve, shattering their collective energy.

John, his eyes focused on the cultists, acted as their shield, their protector. His presence alone was a force to be reckoned with, a bastion of strength that shielded his family from the cultists' desperation and fear. His unwavering resolve, born from love and unwavering loyalty, served as an impenetrable wall against the cult's dwindling power. He was the anchor, the sturdy foundation upon which their shared strength rested.

Mary, seeing the painting complete, took the stones from her pocket. They no longer glowed with ethereal light, but they pulsed with the raw energy of their sacrifice. The stones were not weapons to be wielded, but conduits, vessels through which their shared trauma would be channeled, transformed, and dissipated. She whispered an ancient incantation, one that spoke not of destruction but of healing, of transformation, of forgiveness.

As she spoke, the energy around them intensified, swirling and coalescing, forming a protective shield that enveloped the Millers, deflecting the cultists' waning power. The cultists, overwhelmed by the sheer force of their collective energy, began to collapse, their power dissolving, their desperate attempts at maintaining their hold on reality failing.

The air filled with the sound of screams, not of pain or rage, but of despair, of acceptance, of surrender. The cultists' desperation turned to defeat as they understood the true nature of the Millers' sacrifice. It wasn't a battle of strength against strength, but a confrontation of hope against despair, resilience against desperation.

The forest clearing fell silent once more, the silence now filled not with dread but with an almost tangible sense of peace. The bonfire embers died out, leaving only the glow of the moon and the stars. The cultists lay scattered, defeated, their power broken, their influence eradicated. The threat they had posed was extinguished.

In the aftermath, the Millers stood together, their bodies weary, their spirits worn but unbroken. They had sacrificed their pain, their fear, their trauma, and in doing so, had freed themselves, and the community, from the grip of Blackwood Lane. The sacrifice hadn't been easy; it had been a painful release, a letting go of the burden they had carried, a shedding of their collective wounds.

The unexpected alliance with Detective Harding and Dr. Albright had been crucial, but it was their shared strength, their resilience, their unbreakable bond, that had ultimately triumphed. They understood that true strength lay not in the wielding of power, but in the embrace of vulnerability, in the acceptance of shared pain, and in the unwavering support for each other.

The journey had been long and arduous, filled with peril and loss, but they had emerged victorious. The whispers of Blackwood Lane were finally silenced, forever replaced by the quiet murmur of renewed hope. They had stared into the abyss and emerged, not unscathed, but transformed, their spirits strengthened, their family bond unbreakable, their shared victory a testament to the enduring power of love and resilience. The house on Blackwood Lane remained, but its darkness had been banished, replaced by the quiet strength of a family that had faced its demons and emerged triumphant. They had saved themselves, each other, and their community, their sacrifice a final testament to the human spirit's indomitable strength.

Healing from Trauma

The aftermath wasn't a sudden blossoming of peace; it was a slow, arduous climb out of a deep, dark pit. The immediate relief of vanquishing the Blackwood Lane cult was followed by a chilling emptiness, a void where fear and adrenaline had once raged. The silence of their home, once a source of dread, now felt oppressive, a constant reminder of the horrors they'd endured. Each creak of the house, each rustle of leaves outside, sent jolts of anxiety through their bodies. Sleep became a battlefield, haunted by fragmented images and chilling whispers echoing from the recesses of their minds.

Dr. Albright, a specialist in trauma and cult-related psychological distress, became a pivotal figure in their healing journey. Her approach was holistic, addressing not only the individual trauma each family member experienced but also the fractured family dynamic itself. The sessions were intense, often emotionally draining, forcing them to confront the deepest, darkest corners of their minds. They explored the insidious nature of manipulation, the subtle erosion of their individual identities, and the insidious way the cult had exploited their vulnerabilities.

John, the stoic patriarch, initially resisted therapy. His ingrained sense of duty and responsibility had led him to suppress his emotions, building an impenetrable wall around his vulnerability. He struggled to articulate his feelings, to admit the fear and helplessness he had experienced. Dr. Albright patiently worked with him, using techniques to help him unravel his suppressed emotions, to acknowledge his own pain without feeling weak. She gently guided him to understand that his strength wasn't in his stoicism, but in his ability to acknowledge and process his emotions. He started to open up, his tightly controlled façade gradually crumbling, revealing the deep scars that lay beneath. The weight of his unspoken fears and anxieties, initially suffocating, began to lift, replaced by a growing sense of self-acceptance and inner peace.

Mary, the ever-practical matriarch, wrestled with guilt and survivor's remorse. The weight of their ordeal pressed heavily on her. The knowledge that they'd narrowly escaped, while others had not, haunted her. She questioned her own judgment, replaying every decision, second-guessing every action. Dr. Albright helped her reframe her perspective, emphasizing the importance of self-compassion. Mary's resilience had been instrumental in their survival; her strength, forged in the crucible of their ordeal, was undeniable. She learned to acknowledge her fears and anxieties without letting them dictate her actions. Gradually, she began to accept that survival wasn't a measure of strength but a demonstration of unwavering resilience.

Silas, the artistic son, had suffered the most direct impact of the cult's insidious manipulation. His art, previously a source of joy and expression, had been twisted into a tool of their evil design. The vibrant colours of his paintings had become muted, reflecting the darkness that had consumed him. His therapy focused on reclaiming his art, on reconnecting with his creativity, and on using his artistic talents as a vehicle for emotional expression and healing. He began to paint again, his brushstrokes initially hesitant and uncertain, but gradually gaining strength and confidence. His canvases became a testament to his resilience, reflecting his journey from darkness to light. His art was no longer a tool of manipulation but a powerful force for healing, both for himself and for his family.

Emily, the introspective daughter, had been profoundly affected by the unsettling events. Her connection to the land, once a source of comfort and strength, had become tinged with fear and suspicion. She withdrew into herself, struggling to reconcile her profound sense of connection with the world with the betrayal and manipulation they had experienced. Her therapy focused on re-establishing her trust in herself, her instincts, and the healing power of nature. Dr. Albright helped her to channel her intuitive strengths and understand that her sensitivity was not a weakness but a gift. Through guided meditation and nature-based therapies, she gradually regained her equilibrium, reconnecting with the peace she had once found in the natural world.

Family therapy was a critical component of their healing process. The trauma they'd shared had left deep fissures in their relationships. Mistrust, fueled by paranoia and suspicion, had seeped into their once-harmonious family dynamic. In sessions, they worked to rebuild trust, to communicate openly and honestly about their fears and anxieties. They learned to confront their unresolved conflicts, to address the unspoken resentments and accusations that had festered beneath the surface. They were guided to understand that their shared experience, while harrowing, could also be a source of strength and unity, if they chose to harness it in a positive way.

The healing process was gradual, a slow, steady reconstruction of their lives. It wasn't a linear journey; there were setbacks, relapses, moments of intense emotional pain. But their unwavering commitment to healing, their mutual support, and Dr. Albright's expert guidance ensured they steadily moved towards emotional recovery. They attended support groups with other survivors of cult manipulation, finding solace and understanding in shared experiences. They learned coping mechanisms for managing their anxieties, developing healthy communication patterns, and fostering a stronger sense of self-awareness and self-compassion. They also discovered a new level of empathy for one another; their shared trauma forging an unbreakable bond between them.

Their journey was a testament to the human spirit's capacity for resilience and the power of human connection to overcome even the most devastating experiences. The house on Blackwood Lane remained, a constant reminder of their ordeal, but it no longer held the same power over them. It was just a house, a structure of wood and stone, devoid of the malevolent energy that had once permeated its walls. The darkness had been banished, replaced by the enduring strength of a family that had faced its demons, emerged victorious, and found healing in unity and unwavering support. Their lives were not what they had once envisioned, yet, the strength they had discovered in the face of adversity gave them the foundation they needed to rebuild a future filled with love, hope, and a profound understanding of the resilience of the human spirit. The scars remained, a testament to their journey, but they were now a reminder of their shared strength, a bond that had been forged in the fires of trauma and emerged stronger than before. Their story, a harrowing tale of darkness and survival, became a testament to the power of healing, resilience, and the enduring strength of the human spirit, a story that would forever echo not in fear and dread, but in the quiet strength of a family that had faced the darkness and found the light. They had not only survived but they had transformed. Blackwood Lane was silenced, and the Millers had found their voice.

Rebuilding Relationships

The initial weeks following their escape from Blackwood Lane were a blur of medical checkups, police interviews, and the slow, painstaking process of returning to normalcy. Normalcy, however, felt like a foreign country, a place they could only glimpse from afar. The familiar comfort of their old home, once a sanctuary, now felt sterile and unsettling. Each quiet moment was punctuated by a nervous twitch, a fleeting shadow of fear that threatened to engulf them once more.

John, despite his outward stoicism, found himself inexplicably drawn to the abandoned Blackwood Lane property. He'd drive past it late at night, the dark silhouette of the house a silent reproach against the peace he craved. The weight of his suppressed emotions, the unspoken guilt he carried for not protecting his family sooner, manifested as a relentless, gnawing anxiety. He felt a responsibility to the house, to the victims who had not survived, a weight far greater than the physical toll he'd suffered. Mary noticed his change, his restless nights, his sudden, almost desperate need for control, a need that manifested itself in meticulously cleaning and rearranging their belongings. She began to understand the deep wounds he was trying to conceal, the burden he carried alone.

Mary, in turn, found herself grappling with a crippling sense of helplessness. The images of the cult members, their vacant stares and chilling devotion, haunted her waking moments. She couldn't shake the feeling that she had missed something, that there was more to the story that remained hidden, lurking just beneath the surface of the investigation. Sleep offered little respite, filled with fragmented nightmares of whispering voices and shadowy figures moving through their old home. The guilt she felt for surviving, for escaping while others had not, was a relentless, crushing weight. She found herself constantly questioning her decisions, second-guessing her instincts, blaming herself for their ordeal. Her once-sharp focus became clouded by doubt and uncertainty, and she found it increasingly difficult to cope with even the simplest tasks. She needed John, needed his strength, but his own struggle prevented him from offering the support she desperately craved.

Silas's art became his lifeline. The vibrant colors that had been muted by the cult's manipulation began to flood his canvases again. He poured his fear, his anger, and his grief onto the canvas, transforming his emotions into powerful, evocative images. His art was no longer a tool of manipulation, but a weapon of catharsis, a way to reclaim his identity and express the turmoil he'd endured. He started to use bold strokes, intense colours, showcasing a dramatic shift in his artistic style, a reflection of the dramatic shift in his emotional state. The process was agonizing, cathartic and necessary. The paintings acted as visual representations of his journey from darkness to light, the brushstrokes mirroring his struggle to reclaim his life. He began to exhibit his work, finding solace in the positive feedback from the community, realizing that his art could touch others, and that their reactions reminded him that he wasn't alone in his struggle.

Emily, the most sensitive of the family, retreated into herself, finding solace in the natural world. She spent hours walking through the woods near their new home, seeking a connection to the earth that had been severed during her ordeal. The forest, once a place of comfort and peace, had become a space of emotional reckoning. She spent hours tending to her herb garden, the careful act of nurturing life a counterpoint to the darkness she had faced. The tactile experience and the meditative rhythm of gardening calmed her anxiety. She learned to ground herself in the natural world, harnessing the earth's energy to soothe her troubled mind. Her connection to nature, once a source of comfort, helped her to rebuild her trust in herself and her intuitive abilities. Her healing journey took the form of embracing her sensitivity as a strength. The healing was gradual, but she started to feel herself again, slowly weaving a new narrative of life from the fragments of her old one.

Family therapy became the cornerstone of their recovery. Dr. Albright, a perceptive and empathetic therapist, guided them through a process of painstakingly rebuilding trust and communication. They learned to listen, truly listen, not just to the words spoken, but to the unspoken emotions that lay beneath. They confronted the unspoken resentments and accusations, the buried anxieties that had been simmering for years, unspoken hurts from before Blackwood Lane. They confronted the manipulation and its consequences, understanding the subtle ways the cult had poisoned their interactions. John acknowledged his own failings, his tendency towards emotional suppression and its effect on their family. Mary confronted her self-doubt, realizing the strength of her actions throughout the ordeal. Silas openly explored the impact of the cult's manipulation on his art and his identity. Emily shared her feelings of isolation and betrayal, understanding how her sensitivity had been exploited. These sessions were raw and emotionally charged, but they laid the groundwork for a more authentic, deeper connection.

The therapeutic journey was not without its setbacks. There were days when the progress they'd made seemed to evaporate, when old fears resurfaced, threatening to overwhelm them. Arguments erupted, silences stretched into painful chasms, and the shadow of Blackwood Lane threatened to eclipse the light of their healing. There were tears, anger, frustration, and moments of profound despair. But they learned to navigate these rough patches, to support each other, to recognize that setbacks were a natural part of the healing process. The trust they were rebuilding was fragile, like new seedlings after a harsh winter, requiring tender care and constant vigilance. But slowly, surely, a new foundation of understanding and mutual support began to take root.

They started attending support groups, connecting with other survivors of cult manipulation. Sharing their experiences, listening to the stories of others, helped them to realize that they were not alone, that their trauma was not unique. They found comfort in shared experiences, learning coping mechanisms from each other, and forging bonds with individuals who truly understood what they had endured.

The process of rebuilding their lives was slow, meticulous, requiring patience, forgiveness, and a shared commitment to healing. They learned to communicate more openly, to listen more attentively, to address their conflicts directly and honestly. They celebrated small victories, acknowledging the progress they had made, cherishing the moments of connection and shared laughter that began to weave their way back into their lives. The house on Blackwood Lane remained, a stark reminder of their ordeal, but it no longer held the power to dictate their lives. It was a place they had survived, a testament to their resilience and the strength of their bond as a family. The Millers, scarred but unbroken, emerged from the darkness, their lives transformed, their bonds reforged in the crucible of trauma and adversity. Their story became one not of defeat, but of triumph, a testament to the human spirit's indomitable capacity for healing, resilience, and the enduring power of love. They had not only survived, they had thrived. They had faced their demons, and they had won. Blackwood Lane was a chapter closed, its chilling echoes replaced by the quiet strength of a family healed.

Finding Closure

The final session with Dr. Albright felt strangely anticlimactic. There were no dramatic pronouncements, no sudden breakthroughs. Instead, there was a quiet acceptance, a settling of the dust after the storm. Dr. Albright, her usually vibrant eyes softened with empathy, simply nodded, a small, almost imperceptible gesture that conveyed a depth of understanding that words could not. She had guided them through the darkest depths of their shared trauma, but now, it was time for them to navigate the uncertain terrain of their future alone.

John, ever the pragmatist, was the first to speak, his voice low and steady, betraying little of the turmoil that still simmered beneath the surface. "I don't think we'll ever truly forget Blackwood Lane," he said, his gaze meeting his wife's. Mary's hand instinctively reached across the small table separating them, her fingers intertwining with his. The silent acknowledgment of their shared burden passed between them, a testament to the strength of the bond they had forged in the crucible of their ordeal.

"No," Mary agreed softly, her voice thick with emotion. "But we don't have to let it define us." The words hung in the air, a simple yet profound declaration of their intention to move forward, to reclaim their lives from the shadow of the past. The events of Blackwood Lane had irrevocably changed them, leaving scars on their hearts and minds. But they refused to be consumed by those scars. They would learn to live with them, to integrate them into the tapestry of their lives, transforming them into a testament to their resilience, a reminder of their strength.

Silas, his eyes still holding a trace of the haunted look that had clung to him for so long, spoke next. His voice, once hesitant and unsure, now possessed a newfound strength, a quiet confidence that reflected the progress he had made. "The paintings…they helped," he admitted, a faint blush rising on his cheeks. "Getting it all out… onto the canvas…it was like releasing a caged bird." He gestured towards the stack of canvases leaning against the wall of the therapy room, each one a vibrant testament to his journey through darkness and towards light. His art had become more than just an expression of his pain; it had become a tool for healing, a pathway to self-discovery, a medium through which he had reclaimed his identity and his voice.

Emily, the youngest, remained silent for a moment, her gaze fixed on the intricate pattern of the rug beneath her feet. She had spent the months following their escape from Blackwood Lane reconnecting with nature, finding solace in the quiet rhythm of the natural world. The process had been slow and gradual, but the healing power of the earth had been profound. She had found strength in the resilience of nature, in the cycle of growth and decay, of life and death.

"The forest," she finally whispered, her voice barely audible. "It helped me to understand that even in the darkest places, life finds a way to bloom again. That even after the harshest winter, there is always the promise of spring." Her words held a poetic beauty, a profound understanding that spoke volumes of the healing she had undertaken. The natural world had helped her to find her grounding and to understand that nature's cycles mirrored her own emotional journey.

The following months were filled with quiet acts of rebuilding. They slowly integrated back into the community, attending local events, cautiously rebuilding the relationships that had been strained and fractured by their ordeal. John, his quiet strength a beacon of stability, found solace in his work, the familiar rhythm of his routine providing a sense of normalcy. Mary, her spirit gradually regaining its spark, began volunteering at a local shelter, finding purpose and fulfillment in helping others. Silas continued to create, his art finding its way into galleries and exhibitions, his powerful images resonating with those who had experienced similar struggles. Emily, her spirit invigorated, found a niche volunteering at a botanical garden, her deep connection with the plant world helping her to heal and to foster a deeper connection with herself.

They continued their family therapy, not as patients seeking a cure, but as individuals striving to forge a stronger, more resilient bond. The sessions were less about confronting the past and more about cultivating the present, about understanding and appreciating the complexities of their relationships, their strengths and weaknesses, their individual journeys and their shared experiences. They continued to attend their support groups, finding strength in the shared stories of others who understood their pain. They learned to accept that they would carry the scars of Blackwood Lane with them always, but those scars would not define them. They were more than the sum of their suffering; they were a testament to the resilience of the human spirit, the enduring power of family, and the unwavering strength of love.

The house on Blackwood Lane remained, a chilling reminder of their ordeal. They did not return, nor did they feel the need to. Its presence was a reminder of what they had endured, a testament to their survival. It remained a chapter in their lives, but one that no longer held the power to control their narrative.

One evening, a year after their escape, the family sat on their porch, watching the sunset paint the sky in hues of orange and purple. A comfortable silence settled over them, a silence filled with the quiet contentment of a family reunited, a family healed. There was no need for words; their shared experience had forged a bond stronger than any words could express. They had faced their demons, confronted their fears, and emerged from the darkness stronger and more united than ever before.

Blackwood Lane was a chapter closed, but not forgotten. Its memory served as a constant reminder of their resilience, of the darkness they had overcome, and of the unbreakable bond that had carried them through. The Millers had found closure not in erasing their past but in accepting it, integrating it into the fabric of their lives, transforming their trauma into a testament to their enduring strength and unyielding love. They had survived. They had healed. They had thrived. And in their quiet acceptance, they had found a profound and lasting peace.

Learning to Live

The first anniversary of their departure from Blackwood Lane arrived almost unnoticed. There was no grand celebration, no dramatic pronouncements. Instead, it was marked by a quiet understanding, a shared acknowledgment of the invisible scar tissue that still knit itself across their lives. John, ever the practical one, had meticulously documented every expense related to their therapy, the legal battles over the house, the repairs to their new home – a modest, unassuming cottage far removed from the imposing grandeur of Blackwood Lane. He'd meticulously filed these documents away, a tangible representation of their journey from nightmare to normalcy. Yet, even the precise order of his filing couldn't fully contain the chaos that still lingered within.

Mary, however, found herself drawn to acts of symbolic cleansing. She meticulously purged their belongings of anything that even remotely hinted at their time in the house —the antique mirror that seemed to distort reflections, the ornate music box with its unsettling melody, the worn velvet curtains that seemed to whisper secrets in the dead of night. Each discarded item represented a piece of the past, painstakingly removed to make room for the future. The act of letting go was as much for the physical objects as it was for the memories they evoked. She spent hours gardening, planting vibrant flowers that choked the lingering weeds of their past trauma. Each seed planted, each delicate bloom that unfurled, felt like a tiny rebellion against the darkness that had threatened to consume them.

Silas's art continued to evolve. His paintings, once filled with disturbing imagery of shadows and grotesque figures, slowly transitioned to canvases brimming with light and color. He began to paint landscapes, capturing the breathtaking beauty of the natural world that had played such a vital role in their healing. The trees, the rivers, the mountains – all became symbols of resilience, of the power of nature to endure and regenerate. He no longer painted to exorcise his demons, but to celebrate the triumph of life over adversity. His art was still raw, honest, sometimes even haunting, but it now carried a message of hope, a testament to his journey from despair to peace. Each stroke of the brush was a deliberate act of reclaiming his voice, his identity, his future. His hands, which had once trembled with fear, now moved with a confidence born from facing his deepest fears and emerging victorious. He exhibited his work, not seeking fame or fortune but sharing his experience, offering solace to others who might understand his pain.

Emily's healing manifested in a quieter, more introspective manner. Her quiet strength was a force to be reckoned with. The botanical garden where she volunteered became her sanctuary, a place where she found peace and purpose. She meticulously cared for the delicate plants, nurturing their growth, learning their secrets, understanding their resilience in the face of adversity. The meticulous care she provided to the fragile seedlings seemed to mirror the delicate care she needed to tend to her own emotional well-being. She rediscovered a love for writing, journaling her experiences, translating the silence into poetic words. Her writing was not an attempt to relive the trauma, but a way to understand and process it, to give voice to the silent observations she had made during their ordeal. Each entry became a milestone, a record of her journey toward healing and self-discovery.

Their family therapy sessions transformed, becoming less focused on the trauma itself and more on cultivating a healthy foundation for the future. Dr. Albright played the role of a facilitator, guiding their conversations, gently nudging them towards self-awareness, fostering open communication, and guiding them in developing strategies to deal with the lingering effects of PTSD and their individual coping mechanisms. They learned to identify their triggers, developing strategies to manage their anxiety, their fear and panic responses. They practiced techniques to manage their emotional responses, allowing each other to grieve and heal at their own pace. The sessions shifted from a clinical setting to an emotionally supportive environment, allowing them to connect more profoundly.

The support group continued to be a lifeline, a constant reminder that they were not alone in their struggle. Sharing their stories with others who understood the depths of their pain was a powerful form of validation, a powerful demonstration of the power of collective support. The group provided a sense of belonging, a safe space to openly express their vulnerabilities without fear of judgment or criticism. The bond that formed between the members transcended their individual traumas and became a powerful force of resilience and community.

The house on Blackwood Lane remained, a physical manifestation of their shared ordeal, a constant, albeit distant reminder. They deliberately avoided driving past it, not out of fear, but out of a quiet respect for the intense emotions associated with that place. It represented a chapter in their lives, a challenging and dark period they would never forget, but they made a deliberate choice not to allow its shadow to fall upon their new life. It wasn't about forgetting; it was about acceptance, about integrating that experience into the tapestry of their lives, seeing it as a testament to their collective resilience.

Slowly, tentatively, they began to rebuild their lives. John, ever the anchor of their family, found solace in the predictability of his work. Mary embraced a new role at the local community center, pouring her energy into helping others. Silas's art found a place in local galleries, his powerful images resonating with the community and with those who had experienced similar traumas. Emily continued to work in the botanical garden, finding solace and healing amidst the beauty of the natural world. Their individual journeys interwoven, intertwined, strengthened by their shared experience.

They built new rituals, new traditions, replacing the old ones that had been fractured by their time at Blackwood Lane. Family dinners became a sacred time for them, an opportunity to connect, to share their day's events, to offer each other support and understanding. They learned to communicate openly and honestly, sharing their vulnerabilities and their hopes without fear of judgment. They rediscovered laughter, their shared moments of levity serving as a reminder of the strength of their bond. The lingering trauma cast its shadow at times, but they learned to navigate it together, armed with the tools they had gained through therapy and support, understanding that healing is not a linear process but a journey of ebbs and flows.

The years that followed were filled with quiet joy, punctuated by moments of reflection and quiet contemplation. They had learned to live with the scars of Blackwood Lane, incorporating the experience into the story of their lives, a testament to their resilience, their strength, and the enduring power of their family unit. They didn't erase their past, they integrated it. They didn't forget Blackwood Lane, but they reclaimed their narrative, transforming their trauma into a tale of triumph over adversity, a story of healing and forgiveness, and a profound testament to the resilience of the human spirit. They had survived, healed, and indeed, they had thrived. They had found peace, not by forgetting, but by remembering, integrating, and ultimately, accepting. The quiet peace they found in their new lives was a testament to their journey, to their struggle, and to the enduring power of love in the face of overwhelming darkness.

New Normal

The scent of freshly baked bread, a smell that once held the comforting familiarity of home, now carried a bittersweet undercurrent. It was a deliberate choice, Mary decided, a conscious effort to reclaim the simple joys that Blackwood Lane had stolen. Baking had become her ritual, a meditative act that allowed her to focus on the present, the rhythmic kneading of dough a counterpoint to the chaotic memories that still occasionally surfaced. Each loaf, a testament to her resilience, a tangible representation of her reclaiming her life, one perfectly risen crust at a time. She'd even started a small online business, selling her artisan bread to local cafes and farmers markets, a quiet triumph that spoke volumes about her quiet strength.

John, meanwhile, found solace in the structure of his work, but even the meticulous spreadsheets and financial reports couldn't fully erase the lingering anxieties. He'd begun attending a men's support group, a space where he could openly discuss his fears and anxieties without the weight of his family's needs pressing down on him. The anonymity offered a release, a space to acknowledge the vulnerability he had so carefully masked for so long. The other men, each grappling with their own burdens, shared a silent understanding, a sense of camaraderie forged in the crucible of shared trauma. The conversations weren't always easy, raw emotions often surfacing, but the shared experience fostered a deep sense of connection, proving that even in the darkest moments, support could be found in the most unexpected places. He started taking up woodworking in his spare time, the precise movements, the methodical shaping of raw materials into something beautiful, offering a welcome distraction from the lingering anxieties.

Silas's art continued to flourish, his landscapes now characterized by a breathtaking luminosity, his colors bolder, more vibrant. He'd started teaching art classes at the local community center, sharing his passion with others, finding fulfillment in watching his students discover their own creative voices. The act of teaching, of sharing his skills and experiences, was a powerful form of healing, a way of giving back to the community that had supported him. He found himself drawn to teaching children, their boundless energy and unburdened imaginations a stark contrast to the darkness he'd once wrestled with. The children's artwork, often raw and unfiltered, mirrored his own journey, demonstrating the power of expression as a conduit for emotional release and self-discovery. The children, in their own innocent way, reminded him of his own capacity for joy, for healing, for a life beyond the shadows of Blackwood Lane.

Emily, however, remained more reserved, her healing a gradual, internal process. The botanical garden remained her sanctuary, a quiet retreat where she could connect with nature, allowing the rhythms of the natural world to soothe her soul. She'd started volunteering at a local hospice, finding purpose in providing comfort to those in their final days. The act of caring for others, of witnessing their courage in the face of mortality, served as a powerful reminder of the fragility and preciousness of life, intensifying her gratitude for her own survival and second chance at happiness. She continued to write, but now her journals were filled with observations of the natural world, reflections on human resilience, and explorations of themes of hope and renewal. Her words, once filled with fear and despair, now flowed with a newfound clarity, a quiet strength born from overcoming unspeakable adversity.

The new house, while modest, was filled with light, a deliberate contrast to the oppressive darkness of Blackwood Lane. It was filled with the laughter of children, the murmur of conversations, the comforting scents of home-cooked meals. It was a space filled with the tangible signs of their healing journey, a testament to their resilience, a symbol of their newfound peace. They filled it with vibrant colors, with plants that brought life and warmth into each room. They hung Silas's paintings, each one a step further away from the darkness and closer to the light. Mary's bread-making area became a central hub of the home, the aroma of baking bread a comforting constant, a symbol of their renewed life. The family dinners were no longer strained affairs punctuated by silences, but lively, engaging experiences, filled with conversation and laughter.

The new routines were simple, almost mundane, yet profoundly significant. They were rituals designed to build stability and resilience, to foster a sense of normalcy after the chaos of Blackwood Lane. Regular family game nights replaced the tense silences and unspoken anxieties. Sunday morning walks became a weekly tradition, their feet crunching on the fallen leaves, their bodies enveloped in the crisp morning air, their spirits buoyed by the peace and serenity of their new surroundings. These small, intentional acts played a crucial role in establishing a new emotional foundation. It wasn't about erasing the past, but rather about creating a new narrative, a story that celebrated their courage, their resilience, and the strength of their bond as a family.

They learned to identify their triggers, to recognize the subtle signs of anxiety or panic that once threatened to overwhelm them. They developed coping mechanisms, strategies for managing their emotional responses, ensuring that the lingering shadows of Blackwood Lane didn't cast a pall over their lives. They celebrated small victories, acknowledging their progress, appreciating the milestones achieved on their journey toward healing. The support group remained a constant presence, a reassuring reminder that they weren't alone, that others understood the complexities of their experience, the lingering emotional scars that often remained hidden beneath the surface. They shared their progress, their setbacks, their triumphs with one another, fostering a deep sense of connection and mutual support.

The family therapy sessions evolved, becoming less focused on processing the trauma and more concentrated on developing healthy communication patterns, fostering emotional intimacy, and building a stronger, more resilient family unit. Dr. Albright, their ever-present guide, helped them navigate the intricacies of their relationships, guiding them in developing healthy conflict-resolution strategies, teaching them how to communicate their needs effectively, helping them understand and respect each other's individual emotional journeys. The sessions were no longer characterized by raw emotions and painful revelations but by a sense of hope, of progress, of the steady, unwavering growth of their collective resilience. The sessions morphed from a clinical treatment into a forum for growth, allowing them to celebrate their resilience and move forward, hand in hand.

The quiet strength that had characterized their individual healing processes had now transformed into a shared resilience, a collective force that bound them together. Their new normal wasn't a simple return to the past, but a rebirth, a testament to the enduring power of the human spirit, the ability to overcome adversity, to heal from trauma, and to create a life filled with purpose, joy, and love. They had survived, they had healed, and they had thrived, emerging stronger and more united than ever before. The quiet peace that permeated their new lives wasn't merely an absence of darkness but a conscious choice, a testament to their enduring strength, and the unbreakable bonds of family love. They found their new normal, not in forgetting Blackwood Lane, but in embracing the lessons it had taught them, using its memory to fuel their future and forge a stronger, more vibrant life together.

The Power of Family

The shared trauma of Blackwood Lane, though a scar that would forever remain etched upon their hearts, had paradoxically forged a new depth to their familial bonds. The initial fracturing, the suspicion and mistrust that had threatened to tear them apart, had been replaced by a fragile but growing understanding. They had witnessed each other's vulnerabilities, their fears laid bare in the crucible of their shared nightmare. This shared experience, this collective struggle for survival, had paradoxically strengthened the very fabric of their family.

The weekly family dinners, once tense affairs punctuated by strained silences and averted gazes, had transformed into vibrant gatherings, a testament to their renewed connection. Laughter, once a rare commodity, now filled the air, a welcome counterpoint to the lingering anxieties. The conversations were more open, honest, and deeply personal, a reflection of their newfound ability to communicate their feelings and needs without fear of judgment or recrimination. Even the simplest of activities—a game of cards, a shared movie night, the collective effort of preparing a meal—became opportunities to reconnect, to reaffirm their commitment to one another. These seemingly mundane moments held a profound significance, a silent acknowledgment of their shared journey, of the resilience they had discovered within themselves and within their family.

Silas, ever the artist, found himself translating their collective experience onto canvas. His paintings, once dark and brooding, now possessed a newfound luminosity, a vibrant tapestry woven with threads of hope, resilience, and the enduring power of family love. He began painting portraits of his family, capturing not only their physical likenesses but also the nuances of their personalities, their shared history, and the subtle shifts in their relationships. Each brushstroke was a testament to their journey, a visual chronicle of their healing, a poignant reflection of their renewed strength and unity. These paintings became a focal point in their new home, serving as a constant reminder of their journey, their strength, and their unwavering commitment to one another. The act of painting, of pouring his emotions onto canvas, became a therapeutic process, not only for Silas but also for the rest of the family. The paintings became a shared space for reflection, for conversation, and for the quiet acknowledgment of their collective journey.

Mary's baking, once a solitary pursuit, evolved into a shared family activity. She began teaching Emily and Silas the art of bread-making, sharing her knowledge and passion with them. The rhythmic kneading of the dough, the warmth of the oven, the comforting aroma of freshly baked bread— these sensory experiences became a shared ritual, a tangible representation of their family's enduring strength. The process of baking, like their other shared activities, became an opportunity to connect, to communicate, and to reaffirm their bonds as a family. They baked together, they laughed together, they talked together, the scent of the rising dough intermingling with the aroma of their shared experiences. Mary even started a small catering business, incorporating the family's art and baking into her offerings. This collaborative effort brought another layer of connectedness and financial stability.

John's woodworking hobby also became a familial affair. He began creating small wooden toys for the children in the neighborhood, a way of giving back to the community that had supported them through their darkest hours. He also began creating intricate pieces of furniture for their new home, each piece a testament to his renewed confidence and strength. The rhythmic sounds of the saw and hammer, the scent of freshly cut wood, the meticulous process of shaping raw materials into something beautiful—these experiences helped him process his emotions, his anxieties, his fears. The creation of something tangible, something beautiful, gave him a sense of purpose, a sense of accomplishment, and a tangible way to express his gratitude for his family and for the support he had received. He even began teaching Silas some woodworking techniques, creating another avenue for their bond to strengthen.

Emily's quiet strength was a constant source of inspiration for her family. Her dedication to her work at the hospice, her commitment to providing comfort and support to others, served as a powerful example of empathy and compassion. Her journals, once filled with fear and despair, now reflected a newfound appreciation for the beauty and resilience of the human spirit. She began sharing excerpts of her writing with her family, her words weaving a narrative of hope, healing, and the enduring power of human connection. Her subtle strength and wisdom served as a quiet anchor, a grounding force in the midst of their ongoing journey of healing. She started a small writing group with other women in the community, creating a supportive environment for sharing experiences and encouraging creative expression.

The family therapy sessions continued, but their focus shifted. Dr. Albright, having guided them through the darkest depths of their trauma, now helped them navigate the complexities of their renewed relationships. The sessions became less about unpacking the past and more about building a stronger, healthier future. They learned effective communication techniques, resolving conflicts constructively, and fostering a deeper understanding of one another's individual needs and perspectives. The therapeutic process, once a source of pain and anxiety, transformed into a platform for growth, for self-discovery, and for strengthening the bonds that held them together. The sessions became less clinical and more like a friendly gathering, offering a shared space for introspection and growth.

The Millers' journey was far from over, but they were no longer defined by the darkness of Blackwood Lane. They had faced the abyss, stared into the depths of their own fears and insecurities, and emerged stronger, more resilient, and deeply bonded. The power of family, once tested to its limits, had proven its enduring strength, a beacon guiding them toward a future filled with hope, healing, and love. Their story became a testament to the human spirit's capacity for resilience, to the unwavering power of family bonds, and to the transformative potential of shared trauma. The healing process continued, but now they were unified, each member supporting and strengthening the others, creating a new normal built on mutual respect, trust, and unwavering love. Their story, while tinged with the darkness of their past, ultimately became a tale of triumph, a celebration of family, resilience, and the enduring strength of the human spirit. The family's unity, once fractured and threatened, had become their greatest strength.

Resilience

The months that followed were a testament to the Millers' unwavering resilience. The scars of Blackwood Lane remained, a persistent ache beneath the surface of their newfound peace, but they refused to be defined by their past. Their shared trauma, once a crippling weight, had become the unlikely foundation upon which they rebuilt their lives, stronger and more unified than ever before.

John, ever the pragmatist, focused on creating a sense of normalcy. He meticulously landscaped their new garden, the rhythmic movements of his hands a soothing counterpoint to the turmoil he had endured. The garden became a sanctuary, a vibrant space that mirrored the growth and renewal blossoming within their family. He planted flowers of varying colors and textures, creating a beautiful tapestry that represented the complex emotions they had weathered. The vibrant hues symbolized hope and joy, while the subtle shades of purple and grey acknowledged the lingering shadows of their ordeal. The garden, with its carefully cultivated beauty, became a symbol of their resilience, their dedication to rebuilding their lives, one carefully planted seed at a time. He even built a small, sturdy wooden shed, a space for quiet contemplation and creative pursuits.

Mary, her spirit tempered by the challenges they had faced, channeled her energy into community involvement. She volunteered at the local soup kitchen, finding solace in serving others and using her baking skills to bring comfort to those less fortunate. Her act of giving back became a way to process her emotions, to find meaning in her suffering, and to connect with others on a deeper level. The simple act of kneading dough, once a solitary ritual, now served as a form of therapy, a tangible connection to the restorative power of creation. She found a profound sense of fulfillment in this new direction, and her acts of service became a powerful testament to the healing power of compassion and community engagement.

Silas, his artistic talent ignited by their shared ordeal, embarked on an ambitious new project. He began painting a mural for the local community center, depicting the journey of the Millers and their miraculous recovery from the trauma at Blackwood Lane. The mural, a vibrant symphony of color and emotion, became a communal project, bringing neighbors together to participate in the painting process. This collective endeavor further cemented their reintegration into the community. The mural represented more than just their story; it reflected the resilience and strength of the human spirit. It was a tribute to their courage, a testament to their healing journey, and a testament to the power of community support.

Emily, ever the quiet observer, discovered a newfound passion for writing. She began chronicling their experiences, not as a victim, but as a survivor, her words weaving a narrative of resilience, hope, and the enduring power of family. Her writing became a cathartic process, a way to process her emotions, to make sense of their ordeal, and to share their story with the world. She even started a blog about her journey, creating an online space where she connected with others and offered support and encouragement. Her writing became a powerful catalyst for healing, a testament to the transformative power of storytelling.

Their collective healing wasn't solely dependent on individual pursuits. Their weekly family dinners remained a sacred space. The conversations were less about recounting the trauma and more about sharing their hopes for the future. They discussed their individual projects, offering each other encouragement and support. They planned family vacations, anticipating adventures and experiences that would create new memories and further strengthen their bond. The simple act of sitting around the table, sharing a meal, and conversing about their day became a ritual that reaffirmed their family's strength and unity.

The family therapy sessions, while initially challenging, continued. Dr. Albright guided them through the nuances of their evolving relationships, helping them navigate the complexities of trust and forgiveness. They learned to communicate more effectively, expressing their fears and anxieties without judgment or recrimination. The sessions, once a source of dread, transformed into a safe space for self-reflection and growth, a place where they celebrated their progress and acknowledged the challenges that still lay ahead. The focus shifted from resolving the past to building a brighter, stronger future.

The impact of their experiences extended beyond their immediate family. They became advocates for mental health awareness, sharing their story with others and encouraging them to seek help when needed. Their journey of resilience became an inspiration to others, a testament to the transformative power of human connection and the importance of seeking professional support in times of crisis. They found solace in connecting with other families who had experienced similar traumas, offering support and understanding to those who were still navigating their own journeys of recovery.

The Millers' journey was a testament to the power of human resilience. They had faced their fears, confronted their vulnerabilities, and emerged stronger, more united, and deeply appreciative of the life they had rebuilt. They had faced the abyss and found not just survival, but a renewed sense of purpose, a deeper understanding of themselves and one another, and the unbreakable bond of family love that had weathered the storm. Their story became a beacon of hope, a testament to the indomitable human spirit, and a celebration of the transformative power of shared trauma and collective healing. They were a testament to the fact that even from the deepest darkness, a new dawn can emerge, stronger and more beautiful than ever before. Blackwood Lane would forever be a part of their story, but it no longer defined them. Their resilience, their love, and their unwavering commitment to one another had ultimately triumphed over the darkness. Their journey served as a powerful reminder that while trauma leaves its mark, it does not have to dictate one's destiny. The Millers had not only survived but thrived, demonstrating that resilience is not just the ability to withstand adversity, but the capacity to transform it into a catalyst for growth, understanding, and lasting strength.

Importance of Mental Health

The aftermath of Blackwood Lane left an indelible mark on each member of the Miller family, a silent testament to the insidious nature of trauma. While they had physically escaped the house, the psychological scars lingered, subtle yet pervasive, weaving themselves into the fabric of their daily lives. Sleep became a battlefield, haunted by fragmented memories and unsettling visions. The once-familiar comfort of their home was replaced by a pervasive sense of unease, a constant reminder of the horrors they had endured. Even seemingly mundane activities – the rustling of leaves, the creaking of floorboards, the distant whisper of the wind – could trigger flashbacks, plunging them back into the heart of their ordeal.

It was Dr. Albright, their insightful and compassionate therapist, who first recognized the depth of their collective trauma. She gently guided them through the complex maze of their emotional landscapes, helping them navigate the treacherous terrain of fear, anxiety, and mistrust. The initial therapy sessions were fraught with tension. John, ever the stoic patriarch, struggled to articulate his feelings, his inherent pragmatism clashing with the raw emotional vulnerability the therapy demanded. Mary, her heart still bruised from the ordeal, battled guilt and self-blame, questioning her ability to protect her family. Silas, grappling with the lingering effects of his near-psychotic break, found it challenging to distinguish between reality and delusion, his artistic genius temporarily overshadowed by his emotional fragility. Emily, though outwardly resilient, carried the weight of unspoken fears and anxieties, her silent observations masking a deep-seated emotional turmoil.

Dr. Albright understood the intricacies of their collective trauma. She recognized that their shared experience had created a unique tapestry of emotional wounds, each thread interwoven with the others, making individual healing impossible without addressing the shared trauma. She skillfully employed various therapeutic techniques, weaving together elements of family systems therapy, cognitive behavioral therapy, and trauma-focused approaches. She encouraged them to openly share their experiences, creating a safe space where vulnerability was not a weakness but a pathway to healing. The therapeutic sessions became a crucible where their individual struggles were forged into a shared narrative of resilience, understanding, and forgiveness.

One of the critical aspects of their therapy involved addressing the erosion of trust. The events at Blackwood Lane had shattered their sense of security, causing deep fissures in their relationships. Suspicions and accusations, born from fear and paranoia, had poisoned their interactions, leaving them feeling isolated and vulnerable. Dr. Albright guided them through the painstaking process of rebuilding trust, emphasizing the importance of open communication, active listening, and empathetic understanding. They learned to articulate their fears and anxieties without judgment or recrimination, creating a space where honesty and vulnerability could coexist.

The family gradually learned to identify and challenge the negative thought patterns that perpetuated their emotional distress. Cognitive behavioral therapy proved invaluable in helping them reframe their experiences, shifting from victimhood to survivorhood. They learned to distinguish between factual events and the distorted narratives their minds had constructed, replacing fear-based assumptions with more realistic perspectives. They actively challenged their negative self-talk, replacing self-doubt with self-compassion, gradually rebuilding their self-esteem and self-efficacy.

Trauma-focused therapy proved crucial in addressing the lingering psychological wounds. They gradually revisited their traumatic experiences, guided by Dr. Albright's skillful support. The process was arduous and emotionally demanding, requiring immense courage and patience. But as they revisited the events, they began to reclaim their narratives, transforming the power of their trauma from something that controlled them to something they could understand and integrate into their lives. The act of recounting their experiences, in a safe and controlled environment, allowed them to process their emotions, confront their fears, and reclaim a sense of agency.

The therapeutic journey was not without its setbacks. There were days when the pain felt insurmountable, when the progress they had made seemed to vanish in an instant. They experienced moments of regression, reliving past anxieties and fears, but they persevered, supported by Dr. Albright's unwavering guidance and their newfound strength. They learned that healing was not a linear process but a journey filled with both forward momentum and occasional setbacks. They learned to accept the ebbs and flows of their emotional recovery, understanding that it was a marathon, not a sprint.

Beyond the formal therapeutic sessions, the Millers discovered the importance of self-care. They embraced healthy coping mechanisms, finding solace in individual pursuits and collective family activities. John rediscovered his passion for woodworking, creating intricate pieces that reflected his journey of healing. Mary continued her volunteer work, finding purpose and fulfillment in serving others. Silas channeled his emotional energy into his art, using his canvas as a space to explore his feelings and express his experiences. Emily continued to write, her words becoming a powerful tool for self-expression and emotional processing.

Their weekly family dinners became a sacred space, a ritual that reaffirmed their bond and celebrated their collective healing journey. They shared their experiences, both triumphs and setbacks, offering each other unwavering support and understanding. They created new traditions, creating memories that overshadowed the darkness of their past. They embarked on family vacations, creating new experiences and memories, fostering a deeper sense of unity and appreciation for one another.

The Millers became advocates for mental health awareness, sharing their story and inspiring others to seek help when needed. They actively participated in community events and organizations focused on raising awareness about mental health issues. They shared their experiences publicly, advocating for increased access to mental health services and challenging the stigma associated with mental illness. They believed that their journey could serve as a beacon of hope for others, demonstrating that healing is possible, even from the most profound trauma.

Their journey serves as a powerful reminder that seeking professional help for mental health issues is not a sign of weakness but a testament to strength and resilience. The Millers' story underscores the critical role of therapy and support systems in overcoming trauma and fostering mental well-being. Their unwavering commitment to healing, both individually and as a family, stands as a testament to the transformative power of human resilience and the enduring strength of family bonds. The darkness of Blackwood Lane might have cast a long shadow, but it was ultimately overshadowed by the light of their collective healing and the strength of their unwavering commitment to one another. Their story became a testament to the possibility of healing, a testament to the enduring power of the human spirit, and a powerful message to others struggling in the shadows of their own traumas: hope, healing, and recovery are attainable.

Confronting the Past

The process of confronting their past wasn't a singular event, but a gradual unveiling, layer by painstaking layer. Dr. Albright, ever mindful of their individual sensitivities, carefully guided them through the treacherous terrain of their shared trauma. She started with individual sessions, allowing each member of the family to process their individual experiences and emotions in a safe and supportive environment. John, initially resistant to the vulnerability the therapy demanded, began to crack under the weight of his unspoken anxieties. His stoicism, once a shield against emotional vulnerability, crumbled as he recounted his terrifying experiences within the Blackwood Lane house, the lingering fear of the unknown etched onto his face. He spoke of the unsettling noises, the feeling of being watched, the palpable sense of dread that had consumed him. He described how the house seemed to feed on his fears, amplifying them, twisting them into nightmarish hallucinations. It was a harrowing confession, a testament to the psychological toll the house had taken on him.

Mary's sessions were equally harrowing, laced with guilt and self-recrimination. She relived her inability to protect her children, the feeling of helplessness that had overwhelmed her during the escalating chaos. She berated herself for not recognizing the signs sooner, for not being more perceptive, for failing to shield her family from the malevolent presence that seemed to inhabit Blackwood Lane. Her confession was a torrent of remorse, a waterfall of self-blame that threatened to drown her in a sea of despair. Dr. Albright, with her compassionate understanding, guided her towards self-forgiveness, helping her understand that the events were beyond her control, that no one could have been prepared for the horrors they had endured.

Silas' journey was perhaps the most challenging. His near-psychotic break had left him struggling to differentiate between reality and delusion, his artistic brilliance temporarily overshadowed by the fragility of his mental state. His sessions were a tapestry of fragmented memories, vivid hallucinations interwoven with fleeting moments of lucidity. He painted vivid pictures of the house, portraying its menacing presence, the distorted shadows and grotesque figures that seemed to stalk its hallways. His art became a mirror to his fractured psyche, a visceral representation of his inner turmoil. Through therapy, he gradually started to distinguish between his hallucinations and reality, piecing together his fragmented memories, reclaiming his narrative from the clutches of his trauma.

Emily, the seemingly resilient one, revealed the depth of her unspoken fears and anxieties in her own time. She had silently observed the unraveling of her family, the growing tension, the deepening mistrust. Her diary entries, filled with cryptic observations and unsettling descriptions of Blackwood Lane, became a window into her own mental state. The events of Blackwood Lane had triggered a deep-seated fear that shattered her sense of safety and security, leaving her perpetually on edge. She learned to express her fear, not as a weakness, but as a valid emotion that needed to be addressed. Through therapy, she learned to recognize and manage her anxiety, transforming fear into strength and resilience.

As they progressed, the family sessions began to illuminate the intricate tapestry of their shared trauma. They began to understand how their individual experiences were interwoven, how each person's suffering had impacted the others, creating a complex web of emotional entanglement. The sessions became a crucible, where accusations and mistrust gave way to empathy and understanding. They learned to actively listen to each other, validating each other's experiences, offering support and compassion.

One particularly poignant session involved revisiting the night of the incident. Each family member recounted their individual experiences, their narratives intertwining and illuminating the shared trauma. The fragmented memories began to coalesce, forming a clearer picture of the events that had transpired. As they shared their individual perspectives, they started to see the events not as a series of isolated incidents but as a shared experience that had bound them together. This helped them to heal collectively, to appreciate the strength and endurance of their collective bond.

The process of healing was not without its challenges. There were days when the pain felt overwhelming, when the progress they had made seemed to dissolve into the darkness of their past. There were moments of intense emotion, accusations that had simmered beneath the surface for months erupted into the open, testing the boundaries of their newfound resilience. But through it all, Dr. Albright's guidance, their commitment to honesty, and their shared experiences helped them navigate the challenges.

Confronting the past also meant confronting the shadowy figures that had haunted their lives even before Blackwood Lane. Long-buried family secrets emerged, exposing patterns of dysfunction and unresolved conflicts. They discovered that their family's history was riddled with trauma, a chain of unresolved issues passed down through generations. The house at Blackwood Lane, they came to realize, had merely amplified existing vulnerabilities. Understanding this generational trauma helped them break the cycle, to finally address the underlying issues that had shaped their perceptions and interactions.

The healing process extended beyond the confines of the therapist's office. The family embarked on a journey of self-discovery, each member finding solace in individual pursuits that nurtured their emotional well-being. John took up pottery, transforming clay into beautiful expressions of his inner peace. Mary discovered a passion for gardening, tending to her plants with the same care and dedication she once poured into her family. Silas, his artistic genius rekindled, created a series of paintings that captured the emotional intensity of their experiences at Blackwood Lane, transforming darkness into art, trauma into beauty. Emily continued to write, her words flowing freely, transforming pain into poetry, her prose into a healing process.

Their family dinners became sacred rituals, a time to share their experiences, to celebrate their progress, and to reaffirm their commitment to one another. They started engaging in family activities, creating new traditions, replacing the fear and suspicion with laughter, understanding and the comforting feeling of togetherness. Vacations became a necessary escape and opportunity to create new memories, to forge bonds unburdened by the weight of the past.

Their journey of healing was a long and arduous one, filled with setbacks and moments of profound emotional pain. But through it all, they held onto each other, supporting one another, persevering in their quest for healing. The process was not about forgetting the past, but about understanding it, accepting it, and integrating it into the fabric of their lives, transforming trauma into a catalyst for growth and resilience. They learned that confronting the past is a courageous act, a testament to the strength of the human spirit, and a journey towards a future filled with hope, healing, and renewed strength. Their shared experience transformed them from victims of trauma to survivors, advocates, and inspiration for others who share similar experiences, demonstrating that even from the deepest shadows, there is a path toward healing and a brighter future. Their family emerged stronger, their bond forged in the crucible of adversity, their resilience a testament to the power of love, forgiveness, and the unwavering strength of the human spirit. They learned that home wasn't just a building, but a feeling of belonging, a sanctuary built on trust, forgiveness, and the enduring power of family.

Hope and Healing

The lingering scent of bleach and antiseptic still clung to the air in their renovated home, a constant, faint reminder of the darkness they had wrestled with and, to a large extent, conquered. The walls, once imbued with an almost palpable sense of dread, now seemed to breathe easier, the silence less ominous, more peaceful. The sunlight streamed through the windows, illuminating the carefully arranged furniture, each piece selected not just for its aesthetic appeal but also for the sense of calm and comfort it brought. It was a deliberate act of reclaiming their space, transforming the house from a symbol of terror into a haven of healing.

John, his hands calloused from months spent shaping clay on the potter's wheel, felt a profound sense of accomplishment. Each piece he created was a testament to his journey, a tangible representation of his triumph over fear. The smooth curves and earthy tones of his pottery mirrored the serenity he had found within himself. The rhythmic motion of his hands, once tense and shaky, now flowed with the effortless grace of a seasoned artist. The act of creation had become a form of meditation, a way to channel his anxieties and transform them into something beautiful. He found solace in the quiet solitude of his workshop, the cool clay a soothing balm on his troubled spirit.

Mary's garden, once neglected and overgrown, now flourished with vibrant blooms and lush greenery. The vibrant colors of the flowers seemed to reflect the renewed vibrancy of her spirit. The act of tending to her plants, nurturing their growth, had brought her a sense of purpose and peace. It was a tangible expression of her nurturing instinct, a way to cultivate life and beauty, a stark contrast to the darkness that had threatened to engulf her. Each seed she planted represented a renewed hope, each blossom a testament to her resilience. The garden became her sanctuary, a place where she could reconnect with nature and find solace in its restorative power. She found herself spending hours in her garden, losing herself in the beauty of the flowers, finding peace and serenity in the soil beneath her fingertips.

Silas's canvases, once dominated by grotesque figures and distorted shadows, now showcased a breathtaking array of colors and forms. His artistic genius, temporarily eclipsed by the horrors he had witnessed, had reemerged with renewed intensity. His paintings, still infused with a raw emotional honesty, now radiated a sense of hope and resilience. The darkness remained, but it was no longer the dominant force; it was interwoven with light, creating a tapestry of both pain and healing. He had learned to channel his trauma into his art, transforming it into a powerful vehicle for self-expression and healing. His art became a mirror to his soul, reflecting the journey from darkness to light, from despair to hope. Each brushstroke was a step towards healing, a testament to the transformative power of art.

Emily, her diary now filled with poetry rather than chilling descriptions, had found her voice. She had transformed her fear into a source of strength, her anxiety into a creative force. Her words flowed freely, transforming her pain into beauty, her vulnerability into strength. She discovered that her experiences, once a source of shame and fear, could be shared, understood, and even appreciated. Her writing became a cathartic experience, a journey of self-discovery, and a testament to her resilience. She found a sense of purpose in sharing her story, hoping to inspire others who had experienced similar traumas. Her writing became a source of healing, not just for herself but for others as well.

She learned that vulnerability wasn't weakness; it was a strength, a testament to the human capacity to endure and overcome.

The family sessions with Dr. Albright continued, but their focus shifted. While the past was acknowledged and processed, the emphasis moved towards building a stronger, healthier future. They learned to communicate more effectively, to express their needs and feelings openly and honestly. They established new family rituals – weekly game nights, Sunday brunches, even spontaneous family hikes – creating new memories that gently overlaid the trauma of Blackwood Lane. The shared laughter, the simple act of being together, helped to replace the fear and mistrust with a sense of belonging. The family that once fractured under pressure was now reforming, stronger and more resilient. Their bond, forged in the crucible of shared trauma, was now a source of strength, a testament to their enduring love and commitment to each other.

They understood that healing was not a linear process; it was a winding road with unexpected turns and detours. There were days when the pain resurfaced, when the memories of Blackwood Lane threatened to engulf them once more. But they had learned the tools to manage those moments, to support each other, and to seek professional help when needed. They had discovered the profound importance of self-compassion, of acknowledging their vulnerabilities and accepting their imperfections. They learned to forgive themselves, to let go of the self-recrimination that had weighed them down. The forgiveness extended to each other as well; the accusations and recriminations that once poisoned their relationships were replaced by empathy and understanding.

Their journey wasn't just about overcoming the trauma of Blackwood Lane; it was about confronting their family history, their inherited patterns of dysfunction, and the unspoken hurts that had been passed down through generations. They explored these issues with a newfound openness, acknowledging the impact of their past on their present. This self-awareness helped them break the cycle, creating a healthier and more loving family dynamic. They developed strategies to communicate effectively, to address conflicts constructively, and to support each other through challenges. They learned to appreciate their individual strengths and to acknowledge their interdependence. Their family became a true team, each member playing a vital role in supporting the collective well-being.

Their renewed sense of hope was reflected in their outward lives, too. John's pottery gained recognition; Mary's garden became a local landmark, admired for its beauty and resilience; Silas's art garnered critical acclaim, his paintings telling a powerful story of overcoming adversity; and Emily's writing reached a wider audience, her words resonating with those who had faced similar struggles. Their individual successes became intertwined, a reflection of their shared journey and collective strength.

Blackwood Lane remained, a constant physical reminder of their past. But it was no longer a place of fear, but a place where a significant chapter of their lives had been written, a chapter that ultimately led to healing, growth, and a stronger, more resilient family. They had reclaimed their narrative, transforming their shared trauma into a testament to the enduring strength of the human spirit and the unwavering power of love, forgiveness, and family. They understood that true home wasn't just a house, but a feeling of belonging, of security, of unconditional love, a sanctuary built on the foundation of shared experiences and the enduring strength of their bond. Their story became a beacon of hope, a testament to the transformative power of resilience, a powerful reminder that even from the deepest shadows, healing and hope can bloom. Their story would become an inspiration for others, demonstrating that even the darkest chapters can lead to a brighter future, where love, resilience and unity prevail.

A Year Later

The anniversary of their escape from Blackwood Lane arrived quietly, almost unnoticed in the flurry of everyday life. There were no grand celebrations, no dramatic pronouncements. Instead, there was a shared sense of quiet accomplishment, a collective exhale after a year of intense emotional labor. The palpable tension that had once permeated their home was gone, replaced by a comfortable silence punctuated by the sounds of laughter, the clatter of dishes, and the gentle hum of conversation.

John's pottery studio, once a sanctuary for his simmering anxieties, now overflowed with light. Sunlight streamed through the large window, illuminating his workspace, transforming the dust motes dancing in the air into shimmering specks of gold. His hands, still bearing the faint scars of his struggle, moved with a practiced fluidity, shaping the clay with a confidence born of perseverance. He wasn't just creating pottery anymore; he was crafting narratives, each piece telling a silent story of his journey, a testament to his resilience, a symbol of his triumph over fear. The vibrant colors he now incorporated reflected the kaleidoscope of emotions he had navigated—from the deep blues of despair to the radiant yellows of newfound hope. He had even begun to experiment with incorporating fragments of Blackwood Lane's unsettling history into his pieces, subtly weaving shards of broken glass or rusted metal into his designs, transforming the remnants of their trauma into powerful symbols of their healing. Each piece became a poignant reminder of his journey, and a celebration of the strength he found within himself. His work was no longer solely an artistic expression, but an act of healing, of reclaiming his narrative and forging a path toward a brighter future. The gallery showing approaching the autumn months held the promise of an even larger audience, a validation of his artistic journey and a testament to his healing.

Mary's garden, a vibrant tapestry of life and color, was a testament to the restorative power of nature and the unwavering tenacity of her spirit. The roses, once wilting symbols of despair, now blossomed in profusion, their petals unfurling like the gradual healing of her own soul. She had expanded the garden, adding a small orchard where she meticulously tended to apple and pear trees, their branches reaching skyward like hopeful prayers. The rhythmic act of planting, nurturing, and harvesting offered her a sense of control, a counterpoint to the overwhelming chaos she had previously endured. The garden had become more than just a place of beauty; it was a place of healing, a sanctuary where she could reconnect with the natural rhythms of life and find solace in the tangible growth around her. The community garden project she had embarked on brought additional healing, the shared work with others reinforcing her connection and belonging. She helped those who had also struggled with their mental health, building a community around shared experiences, offering support and fostering mutual healing.

Silas, his studio a whirlwind of activity, had transformed his canvases into vibrant windows into his soul. The darkness, once omnipresent in his work, was now tempered with light. He had found a new palette, incorporating vivid blues and greens, representing the peace and renewal he found in nature after his ordeal. While he still explored the darker themes of human experience, he no longer seemed consumed by them. His paintings were more nuanced, reflecting a deeper understanding of his own emotions and a newfound capacity for empathy. His art had become a conversation, a dialogue between darkness and light, pain and hope, a testament to the human spirit's capacity to endure and ultimately thrive. His art became a meditation on healing, exploring not only his personal journey but the broader human experience of trauma and recovery. He began giving art therapy sessions, sharing his transformative journey with others who had experienced the effects of severe trauma.

Emily, her pen now a potent instrument of healing, had found her voice. She continued to write, her words flowing like a river, carrying with them the weight of her experiences, the pain of her past, and the hope of her future. Her writing evolved beyond the diary entries that chronicled the nightmare of Blackwood Lane. She was now crafting short stories, each a microcosm of the human experience, exploring themes of resilience, family, and the complex tapestry of human emotions. She was telling stories not only of overcoming adversity but of the quiet strength found in everyday moments, the resilience of the human spirit in the face of impossible odds. She published her work; the validation further spurred her creative energy, allowing her to share her experiences and provide comfort and hope to other survivors.

Dr. Albright's sessions continued, but they were no longer dominated by the trauma of Blackwood Lane. The focus shifted to maintaining the gains they'd made, to cultivating strategies for dealing with recurring anxieties and developing healthy coping mechanisms. They worked on building stronger communication skills, fostering open and honest dialogue, and cultivating a deeper understanding of each other's needs. They explored family dynamics, addressing any lingering resentments and fostering mutual empathy. Dr. Albright helped them to establish rituals and routines that promoted connection and stability, creating a solid foundation for their continued healing and growth. The sessions became less about therapy and more about ongoing support, a check-in on their collective well-being.

The family, once fractured and broken, was now a tapestry woven from strength, resilience, and a profound love. They had established new traditions – weekly family dinners, weekend hikes in the nearby mountains, spontaneous movie nights. These shared experiences helped to replace the fear and mistrust with a sense of belonging. They supported each other's endeavors, celebrating each other's successes and offering comfort during setbacks. Their bond, once strained almost to breaking point, was now unbreakable, forged in the crucible of shared trauma and strengthened by their collective journey through healing. The laughter that echoed through their home was no longer tentative; it was genuine, unrestrained, a testament to their shared journey and enduring love.

Their home, meticulously renovated, was not merely a place to live; it was a sanctuary. The lingering scent of bleach and antiseptic had faded, replaced by the comforting aromas of freshly baked bread, simmering soups, and the gentle fragrance of Mary's garden. The house, once a symbol of fear and uncertainty, was now a haven of peace and serenity. The family spent time reminiscing about their past; it was no longer a story of horror but a tale of resilience, and the discovery of strength within themselves. They had faced darkness and emerged into the light, stronger, wiser, and more deeply connected than ever before. Blackwood Lane remained, a constant reminder of their past, but it held no power over them now. They held the power; they had reclaimed their narrative, transforming their trauma into a source of strength and understanding. Their story was a testament to the enduring strength of the human spirit, the power of love, forgiveness, and the unbreakable bonds of family. Their journey, though arduous, served as a beacon of hope for others, proving that even the deepest shadows can give way to the light of resilience and healing.

Looking Ahead

The following autumn, the Miller family stood on the precipice of a new beginning. The gallery showing of John's pottery was a resounding success. Critics praised his raw, emotional pieces, recognizing the depth of feeling woven into each curve and crack. The vibrant colors, once a shocking juxtaposition against the muted tones of his earlier work, now resonated with a powerful sense of catharsis. The pieces, imbued with fragments of Blackwood Lane's unsettling history, served not as reminders of trauma, but as testaments to survival. One particularly striking piece, a large ceramic vessel incorporating shards of broken glass and rusted metal, was titled "Phoenix," a silent declaration of their collective rebirth. The piece became a symbol of hope, a powerful metaphor for the family's journey from devastation to renewal. The success of the show wasn't just artistic validation; it was a powerful affirmation of John's healing process, a tangible manifestation of his resilience. The proceeds from the sale allowed him to further invest in his studio, solidifying his new path.

Mary's community garden project continued to flourish. It had expanded beyond its initial scope, becoming a vital hub for emotional support and community building. She collaborated with local therapists and social workers, offering workshops on horticultural therapy and stress reduction. The garden, once a personal sanctuary, became a space where others could find solace and cultivate their own inner strength. The vibrant colors of the flowers, the rhythmic act of planting and tending, and the shared experience of creating something beautiful fostered a profound sense of healing and connection. The sense of community provided Mary with a renewed sense of purpose, filling the void left by the trauma of Blackwood Lane. She realized the power of shared experience and mutual support in overcoming adversity, a lesson deeply rooted in her own family's healing journey. This project proved to be more than just a garden, it was a testament to her remarkable resilience and the powerful influence of community.

Silas's art continued to evolve, reflecting his deepened understanding of the human condition. He received a commission for a large mural in a local hospital, depicting scenes of hope and healing. He incorporated elements from his Blackwood Lane paintings, but recontextualized them, framing the darker themes within a larger narrative of resilience. The mural, a vibrant tapestry of light and shadow, became a powerful symbol of hope for patients and visitors alike. He embraced the complexities of human experience, creating art that was both thought-provoking and profoundly moving. The art therapy sessions he now led provided him with a profound sense of purpose, allowing him to share his healing process with others and contribute to their own recovery. He found purpose in helping others navigate their traumas and discover their own inner strength. His art had become a platform not just for self-expression but for collective healing.

Emily's writing flourished. Her first short story collection, a series of interconnected narratives inspired by her experience, garnered significant attention. Reviewers praised her evocative prose and her unflinching portrayal of trauma and healing. Her work resonated deeply with readers, many of whom shared their own stories of overcoming adversity, providing a powerful testament to the universality of human experience. Emily's journey had transformed her from a victim to a storyteller, her voice echoing the strength and resilience of the human spirit. The validation from her writing career, her acceptance in the literary community, and the connections she made with other writers were transformative experiences in her healing journey. She felt a sense of empowerment, which was a marked difference from the helplessness she felt during her time at Blackwood Lane.

Dr. Albright's sessions continued, but their focus shifted towards long-term emotional well-being and preventative strategies. They discussed healthy communication techniques, strategies for managing stress, and techniques for identifying and addressing early warning signs of relapse. The sessions became less about unpacking the trauma of Blackwood Lane and more about building a strong foundation for lasting mental health and well-being. The Miller family had learned the importance of open and honest communication, a stark contrast to the simmering resentments and unspoken anxieties that had plagued them before. Dr. Albright helped them establish new family rituals and traditions, creating a sense of normalcy and security that was essential for their continued recovery. These routines weren't just about structure; they were about connection, about fostering a shared sense of belonging and mutual support.

The Miller's life together continued to evolve, not without its challenges. There were moments of lingering anxiety, fleeting flashbacks, and the occasional bout of melancholy. But these moments were less frequent, less intense, and far easier to manage. Their collective strength, forged in the crucible of adversity, allowed them to face these challenges together, supporting each other through the difficult times and celebrating the victories, both big and small. They learned to view their past trauma, not as a defining characteristic, but as a shared experience that deepened their bond and strengthened their resolve. The family embraced the healing power of laughter, of shared meals, of spontaneous adventures, and of simply being present in each other's lives. The rebuilding of their lives was a process, not an event, a testament to their enduring resilience.

Christmas that year was filled with warmth and laughter, a stark contrast to the previous year's shadowed anxiety. They decorated their home with joyous exuberance, filling it with the scent of pine and cinnamon. Their laughter echoed through the rooms, a tangible manifestation of their renewed hope and optimism. The children, once burdened by the weight of their parents' fear, now revelled in the joy of the season, their innocence restored. The family dynamics had fundamentally shifted; trust, understanding, and mutual support had replaced suspicion and fear. Their collective healing was a testament to the unwavering strength of their familial bond, their shared journey through trauma, and their unwavering commitment to a future filled with hope. They cherished the memories of their ordeal, not as a source of pain but as a reminder of their indomitable spirit and capacity for resilience.

As the years went by, the memory of Blackwood Lane faded, not in the sense of being forgotten, but in the sense of losing its power to define them. It became a chapter in their family history, a powerful story of overcoming adversity, of rediscovering resilience and of the enduring strength of human connection. They embraced the present and looked forward to the future with renewed hope and optimism. They understood that trauma is not something to overcome once and for all; it is a process, a continuous journey of healing and growth. But they had learned that with support, compassion, and unwavering determination, it was a journey that could lead to a brighter future, to a life filled with joy, laughter, and the unwavering strength of family. Their story serves as a testament to the enduring human spirit and its capacity to triumph over adversity, transforming trauma into strength, loss into love, and darkness into light. Blackwood

Lane was no longer a place of terror; it was a place of profound transformation, a foundation for their healing, and a powerful reminder of their collective strength. Their story, a beacon of hope, serves as a reminder that even the darkest chapters can lead to the most extraordinary resilience and growth.

Lasting Scars

The years that followed unfolded like a tapestry woven with threads of both sorrow and joy. The Millers' lives, once consumed by the chilling presence of Blackwood Lane, slowly began to reclaim their vibrancy. The house itself, now empty and awaiting a new family, remained a silent testament to their ordeal, a distant echo in their shared history. Yet, the family understood that its spectral grip no longer held them captive. They had wrestled with its demons and emerged, scarred but unbroken.

John's pottery continued to evolve, reflecting a newfound serenity and acceptance. The raw emotionality remained, but the jagged edges had softened, replaced by a gentler grace. His pieces, once imbued with the chilling atmosphere of Blackwood Lane, now conveyed a sense of peace and resilience. He began to incorporate natural elements into his work – smooth river stones, delicately preserved wildflowers, and polished wood – each piece a quiet meditation on the healing power of nature. He established workshops for troubled youth, sharing his craft and his story, offering them a safe space to explore their own creative expression and to find solace in the transformative power of clay. His success went beyond financial security; it represented a complete integration of his past trauma into his present purpose, transforming his pain into a source of healing for others. He found a profound sense of fulfillment, a profound gratitude for the life he had painstakingly rebuilt.

Mary's garden, once a refuge, had blossomed into a thriving community center. It was a testament not only to her horticultural skills but to her ability to nurture and heal others. She organized annual fundraising events, attracting local businesses and charitable organizations. The money raised went towards expanding her community programs, providing mental health resources and supporting families in need. She continued to collaborate with therapists, integrating the garden into their therapeutic approaches. She saw firsthand how the simple act of connecting with nature could soothe the soul and foster resilience. The garden became a symbol of her strength, a reminder that even from the darkest soil, beauty and hope can flourish. The enduring legacy of her work was in the countless lives she touched, in the small acts of kindness that bloomed from the fertile ground of her heart.

Silas's art took on a new dimension, moving beyond the stark depictions of fear and paranoia that had characterized his Blackwood Lane series. His paintings now explored the complexities of human resilience, the delicate balance between fragility and strength. He received numerous commissions, his work displayed in prestigious galleries across the country. He established an art therapy program for veterans, using his art as a medium to help them process their trauma and rediscover their inner peace. His work became a bridge between the visible and the invisible worlds, a testament to the enduring power of art to heal and transform. The recognition and acclaim he received wasn't simply about personal success, it was a powerful symbol of his evolution, of his journey from victimhood to triumph. The depth of his creativity served as a testament to the enduring human spirit's ability to transcend adversity.

Emily's writing career soared. Her short story collection became a bestseller, translated into multiple languages and optioned for a film adaptation. She continued to explore themes of trauma, resilience, and family dynamics, but with a growing focus on hope and healing. Her next novel, a powerful exploration of intergenerational trauma, further solidified her reputation as a compelling and empathetic storyteller. She used her platform to advocate for mental health awareness and to support organizations dedicated to helping survivors of trauma. She received countless letters from readers sharing their own stories, finding solace and connection in her words. Her journey had taken her from a place of deep vulnerability to one of profound strength and empowerment. Her books became a beacon of hope, reminding readers that even in the darkest of times, healing and recovery are possible.

Dr. Albright's role evolved from therapist to trusted advisor and family friend. The Miller family's sessions gradually decreased in frequency, the focus shifting to preventative strategies and ongoing emotional well-being. He became a valuable resource for them, a wise guide helping them navigate the complexities of their post-trauma lives. He was instrumental in helping them establish healthy coping mechanisms and create a strong foundation for their ongoing emotional resilience. Dr. Albright's presence in their lives remained a testament to the enduring power of human connection and the importance of professional guidance even after the acute phase of trauma has passed. His commitment to their well-being extended beyond the therapeutic setting, creating a lasting impact on the family's healing journey.

The scars of Blackwood Lane remained, etched subtly into their memories. There were moments when the shadows of the past threatened to engulf them – fleeting glimpses of fear, the echoes of unsettling sounds, a chilling sense of déjà vu. But these moments were now manageable, the power of their trauma diminished by the strength of their collective healing. They learned to identify the triggers, to approach these moments with awareness and compassion, and to support each other through them. Their shared experience became a bond, a source of both empathy and strength. Their resilience grew not in spite of their trauma, but because of it.

The family found healing in the most unexpected places. A spontaneous weekend trip to the coast, a shared laughter during a family movie night, a simple act of kindness extended to a neighbor – these seemingly ordinary moments became potent antidotes to the lingering shadows of the past. They cultivated a culture of open communication, ensuring that every member felt safe to express their feelings, anxieties, and vulnerabilities. This transparency fostered trust and a deep sense of mutual support, creating a safe space for everyone to heal at their own pace. The family learned that healing wasn't a destination but an ongoing journey, and that true strength comes not from suppressing the past, but from accepting it, integrating it, and growing beyond it.

The narrative of the Millers' journey is not one of complete erasure but one of transformative integration. The haunting events of Blackwood Lane will forever hold a place in their collective memory, a stark reminder of their vulnerability and resilience. It was a chapter, not the entire story. Their resilience was not the absence of scars, but the conscious choice to live a life that honored both their past and their future. They learned to embrace their newfound strengths, to appreciate the simple joys, and to cherish the precious gift of their family bond. They were living proof that the human spirit, even when fractured, possesses an extraordinary capacity for healing and renewal. Their story became a testament to the remarkable power of human resilience, an enduring narrative of triumph over adversity. Blackwood Lane might have left its mark, but it did not define them. They, in their strength, redefined what it meant to overcome trauma, to live, to love, and to flourish.

New Beginnings II

The first spring after leaving Blackwood Lane felt different.
The air, instead of carrying the chilling whispers of the past,
hummed with the promise of new life. John, his hands still
bearing the faint traces of clay, planted a small orchard
behind their new home. The saplings, fragile yet determined,
mirrored their own journey of recovery. He found a quiet joy
in nurturing them, watching them grow, a tangible
representation of the life they were rebuilding. The scent of
blossoms replaced the lingering stench of decay that had
clung to their memories, a subtle but potent shift in their
emotional landscape. He no longer sculpted figures burdened
by fear; his work now explored the themes of growth and
resilience, the intricate dance of life and death represented in
the twisting branches of ancient oaks or the delicate petals of
a newly opened rose. His pottery, once a vessel for his
anguish, transformed into a medium for celebrating his
healing. He found solace in the rhythmic turning of the
wheel, a meditative act that grounded him in the present,
allowing him to shed the lingering ghosts of Blackwood
Lane.

Mary's garden, though significantly smaller than the
sprawling expanse at Blackwood Lane, became her
sanctuary anew. It wasn't simply a collection of flowers and
herbs; it was a carefully curated space reflecting her inner
peace. Each plant, selected with meticulous care, held a
specific meaning. A resilient lavender bush, symbolic of
healing and serenity, stood sentinel near the entrance.
Sunflowers, their faces perpetually turned toward the light,
reminded her of the importance of hope and optimism. And
the delicate jasmine vines, climbing the walls of her new
garden shed, represented the slow, persistent growth of her

emotional recovery. She found herself sharing her knowledge with the community, establishing small workshops on sustainable gardening practices, fostering a sense of connection and shared purpose. The garden wasn't just a source of personal healing; it was a tool for helping others find their own path towards restoration. The aroma of herbs and flowers replaced the scent of damp earth and decay, transforming the physical space into a haven of serenity and renewal.

Silas, away from the oppressive weight of Blackwood Lane's history, found his artistic voice evolving. He abandoned the bleak, claustrophobic scenes that had defined his previous work, shifting towards vibrant landscapes and portraits brimming with life. His paintings, once filled with a palpable sense of unease and dread, now radiated warmth and serenity. He began experimenting with brighter colors, bold strokes, and abstract forms, expressing the multifaceted nature of his emotional healing. The shadows and darkness remained, but they were now interwoven with streaks of light, representing the enduring strength of the human spirit to overcome even the most daunting adversity. He created a series of paintings reflecting the beauty of nature's resilience: trees bending in the wind, birds soaring through the sky, wildflowers pushing through cracks in the pavement. These paintings became a visual representation of his own capacity for growth and adaptation. He dedicated a portion of his earnings to supporting emerging artists from underprivileged backgrounds, recognizing the transformative power of art as a tool for self-expression and healing.

Emily, fueled by her experience, produced a memoir that resonated with readers worldwide. It wasn't merely a recounting of their ordeal at Blackwood Lane; it was a nuanced exploration of family dynamics under extreme pressure, a testament to the resilience of the human spirit, and an insightful look into the complexities of trauma and healing. The book didn't shy away from the darkness, but it focused on the light that emerged from it. It became a source of comfort and hope for countless readers who had experienced similar struggles. Her newfound fame brought opportunities to advocate for mental health awareness and to support survivors of trauma. She used her platform not for personal gain, but to create positive change, transforming her pain into a catalyst for healing in the lives of others. She established a writing workshop for young adults, offering guidance and support to aspiring writers, creating a supportive environment where they could share their stories and find their voices.

The family's therapy sessions with Dr. Albright continued, but the focus shifted. They no longer dwelled on the horrors of Blackwood Lane; instead, they explored strategies for maintaining emotional well-being, building healthy coping mechanisms, and preventing future trauma. Their meetings transformed into a forum for self-reflection, a space where they could honestly assess their progress and celebrate their achievements. Dr. Albright became a trusted advisor, a friend who offered guidance and support even as their individual therapies concluded. He celebrated their accomplishments, acknowledged their struggles, and helped them develop strategies for navigating challenges with grace and resilience. His ongoing involvement symbolized the enduring importance of mental well-being and the profound value of support systems in the journey of healing.

Their new home, a modest but comfortable house nestled in a quiet neighborhood, became a haven. It lacked the imposing grandeur of Blackwood Lane, but it overflowed with warmth, laughter, and a tangible sense of peace. They filled it with new memories: family game nights, spontaneous dance parties in the living room, quiet evenings spent reading together. These seemingly simple moments, unburdened by the specter of the past, became the foundation of their renewed lives. The house held no echoes of the past; only the soft sounds of life, gently erasing the chilling whispers that had once haunted them. They decorated it with artwork created after Blackwood Lane— vibrant canvases, delicate pottery, and hand-stitched quilts, each piece a testament to their journey of healing and growth. The walls didn't just hold pictures, they held a narrative of resilience and growth, a visual representation of their collective transformation.

The scars of Blackwood Lane, however, were not erased. They remained etched on their hearts, subtle reminders of their shared ordeal. But these scars were no longer sources of pain or fear; they became badges of honor, testaments to their strength, resilience, and unwavering love for one another. They found ways to integrate these memories into their present lives, acknowledging their impact without allowing them to define their future. They commemorated their journey with a private ceremony near a tranquil lake. They shared their memories, spoke about their deepest fears and their greatest triumphs, and reaffirmed their commitment to living a life filled with hope, joy, and unwavering love.

Years later, the Millers gathered together, not in fear, but in celebration. They had built a life filled with joy, love, and a deeper understanding of themselves and one another. The memories of Blackwood Lane were present, but they no longer cast a shadow over their lives. Instead, they served as a constant reminder of their extraordinary resilience, a testament to the human spirit's ability to heal and to find happiness even after surviving the unthinkable. They stood together, stronger than ever, a family forever bound by the shared experience of overcoming adversity, a family that found its strength in their collective healing. Their story, a narrative of trauma, resilience, and the transformative power of family, became a beacon of hope, reminding others that even in the face of unimaginable darkness, the light of recovery and the enduring power of love can prevail. The house on Blackwood Lane remained, a silent monument to a chapter in their lives, but it no longer held any power over them. Their future, bright and filled with promise, was a testament to their unwavering strength and the indelible power of family bonds. Their story was a testament to the enduring strength of the human spirit, a beacon of hope in the face of unimaginable adversity.

A Testament to Resilience

Ten years later, the scent of pine needles and damp earth replaced the lingering memory of decaying wood and mildew. The Miller family, gathered around a crackling fire in their new cabin nestled deep within the Redwood National Park, felt a profound sense of peace. The rhythmic crackle of the flames mirrored the steady beat of their collective heart, a heart that had mended, though the scars remained. Emily, her face etched with the passage of time but her eyes sparkling with a newfound wisdom, stirred the embers with a long, sturdy branch. The firelight danced across her face, illuminating the lines that spoke of resilience and strength.

John, his hands now roughened by years of working the land, leaned back against a large redwood log, a contented sigh escaping his lips. The lines on his face told a story of hard work and perseverance, a reflection of the challenges he had overcome. His presence radiated warmth and unwavering support, a silent testament to his role as the family's steadfast anchor. He looked at his family, his heart swelling with a love so deep it transcended the horrors they had endured.

Mary, her hands delicately cradling a steaming mug of herbal tea, watched the flames with a serene smile. The garden she had painstakingly cultivated at their new home, a riot of color and fragrance, flourished under her careful attention. It was a testament to her healing journey, a vibrant representation of the growth and peace she had found. The lines on her face spoke of a woman who had faced unimaginable fear, but emerged stronger and more compassionate. Her quiet strength was a beacon of hope for the family.

Silas, his artistic spirit now flourishing, sketched in his worn leather-bound journal, the firelight casting an ethereal glow upon his thoughtful face. He had established a successful gallery in a nearby town, his paintings a fusion of darkness and light, representing the journey they had traversed together. His work reflected the depths of their experience, yet celebrated the enduring power of hope and the transformative nature of art. The intensity in his eyes had softened, replaced with a gentle peace.

Even little Thomas, once a child haunted by the whispers of Blackwood Lane, was now a young man, his laughter ringing out in the crisp night air, untainted by the shadows of the past. He had excelled in his studies, his passion for nature reflecting the serenity of their new surroundings. He was a living testament to the family's ability to overcome adversity and cultivate a nurturing environment for their children.

The silence that fell between them wasn't heavy with unspoken words, but filled with a shared understanding, a silent acknowledgment of their shared journey. It was a comfortable silence, a comforting rhythm in their newly found harmony. Their conversation drifted to the events of Blackwood Lane, but the tone was devoid of fear. They spoke of their experiences with a detached clarity, acknowledging the trauma without being consumed by it. The memories were part of their history, not their identity.

Emily recounted the painstaking process of writing her memoir, the cathartic experience of pouring her emotions onto the page. The book had become a bestseller, not because it dwelt on the gruesome details, but because it offered a message of hope, a testament to the human spirit's ability to overcome adversity. It was a story of survival, resilience, and the unwavering power of family bonds. The process had allowed her to confront her fears and to help others find healing through their shared experiences.

John spoke of his return to pottery, the therapeutic rhythm of the wheel grounding him in the present moment. He no longer sculpted figures of fear and despair, but created pieces that reflected the beauty of nature and the enduring strength of the human spirit. His work became a means of expressing his healing process, a visual journey of transformation. The process was not without its emotional upheaval, but it was a cathartic experience that led him to a new creative outlet.

Mary shared how her garden, initially a therapeutic sanctuary, had blossomed into a community project. She had established a local gardening collective, nurturing not only plants but also the spirits of others. It provided her with a sense of purpose, a way of giving back to the community that had supported them during their darkest hours. Her ability to share her knowledge and expertise had transformed her trauma into a catalyst for positive change.

Silas described his artistic evolution, the way he had channeled his trauma into vibrant, life-affirming landscapes. His paintings now sold at prestigious galleries, showcasing his ability to transform darkness into light, showcasing the complexity of their collective trauma and the triumph over it. He had found a way to use his art as a vehicle for self-expression and healing, to showcase his profound journey of transformation.

Thomas spoke of his future aspirations, his desire to use his education to work towards environmental conservation, inspired by the beauty and serenity of their new surroundings. He spoke of the peace he found in nature, in the quiet solitude of the Redwood forests. He was no longer defined by the shadows of his past, but rather inspired by the beauty of the world around him. He was a symbol of hope and a promise of the family's bright future.

They talked about Dr. Albright, their therapist, and the continued support he had offered, even after their formal sessions had ended. They acknowledged the importance of his guidance and his belief in their resilience. His presence in their lives was a testament to the value of mental health support and its impact on their recovery process.

As the flames died down, embers glowing like distant stars, they held each other close, a silent understanding passing between them. The scars remained, faint but visible, reminders of their shared ordeal. But they were not scars of defeat, but of survival, etched into the tapestry of their lives as badges of honor. Blackwood Lane was no longer a source of fear, but a chapter in their story, a testament to their resilience, their strength, and the enduring power of family love.

Their future was not defined by the horrors they had endured, but by the love they shared, the healing they had achieved, and the unwavering hope that burned within their hearts. The years spent reconstructing their lives had been difficult, demanding, and emotionally draining. Yet they had emerged stronger, their bonds forged anew in the crucible of trauma. They stood together, a family bound not by fear, but by a shared understanding, a profound appreciation for life, and an enduring commitment to each other. They had learned to live with their scars, not as symbols of their past suffering, but as testaments to their unwavering resilience, their capacity for love, and their collective strength. Their journey had transformed them, making them not only survivors, but advocates for healing, beacons of hope for others who had walked similar paths. Their story, a tale of darkness and light, trauma and recovery, would continue to inspire others, reminding them of the enduring strength of the human spirit and the transformative power of love and resilience. Their new life, in the heart of Redwood National Park, was a testament to their enduring strength. The whispers of Blackwood Lane were silenced by the symphony of life surrounding them, a symphony of nature's grandeur, family's unwavering love, and the resilience of the human spirit. Their story was a testament not just to their survival, but to the power of healing, hope, and enduring love. It was a beacon of light in the face of unimaginable darkness, a testament to the indomitable human spirit, and a hopeful narrative for all who dared to embrace their journey towards healing and wholeness.

Acknowledgments

First and foremost, I extend my deepest gratitude to my family and friends for their unwavering support and patience throughout the arduous process of writing this novel. Their belief in my vision fueled my perseverance through countless hours of research, writing, and revision. Finally, I want to thank all those who shared their personal stories of overcoming adversity; their courage and resilience inspired the heart of this novel.

Appendix

This appendix contains supplementary material related to the research conducted for this novel, including excerpts from historical records pertaining to Blackwood Lane and its previous inhabitants, as well as relevant articles on psychological trauma and family dynamics. [Details of supplementary materials, perhaps with page numbers or a brief description of each].

Glossary

This glossary provides definitions for key psychological terms and concepts used within the narrative, aiming to enhance the reader's understanding of the complex emotional landscapes explored.

Dissociation: A mental process of disconnecting from one's thoughts, feelings, memories, or sense of self.

Gaslighting: A form of psychological manipulation where a person seeks to sow seeds of doubt in a victim's mind, making them question their own sanity.

Trauma: A deeply distressing or disturbing experience that overwhelms an individual's ability to cope.

PTSD (Post-Traumatic Stress Disorder): A mental health condition triggered by a terrifying event—either experiencing it or witnessing it. Symptoms may include flashbacks, nightmares and severe anxiety, as well as uncontrollable thoughts about the event.

References

[List of any books, articles, or other sources consulted during the writing process. Use a consistent citation style, such as APA or MLA.]

Author Biography

Emily Via is a psychological thriller writer with a fascination for the complexities of family relationships and the fragility of the human mind under pressure. Their background in e.g., psychology, social work, etc. informs their nuanced exploration of mental health and interpersonal dynamics.